D0467652

Murder by Kindness

A QUILTED MYSTERY

MURDER BY KINDNESS

THE GIFT QUILT

BARBARA GRAHAM

FIVE STAR
A part of Gale, Cengage Learning

GALE
CENGAGE Learning

Farmington Hills, Mich • San Francisco • New York • Waterville, Maine
Meriden, Conn • Mason, Ohio • Chicago

GALE
CENGAGE Learning®

Copyright © 2016 by Barbara Graham
Five Star™ Publishing, a part of Cengage Learning, Inc.

ALL RIGHTS RESERVED.

This novel is a work of fiction. Names, characters, places, and incidents are either the product of the author's imagination, or, if real, used fictitiously.

No part of this work covered by the copyright herein may be reproduced, transmitted, stored, or used in any form or by any means graphic, electronic, or mechanical, including but not limited to photocopying, recording, scanning, digitizing, taping, Web distribution, information networks, or information storage and retrieval systems, except as permitted under Section 107 or 108 of the 1976 United States Copyright Act, without the prior written permission of the publisher.

The publisher bears no responsibility for the quality of information provided through author or third-party Web sites and does not have any control over, nor assume any responsibility for, information contained in these sites. Providing these sites should not be construed as an endorsement or approval by the publisher of these organizations or of the positions they may take on various issues.

LIBRARY OF CONGRESS CATALOGING-IN-PUBLICATION DATA

Graham, Barbara, 1948–
Murder by kindness : the gift quilt / Barbara Graham. — First edition.
pages ; cm — (A quilted mystery)
ISBN 978-1-4328-3097-7 (hardcover) — ISBN 1-4328-3097-X (hardcover) — ISBN 978-1-4328-3091-5 (ebook) — ISBN 1-4328-3091-0 (ebook)
1. Sheriffs—Tennessee—Fiction. 2. City and town life—Tennessee—Fiction. 3. Quilting—Fiction. I. Title.
PS3607.R336M858 2015
813'.6—dc23 2015022039

First Edition. First Printing: February 2016
Find us on Facebook– https://www.facebook.com/FiveStarCengage
Visit our website– http://www.gale.cengage.com/fivestar/
Contact Five Star™ Publishing at FiveStar@cengage.com

Printed in the United States of America
1 2 3 4 5 6 7 20 19 18 17 16

For Tiny Miranda

ACKNOWLEDGMENTS

As an author, I have to thank many people for their patience and assistance. It cannot always be fun to wonder if you are about to be my next victim. Thanks to all of you who have cheered me on, corrected my work and tolerated my mental lapses and excursions. Many of you have answered, more or less politely, any number of odd, inane and frankly murderous questions.

As usual, there are those who must be mentioned by name.

My friend Michelle for testing another mystery quilt pattern for me. In spite of not enjoying them, or maybe because of it, she does a wonderful job.

My husband for proofreading, providing a dose of reality and the willingness to play dead on command (the dogs won't cooperate). My request usually begins with, "You don't need to know why, but . . ." Doesn't he realize what runs through my brain? What bravery!

Alice Duncan, of course, editor extraordinaire, who sees things invisible to me. She tells me what I have left out and what needs fixing. Now.

Thank you all.

The Gift Quilt
A Mystery Quilt by Theo Abernathy
The First Body of Clues

Finished quilt size is approximately 59 by 76 inches. Fabric requirements given are generous and are based on useable fabric widths of 40 inches. (The useable amount seems to have been shrinking.) This quilt pattern assumes familiarity with basic quilt construction, quilting terms, rotary cutting skills and sewing with an accurate 1/4″ seam throughout.

This project makes a large lap-sized quilt.

Fabric requirements:

Fabric A—2-1/4 yards of a print. It can be a floral, novelty, juvenile, frogs, it should not be directional.

Fabric B—1 2/3 yards of complementary color

Fabric C—1-1/2 yards of second complementary fabric

Fabric D—1 yard of a higher contrast fabric

Cutting Instructions

As you cut, remember to label each stack with color letter and size.

Cut from fabric (A):

4 strips—4-1/2″ by LOF (length of fabric)

48 squares 3-7/8″

48 squares 3-1/2″

Cut from fabric (B):

48 squares 3-7/8″

96 squares 3-1/2″

Cut from fabric (C):

31 strips 2″ by 15-1/2″

48 squares 3-1/2″

Cut from fabric (D):

4 squares 4-1/2″

12 squares 3-1/2″

20 squares 2″

8 strips 2-1/2″ by WOF (width of fabric)

Because of the variety of fabric widths on the market, be sure to save the remaining pieces of fabric after cutting in case you need to cut a few extra bits as the quilt is being constructed.

Chapter One

Theo Abernathy thought, and not for the first time this year, "It seemed like a good idea at the time" would probably be her epitaph. She was feeling a bit put upon and, to be fair, the year was only about a month and a week old. The "it" of the moment was her involvement in a silent auction and pie sale being planned as a fund raiser. The words of the phrase "silent auction and pie sale" rang in her head like a tune sung as a round, one continuous loop.

In a moment of madness, Theo had allowed Jane, her mother-in-law, to convince her to create a raffle quilt for the event. Theo was certain she had tried telling Jane she was too busy to do it. Although, to be fair, she had not tried very hard. Her mother-in-law was irresistible. A lack of willpower on Theo's part when Jane was involved was actually the major problem. The second worst problem was Jane knew her power and wielded it often.

Jane had smiled and even managed a somewhat sympathetic smile. "You can have the crew hand-quilt it for you." Jane had been referring to the numerous people who gathered in Theo's quilt shop on a daily basis and who enjoyed the social diversion of working together on community quilts. The smallest county in Tennessee did not suffer from a lack of volunteers.

Again, Theo attempted to resist. After all, she had a shop to run and four children and a husband. She was busy. And then, Jane had delivered the winning blow: "You *do* know what it's for, don't you?"

Theo's fate had been sealed by her mother-in-law's simple statement because Theo did know who the proceeds would benefit. Thinking of it made her feel sad and guilty at her selfishness. It was in support of a very good cause. All of the proceeds were to go to a project begun by Mrs. Dixon, the local veterinarian's wife. A project nicknamed Dixon's Dogs.

Once Theo was over her initial hesitation, she jumped in to help. Moments later she decided to make a very special quilt for the silent auction at the planned Valentine's Day gala.

The goal of Mrs. Dixon's project was meant to do more than to train shelter dogs as companion and service dogs, giving them a better life. It was also designed to help transition a small group of veterans including Boston Quist, Kenneth Proffitt and Dillon Teffeteller, who had returned to civilian life but who no longer fit into their previous niches, into becoming the dogs' trainers.

Tony, Theo's husband and Park County's sheriff, hoped they would even find a dog they could train to search as well as Dammit, Deputy Mike Ott's bloodhound. Tony believed it was always good to have a backup plan, and Dammit and Mike had other things they needed to do.

At the very least, the group hoped to supply trained dogs to flip light switches for a disabled person, open doors, carry items and do other similar simple services for their human. Providing companionship was to be their major role.

Donations for the silent auction were pouring in. There was a wide variety, from inexpensive used books and homemade jams to larger and costlier items like a full day of pampering at Prudence Sligar Holt's new "day spa" where the lucky "winner" would be treated with a massage, a facial and a pedicure. Theo thought the prize sounded divine. What a welcome escape from her frantically busy everyday life it could be. She had hinted to

Tony how she thought it would be a lovely anniversary present but wasn't able to tell if he was listening to her. Of course, if the cost went too high, she wouldn't enjoy it.

One of the more interesting tidbits she'd heard had to do with bedbugs in old books. At first those collecting books to sell had been happy about the generous number of donations. And then bedbugs were found in a few of them and a great debate ensued about whether or not to sell them or refuse to accept them or call Claude Marmot, trash guru, to collect them.

"Put each book in a sealed plastic bag and pop it in the freezer overnight." The advice came from Queen Doreen.

Most of the event's workers, Theo included, decided if it worked for the fastidious Queen, it was worth a try. They doled books out to as many volunteers as possible so no one was overburdened. After all, who had space in their freezer for a lending library?

Theo had already put many hours into the design of the new quilt. She knew she could have created a perfectly acceptable, traditional quilt made from simple squares, rectangles and perhaps a few triangles. Predictably, once she began working on the project, Theo had not only begun to enjoy the new design but made one complicated to construct.

The pie sale, which was expected to bring in most of the money, promised to be very competitive. In a rare moment of genius, the committee had asked Blossom Flowers Baines to be in charge of the pie event. Taking Blossom, the hands-down absolutely best baker in the county, out of the running had opened the door wide for the field of amateur competitors. Many cooks promised to deliver everything from peach pies to chess pies to lemon meringue.

Tony's mom, Jane, and his aunt Martha could both make a pie worth buying.

Theo overheard Jenny Swift and Eunice Plover, best friends

and very good, if not great, pie bakers, talking. They were excited to participate but were keeping quiet about their plans. The two women were ardent competitors, especially against one another, and equally ardent in congratulating the other one. There was a fair age difference between the two, Mrs. Plover being the older one by fifteen years, but they were inseparable. Their arrival in any place was usually accompanied by gales of laughter.

Queen Doreen, who was rumored never to eat because of her stylish, slender frame, had promised to make a couple of her family's favorite pies. According to Doreen, it was a secret recipe handed down from generation to generation. Her husband, Mayor Calvin Cashdollar, was on record promising to buy one of them for himself, no matter how much he had to bid. The other one would be truly up for another bidder. He was quoted as saying, "It *is* an exceptional pie."

Various other well-known cooks in the county were busy trying to decide their most competitive or desirable recipes. Voting, which was separate from gaining ownership, would be monetary. The more money the pie received in its voting jar, the higher its ranking would be. Because ownership of an entire pie would be auctioned separately, the voting was based on samples supplied from a second, identical pie.

Theo was not participating in the pie-baking contest. She hadn't ever actually killed anyone with her cooking, but even she had to admit it was probably more from luck than anything else.

Not everyone in the community was happy about either the dog training or the Valentine celebration. The grumps didn't cause a problem for those who were looking forward to it. There were always a few sour grapes and naysayers, the ones who hated all celebrations and any form of change, but the general sense in the community was one of excitement. February in

Silersville was not well known for its entertainment. This would give the residents of Park County something fun to do.

Part of Theo's reluctance to get involved with the Valentine event had been her concern about an upcoming event involving her business. Maybe she was insane. Caught off guard, she had agreed to be one of the East Tennessee quilt shops involved in a daylong shop hop. A charter bus was going to deliver forty fabric-crazed quilters to her shop, all at the same time. The plan was for the shoppers to spend an hour in each shop on the route and enjoy a catered lunch halfway through the trip. As it turned out, lunch time was when the quilters would be in her shop. Theo didn't consider the lunch a problem, mainly because it was being catered by Ruby's Café.

Everything else about it, though, was turning into an epic headache. She had designed a special quilt-block pattern as a gift for the shoppers. Now she had forty small bags to fill with candy, the pattern and several small pieces of fabric. Theo had to make arrangements for extra seating and find a way to accommodate many extra people in her workroom. She needed extra employees and makeshift cutting stations for the hoped-for banner day.

Theo's frequent nightmares involved either no one buying anything so she would lose money, or everyone clamoring for service at once, leaving Theo and crew unable to keep up and thereby upsetting the shoppers. They would lose customers. Somehow in the early hours of this particular morning, Theo became convinced the shop hop was going to be a disaster, a losing situation.

The giveaway block pattern had not been too difficult to decide upon because each shop started with a holiday theme drawn from a hat. Theo, as luck would have it, got Christmas. It was easy enough for her to design a simple Christmas tree block. Several people had tested it for her and assured her it was a simple block and foolproof. Nothing else had been simple.

The shopping bus was due on Saturday. Knowing Tony would probably be called into work, Theo had already made arrangements with Maybelle to keep the twins all day at the Abernathy house instead of her usual half day. The one-year-olds were into everything. Not for the first time, Theo gave thanks for the kindhearted woman and thought their meeting some months earlier at the grocery store had proven to be providential. In short, they needed each other.

Through the receiver of his cell phone, Park County sheriff Tony Abernathy had been listening to Theo detailing all the disasters she could imagine, including the upcoming Valentine's party and her involvement with the shop hop. He knew Theo tended to be excitable and because she couldn't say no, she often got involved in things she had no time for. She had been particularly distressed this afternoon. While listening to her chatter on, he had gotten some paperwork done.

"Sheriff?" The voice of his favorite dispatcher, Rex Satterfield, came through the intercom. "Can you take a moment to talk with Jimmy Zink? He's out front here."

"Sure, send him on back. Oh, and Rex, could you have Wade come in here, too." Tony explained to Theo and hung up.

His deputy and the schoolteacher arrived at the same time.

Jimmy Zink started talking before any greetings were exchanged. "I got a weird phone call in the middle of the night and thought I'd come by your office because I found the conversation so disturbing," Jimmy said. "It's bothered me all day."

"Have a seat." Tony thought Jimmy looked like he was trying to act casual about the call in the middle of the night. It wasn't working out. Jimmy's skin looked waxy and pale and his breathing was quick and shallow. "Take a deep breath and then start with the ringing of the telephone."

Jimmy nodded his understanding. He perched on the very edge of a chair facing Tony and forced himself to take a couple of slow breaths. "The land-line phone rang. It took me a few moments to answer. Most people I would expect to hear from in the night have my cell number, and I had been sleeping so hard that I even tried turning off my alarm in the dark."

"So you answered, how? 'Hello'? Or, 'This is Jimmy'?" Tony wanted to keep the man talking.

"I think it was more like ' 'lo'?" A faint smile did cross Jimmy's face. "The first time I said it, I had the receiver upside down. The second time, I was wider awake." He shivered. "Then this weird voice, maybe male, maybe female, says, 'Have you found her body?' "

Tony knew Jimmy well enough to know that on a good day, when he was clear-headed and well-rested, the man was a solid average in intelligence. Jimmy was a competent, popular third-grade teacher. At the hour of the phone call, and clearly distracted, he sounded semi-catatonic. "Who is 'her'?"

"That's exactly what I asked." Jimmy blinked several times and swallowed hard. "Then there was a sound like muffled laughter and then the voice said 'Louise'. I don't know anyone named Louise, so I asked my wife if she did and she said no."

"Have you considered it might have been a prank call from one of your students? Or another teacher?" Tony didn't think it sounded like any of the classic ones but it didn't hurt to ask.

"No. It didn't sound like someone playing a joke." Jimmy did smile a bit. "You know, like asking if your refrigerator is running and then telling you to go catch it."

Tony was baffled. He didn't know a Louise either. He couldn't imagine why anyone would call Jimmy asking about a body. The idea of a body being hidden somewhere he didn't know about made Tony slightly uneasy. A few years ago, he never would have considered the possibility someone might have found a body, but in the past few years there seemed to have been an unusual number of deceased persons in his county.

"What should I do?" said Jimmy. "Do you think this person will call again?" He was calmer now but not relaxed.

Tony wondered if somewhere there would be a record they could check. The call had come in on a land line. Some phones kept records of recent calls and some didn't. "Do you have caller ID of any kind?"

"Oh, yeah, I do. It's on my fax machine." Jimmy's eyes brightened at the question. "It's not far over to my house from here. I could run over and print out the list."

"I think we have time to go with you and check it out." Tony glanced at Wade. Wade nodded his understanding and rose to his feet.

Minutes later, they parked in front of Jimmy's house. It was an average, small, frame house. The soft yellow paint looked fairly fresh. After unlocking the front door, Jimmy led them to the answering machine, pressed a few buttons and printed a list of the twenty most recent incoming calls.

Tony studied the list. Nothing useful. The only call received at the time they were interested in had a blocked number. "There really doesn't seem to be anything we can do at this time. Call me immediately if you hear from this person again."

"You know, Sheriff." Wade looked up from busily writing in his notebook. "The caller could've dialed a wrong number. Maybe we could check numbers around this one."

"That's not a bad idea." Tony wondered about the most efficient way to determine what the correct phone number might have been. "Let's assume the prefix is correct. Why don't you start changing numbers with the last digit and work your way forward."

"Sounds like a reasonable plan." Wade smiled. "If nothing

else, some of our citizens will know we are on the job."

Tony doubted it would prevent them from complaining about a nuisance call from his department. Some days you were wrong, no matter what you did.

"Theo!"

Hearing her name being shouted from the phone's receiver before it was halfway to her ear startled Theo. Her best friend, Nina, sounded like she was about to have a stroke. "What's wrong?"

"Gray hair! I have gray hair!" Nina's voice rose in a crescendo until it sounded like a shriek.

"So, I have some, too. What's the panic?" Theo wasn't really proud of her gray hairs, but they still blended fairly well with the blond ones. "The last time I saw you, which hasn't been that long ago, I didn't notice that you were going gray." Theo wasn't sure if her best friend was freaking out because there was gray in her hair or if it was because Dr. Looks-So-Good might realize, assuming he did not have enough brains to do so already, he was dating an older woman, by maybe five whole years.

Nina's soft moan was the only response.

"Aren't you in Washington, D.C., with the school group?" Theo had to laugh. Nina was not normally a vain woman, although she certainly had the looks to give her cause to be. With her glossy auburn hair, unwrinkled complexion and brilliant green eyes, Nina was still a beautiful woman. Theo had no sympathy for her. "It can't be a surprise to get a few gray hairs when you're a field-trip chaperone. I have to hang up now."

"The kids are all in their workshop and I don't have time to run off sightseeing without them. What's more important than listening to your best friend have a nervous breakdown?" Nina made it sound like a soap opera announcer trying to convince viewers to tune in for the next installment.

"It's not as if I'm ignoring your obviously important, maybe even critical, mental medical issues." Theo couldn't believe she got the whole sentence out without Nina interrupting. "I'm supposed to teach a quick Valentine's project."

"Oops," Nina whispered. "I'll get off the phone. I didn't realize you are teaching a class today."

"It's not a full-day class, and it really is just a quick project . . . well it's quick to teach, longer to sew. We're piecing simple flannel hearts to make a snuggle quilt big enough for two."

"Why don't you make one for me and Doctor Looks-So-Good?"

Nina's comment startled a laugh out of Theo. Until now, Nina had been insisting her relationship with the Knoxville dentist was nothing serious. "Aren't you afraid that such a gift would jinx your friendship?" Theo deliberately stressed the "friendship."

"I know, I know. Never mind. I didn't say a word." Nina disconnected.

Chapter Two

Tony stood on the sidewalk outside Theo's shop enjoying the sunshine. This early in the year, the warm rays could vanish as quickly as they arrived. Lulled by the pleasant heat, it took Tony a moment before he realized he was openly staring at Mr. Anderson's toupee.

As they conversed, the man's forehead rose and wrinkled and moved in all the usual manners and directions, but his hairpiece remained immobile. His bushy eyebrows were as busy as the forehead: lifting, lowering and evidently growing, because they needed to be trimmed. A few wild eyebrow hairs met over the bridge of the man's nose and another one seemed to be stabbing the man's right eye. It was mesmerizing to watch his face.

Years earlier, when it became obvious to Tony at a very young age he was quickly going bald, he had made a study of hair replacements. Unlike his middle brother, Tiberius, whose hair was thick and dark, Tony's oldest sibling, Caesar Augustus, and he had the same hair-loss pattern, although Tony's had progressed faster than his brother's. One day, Gus and he had been all but escorted from a hairpiece and wig shop. They had both started trying on some extravagant Pompadour wigs and hairpieces, and when Gus tried to pull a ball cap over it they had both gotten the giggles as badly as any teenage girl. Maybe worse.

Not only had the pair been disruptive, but a middle-aged man with more hair strands on top of his head than Tony had on his entire head now had surreptitiously watched the brothers. After he strode out of the shop, apparently more confident in his worth without a hairpiece, Tony and Gus had been gently, but firmly, asked to leave.

Unfortunately now, Tony realized he had spent more time watching the motionless toupee than he had listening to the man wanting to discuss something with the sheriff. Thankfully it didn't seem to be an emergency. "I'm sorry. Would you mind starting over?"

"You weren't listening?" Mr. Anderson frowned.

"I'll admit that I was a bit distracted by the sunshine." Tony smiled. "Please forgive me."

"You have to do something." Mr. Anderson fiddled with his sideburns, which were as shaggy as the eyebrows and only made Tony stare at the toupee again. "One of my neighbors has been extremely loud and has lights shining from his house all night long. I want it stopped."

"I can ask your neighbor to be quieter, especially, shall we say, after nine in the evening? I don't think I can ask him to turn his lights off though." Tony was surprised to see the smaller man puff up like a sponge absorbing water.

"Why not?" Mr. Anderson narrowed his eyes again. "Isn't that why we pay you?"

"Not to force people to sit in the dark." Tony forced himself not to respond to the question about his salary. It was made easier by the approach of a tall, muscular man neatly dressed in a black suit. He was completely unfamiliar to Tony, but Tony recognized the type. A bodyguard. The bulge under the jacket was probably a handgun. He stopped near Tony and Mr. Anderson but did not interrupt. He stood quietly with both hands visible and crossed near the center of his body. Waiting. Sunglasses covered his eyes.

Mr. Anderson stomped away in a huff and ran directly into

the stranger. He bounced off the larger man like he'd run into a wall. He was fussing loudly about it as he made his way down the sidewalk.

"Sheriff?" The large man pushed his sunglasses up onto his hair and spoke softly. "They call me Bear."

"Yes?" Tony was curious. The nickname looked appropriate for a man that size. "Can I help you?"

"No, sir." Bear extended a huge hand and looked into Tony's eyes. His own were a dark brown. "I always like to introduce myself to law enforcement, just so there are no questions about my job and intentions. I'm one of the private bodyguards for Karl's Bad. He's renting a large cabin just out of town for a few weeks."

Tony shook the bodyguard's hand. He had heard rumors about Karl's Bad. Most of them were unpleasant. The young movie star with the hokey name had a knack for being in the news detailing his almost endless bad behavior. "Are you expecting trouble?"

"Yes, sir. He's almost always surrounded by it." Apparent disgust clouded the bodyguard's face.

"You don't like your job." Tony couldn't see why the man would risk his own life to protect someone he so clearly disapproved of. "Why do you do it?"

Something like pain flickered across the bodyguard's face. "I have two children who live with their mother. One has special needs." Bear glanced around as if checking for someone listening to their conversation. "I can't make this kind of money any other honest way. The little prick pays very well."

"And just what do you do for him?" Visions of some of the lurid activities so prevalent on the news ran through Tony's brain. He doubted he was going to like the situation.

Bear frowned. "My job is to keep what he calls 'the trash' away from him. That's all. I protect the shell. What's inside of him is not in my line of work. Frankly, I'd enjoy tossing him off the mountain and moving into your county. Maybe work for you." Bear looked a bit surprised he'd said all of that out loud. He stopped talking but didn't look away.

Tony smiled. He understood this man. "Thanks for checking in with me. I always like to have a heads-up before any trouble begins. It's easier to control than it is to stop."

Bear nodded. "I'll give you a call if I think he's going to cross the line."

"Anonymously?" Tony thought he'd better warn dispatch about their new informant.

"No, sir, you'll know it's me." Bear grinned. "Here's my card."

"Sheriff? There's some sort of incident at the Okay Bar. Are you available?"

Tony heard Flavio Weems's voice come through his radio. The dispatcher sounded concerned. Tony knew it wasn't always an easy job balancing the few deputies on duty at any given time and the number of calls. Park County, Tennessee, might be the state's smallest county by population, but its proximity to Great Smoky Mountain National Park often kept his small staff busy with accidents, burglary, even murder. Or there might be a week when a missing pet was their most urgent call. The department didn't have the money to keep extra deputies. Tony had been out on another call and had missed the shift change.

"Yes. I'm available, but I don't like it when you say incident, Flavio," Tony rubbed the back of his neck. "You know that can mean any number of things—serious to comical. What's happening?"

Flavio cleared his throat. "According to the call from Mom Proffitt, at least two guys got into a fight, and one of them bit the other one's ear off. I have an ambulance on the way and

Mike and Sheila are both heading for the Okay. I just thought you would want to know."

"Thank you. Tell Mike and Sheila I'm on my way." Tony headed for the Blazer. He was surprised by the location of the brawl. There usually wasn't much trouble at the Okay, not like at the Spa, the other town bar. There was often enough bad behavior, and gnawed ears, at the Spa to make him consider having a full-time time deputy on duty there. At the Okay, Mom Proffitt ran the bar with an iron hand and she didn't sell bait. She kept everyone's keys, even if they were drinking iced tea. She definitely did not allow fighting. Over the years, a few patrons hadn't agreed with her rules and had been banished for life.

As Tony reached the top of one of the higher hills in town and looked down toward the bar, he could see the flashing lights on two patrol cars and the arriving ambulance. They lit up the landscape for a mile. It might not have been so impressive if the interested observers passing by would simply keep driving. But, as always seemed to be the case in Park County, a crowd was already gathering to watch the show. Tony was careful to park the Blazer where it wouldn't be in anyone's way and made his way to the bar's front door. The owner, known to everyone as "Mom," stood waiting for him under the sign that still read "Okay Bar and Bait Shop," in spite of the lack of fishing supplies.

"Sheriff." Mom's voice held a mixture of anger and worry.

Tony thought Mom's face looked strained. And no wonder. If the man on the stretcher, whose head was tightly bandaged, and the expressions on the paramedics' faces meant anything, this was a serious matter. Deputy Mike Ott stood between the stretcher and Deputy Sheila Teffeteller, who was involved in an earnest conversation with two men sitting at a nearby table. Another man stood near Sheila, his hands cuffed behind his back. He was yelling for his attorney at the top of his lungs. Tony wanted silence but knew it was out of the question. He bent over to ask the tiny bar owner, "What happened here?"

"I don't know." Mom's head moved from side to side to side, almost vibrating. "I swear I've never seen anything like it. One minute four men were sitting together at that round table." She indicated the empty table behind Mike. "And all of them seemed to be having a good time, and the next minute one of them lunges across the table and bites the other one's ear off."

"There was no arguing?" Tony had seen few fights that didn't start with some buildup and had been gradually brewing until someone finally exploded. "Had they been here together before?"

The movement of Mom's head switched from shaking to nodding. "They've been part of a larger group for several months. But they weren't interactive with me, so I don't know much more about them than their names. They always handed over their keys, they just didn't talk, you know, chat with me. I don't force my customers to talk." Mom still hadn't blinked. "I just don't understand."

"I presume the man in Sheila's handcuffs did the biting. Where are the men who were sitting with them?"

Looking confused, Mom studied the faces surrounding them.

For a moment, Tony thought maybe their closest witnesses had vanished.

"Oh, thank goodness, there they are." Mom whispered. "Do you see the two men standing near the back door? The stubby redhead and the taller guy with graying hair."

Just as Tony murmured that he did see the men, Wade arrived and Tony nodded for his deputy to join him. For a second, Tony thought the two men he wanted to talk to were going to try and slip out the back door, but whether it was because they decided to cooperate or knew they wouldn't get their keys back from Mom until they did, they waited. Tony made his way toward them and smiled as he said, "I understand you were sitting with the biter and the bitten."

The men nodded. They didn't have to say they preferred not to be involved; it was written all over their faces. Tony guessed that neither man had mentioned to his wife the reason he wasn't home yet for dinner. They weren't intoxicated. "Why don't you call home and tell your wives that I need to talk to you about a crime you might have witnessed. I'm the one delaying you."

Almost identical expressions of relief ran across their faces. They wasted no time pulling out their cell phones as they immediately complied.

Once the calls were done, Tony gestured for the pair to join himself and Wade outside.

This February evening was neither bitterly cold nor pleasantly balmy, but in the fresh air was a better place to talk. Quiet and private. "We would like to talk to each of you separately."

"Why?" asked the older of the two.

"Sometimes, without meaning to, one person's story will affect the other person's story. After we're through, we can all compare notes."

Tony tossed a coin into the air and slapped it onto the back of his hand and looked at the older man. "Heads or tails?" The man called heads. It was tails. "Okay, you wait right there."

The man nodded and wandered over to his designated spot.

"Your name is?" Looking at the remaining witness, Tony opened his notebook and Wade did the same with his.

"Smith." He pulled his wallet from his pocket. "Do you need my driver's license?"

"No, but thank you for offering." Tony smiled. "Do you know the man who is now missing part of his ear?"

"Not well. The four of us have had a few beers together in the past. We all work at the fertilizer plant." Smith shook his head. "I never saw anything like that before. Just all of a sudden Cliff jumped across the table and took a big bite of Paul's ear."

Tony noticed that by the time Smith finished his recitation he was sucking big gulps of air in between each word and he looked a bit shocky. Tony pointed to a nearby picnic table. "I want you to go sit on that bench for a few minutes and try to relax. Take some slow breaths."

They signaled the other man to join them. His version of the events did not sound rehearsed. It simply sounded like both men had witnessed the exact same event. George Ramsey—Tony dubbed him witness number two—had worked at the plant for about a year longer than any of the others. He said that he knew of no problems among any of his coworkers, except the usual differences created by liking different sports teams and so forth, but especially not a problem likely to culminate in such an attack.

Thanking them, and after getting all of their contact information, Tony sent them home. He watched the pair reclaim their car keys before he looked at Wade. "What do you suppose it would take to make you lunge across a bar table and bite off Mike's ear?"

Wade's dark-blue eyes went wide. "I can't imagine. If it was something like him asking my wife out on a date, I doubt I'd be sharing a table in the first place." Wade considered the situation for a minute. "I thought they were all friends together, but maybe the biter wasn't expecting to be sitting with the extra guys. But still, if you were that angry at someone, how would you be able to put up with it as long as he did?"

"The biter was yelling for his attorney when I arrived." Tony wasn't surprised. If it was himself, he'd be asking for his attorney as well. "So we won't be able to learn much from him for a while."

"And the bitee, or whatever you'd call him, will probably be in surgery and then recovery for quite a while before we get to talk to him." As Wade spoke, the ambulance pulled out of the parking lot, headed for Knoxville.

"I'm not sure I want to wait that long to get some information." Tony studied the small clumps of interested onlookers still gathered. "Let's go from group to group and ask general questions."

Wade nodded. "Someone at a nearby table could have overheard some comment or maybe a threat that created the problem."

They worked their way from cluster to cluster asking general questions, knowing Sheila and Mike were doing the same. "Have you seen the men here together before?" And, "Were you aware of any friction between the two men?"

It was not a particularly busy night at the Okay, and no one they talked to seemed to know anything relevant, no one that is except Quentin Mize. Two years ago, Tony wouldn't have believed anything Quentin said, but the young man had come a long way from his drug days. Now Quentin worked hard for Tony's brother Gus in construction, and although Quentin still occasionally over drank, and spent the night in the tank, he had managed to stay clean of drugs. His overall appearance had improved along with his health.

"Tell me, Quentin, do you know the men involved in the ear-biting episode?" Tony asked.

"Kind of."

Tony watched as Quentin's long limbs twitched a bit. Normal for Quentin. "Kind of how?"

"We was all in high school at the same time," Quentin finally answered. "None of us was bright enough to pay enough attention to learn anything." He peered through the darkness as if looking for answers to life's bigger mysteries. "How long is that statue?"

"Statue?" Tony repeated. A half second later it hit him. "You mean the statute of limitations? Is that it?"

"Yes." Quentin turned back to look at Tony and Wade. His thin face drooped under a mournful expression. "That's the one."

"It depends on the crime and how long ago it happened." Tony wasn't sure what to tell Quentin. "If it's not heinous—you know, really bad, like murder—I would guess you'd get credit for being a witness. It might not even go on your record."

"Back in the old days, me and some friends all worked together doing a bit of wrong, selling booze to friends. We also boosted a couple of cars." Quentin looked uneasy and shifted from side to side, rubbing first one foot against the opposite ankle and then changing his weight, switching, doing an odd march in place. "We got away with it. I'm sorry." He fell silent and seemed to study his feet.

Tony thought his expression said it all. Guilt and regret. Tony had heard quite a few confessions over the years. He had also seen a lot of guilty parties who refused to confess no matter how much evidence had been collected against them, but he never was quite sure what to say to someone expressing true remorse. "When was the last time you saw them?"

"Maybe a couple of days ago. The guy what lost his ear was yelling trash at the other one about some hooch they'd brewed. Sounded like some of it went missing."

None of this made sense. Tony thought he would know if the two men had not been reasonably law-abiding since they were in high school. Why pay for booze if they had moonshine? Bootlegging and car theft as juveniles did not, on the surface, have any connection with the current outbreak of interpersonal violence.

Bootlegging. He thought the word might hold some promise in this situation. "Back when you were in school, where did you get the alcohol you sold?" Tony gestured for Quentin to sit down.

Quentin carefully folded his hands together even as he settled onto the folding patio chair. "We were small time. It's not like we had a still. Mostly, we stole it from our own folks. You know, we'd pour out some whiskey from the bottle, and replace it with water. We just didn't want anyone to see the level go down."

"Your dad didn't mention anything about the taste being different? You know, weak or watery?" Tony remembered that Quentin's late father had been a heavy whiskey drinker. His short life had ended with his becoming a drunken-driving statistic who had killed not only himself but also his wife and his younger son, leaving Quentin to fend for himself.

"You remember how he was." A sad shake of his head accompanied Quentin's response. "I doubt he ever could taste anything."

Chapter Three

Tony was working his way through some paperwork and a large sandwich at his desk when a call came in about a multiple-vehicle collision. He would not normally go out on a simple traffic call, but they were shorthanded and the accident had taken place only a couple of blocks away from his office.

Although it would have been quicker to walk, he drove the two blocks so he would have access to his emergency equipment and could use the Blazer to cordon off part of the accident scene. At first glance, it was hard to tell where one piece of wreckage ended and the next began. He could see one driver, a woman, trapped inside the damaged remains of a small green car. There was little left of the vehicle. It looked like someone had taken a giant can opener to it and peeled it open. Above the sound of a car horn blaring, Tony could hear someone calling for help. The front bumper of a white pickup jammed into the wreckage. With the hood crumpled up to the windshield, it didn't look much better than the car.

Out of habit, he quickly moved toward the more damaged vehicle, the car. The female driver was unconscious and bleeding from her temple. Getting her out without injuring her further was going to require special equipment and a medical professional. He keyed the radio microphone hanging on his shoulder. "We need the jaws of life, at least one ambulance. And we need them now." Tony gave the location as he hurried to look in the driver-side window of the pickup. At first, he didn't

see anyone. A movement caught his eye and then he r that the driver must have slid off the seat and was fol under the steering wheel. Only a very small driver coul there. Terrified brown eyes stared up at him. Blood ran gash on the forehead, painting a large portion of the fac knew that nothing bleeds like a head wound but when l the door, it was locked, and the window was closed.

Tony heard the wail of two approaching sirens at exactly the same time. A fire rescue vehicle parked beh Blazer. Before the driver was even out of the truck, Tony telling him what he had seen. Half of the firemen startec apart the car to gain access to the driver. The other went to work opening the pickup. It was easier than because all they to do was pop a lock. They checked the condition before trying to move him.

Tony stayed out of their way and took lots of pictures

Once the driver was safely out of the pickup, Tony rea couldn't be more than ten years old, about the same ag younger son, Jamie. This boy was considerably small Jamie. Pale and shaking, the boy kept saying over a again, "My dad's going to kill me."

Tony's unsympathetic thoughts were along the same his dad didn't take action, he would. Killing wasn't the but Tony wasn't above handing the boy a broom and him sweep sidewalks and parking lots for an indefinite p

Unless they learned something dramatically differe talking to the drivers and witnesses and following the ev the unlicensed boy had caused the accident.

In the meantime, the paramedics were still working fe on the young woman. By the time they managed to get the stretcher, she still had not regained consciousne shape of her bulging belly told Tony she was pregnant. W wasting a moment or a motion, they packed her

ıbulance and sent it away.

One of the paramedics had checked the boy for damage but und nothing more than a knot on his forehead and a bruise his back from sliding under the steering wheel.

Tony retrieved the woman's purse from the car and dropped in an evidence bag. He labeled it with the time, the date and of the information he had at hand. He wasn't in a good ood when he put the ten year old in the cage in the back seat his vehicle. "Who's your family, and what's the phone numer?"

The stunned expression remained on his face as the boy ırled into a ball after giving Tony the information he asked for. 'm sorry. I never meant to, you know, hurt anyone."

Tony wasn't surprised. It simply wasn't an excuse he ɔnsidered valid. He hated senseless accidents.

heo didn't have a police-band radio. She didn't need one of er own. Her only full-time employee, Gretchen, kept a small ne near the cash register. While Theo didn't want to know hat kinds of calls went out, Gretchen, whose husband was a olunteer with the search and rescue group, was an addict. She as only allowed to listen with a headset and only if there were o customers in the shop.

The bell over the front door of the shop rang as a woman ntered, interrupting Gretchen's summary of a recent traffic acident. Theo was surprised to realize the time. The day was lmost over, but Miss P had arrived on schedule.

Almost every day, at exactly four o'clock, the front door of heo's shop opened just a bit. Miss P would poke her head nside and glance around as if she were a mouse checking for a angerous cat. Once she was apparently assured of her safety, he would straighten up and march confidently inside. With a od of greeting to whoever was at the counter, usually Gret-

chen, she made a beeline for the workroom. She didn't stop to talk. She didn't shop. She didn't come to quilt.

If there was a class going on, Miss P would make a token display of admiring the projects in process. It wasn't unusual for her to pat the charity quilt when she trotted by, as if it were a pet. By this time of day, most of the ladies who quilted on it would be at home.

Having performed her small ritual, Miss P would open the refrigerator and remove the foil wrapped plate waiting for her on the middle shelf. After claiming her personal silverware from an empty souvenir mug from St. Louis, she would sit down at a small table positioned far away from the quilt and sewing areas. It was her table.

If other people were in the room, she would look them in the eyes, her dark eyes bright but wary, and bob her head three times in quick succession. She never spoke. After peeling off the foil cover, she would study the food for a moment and then, with exquisite care and no rush, she'd eat her daily meal. Then she would wash the plate and leave it on the counter.

The plate would be returned to the senior center the next day by one of Theo's regulars and exchanged for a fresh, full one. The procedure was well established and never discussed. It was like unlocking the shop's front door signaled they were open for business. It simply was the way it was.

For a while, Theo had worried about Miss P's lack of food on Sunday. The senior center was closed on that day, as was the shop. Miss P did not get two plates on Saturday. Theo knew the woman had filler foods like cereal and bread, but it wasn't enough to supply all the nutrition she required. Theo knew about those groceries only because she could see them in the bag resting near Miss P's feet. Theo had no way of knowing what else was in the bag, maybe a steak or string cheese or food for a pet.

One Sunday, just by chance, Theo saw Jenny Swift talking with Miss P in the church parking lot. Jenny Swift handed Miss P a foil-wrapped plate of something that quickly went into Miss P's omnipresent bag. When Miss P glanced at Theo, Theo pretended to have seen nothing. Surprised by the depth of her relief, Theo continued on her way, curious what it would take for the woman to speak to her. She tried to remember how her shop had become Miss P's personal dining room but failed. It had been going on for as long as the shop had been open.

Not paying close attention to anything but the people in her shop, Theo stepped out onto the sidewalk, planning to have a quick chat with the owner of the coffee shop next door, hoping the upcoming shop hop could benefit both of their businesses. Before she realized what was happening, she felt herself being shoved aside by a man in a suit. Beyond him a skinny, young man with long straight hair was surrounded by several more large men. Whether they intended to or not, another man pushed her and she ended up crashing into the coffee shop's sidewalk sign listing the specials of the day. Out of balance, she ricocheted toward the street.

Just before Theo was trampled or fell, which would have her either landing completely in the street or crashing through the coffee shop's picture window, a large man in a dark suit grasped her like she was an errant toddler and set her on her feet, out of danger.

"Th-thank you," Theo said, but she wouldn't have known if he'd heard her except for a slight nod. She was appalled by names the skinny young man called her protector. The gist of the man's diatribe was it wasn't the bodyguard's job to protect anyone but him.

The coffee shop owner stepped outside. "Can you believe we have a movie star in our midst?"

Theo had to admit she had no idea who he was.

"He's Karl's Bad. You know, like the caverns with all the bats only he spells it different." She grimaced. "My daughter thinks he's amazing."

"And you?" Theo examined her arms. She was amazed the bodyguard hadn't even bruised her when he moved her. "What do *you* think about him?"

"I think he's bad all right. Bad news."

Chapter Four

"Dad, look what we found."

Tony raised his eyelids and focused on his two older children. He was comfortably stretched out on his oversized recliner. He felt a bit sluggish, but the boys stood side-by-side, almost identical expressions of excitement and curiosity on their young faces. "Okay, what is it?"

"This." Chris held out a fuzzy, gray, plush hippopotamus.

Tony didn't touch it. The toy was dirty and wet but otherwise intact. "Okay. I see it."

"No, Dad, you have to look inside." Chris's long fingers pulled the hippopotamus open. Inside was a tangle of jewelry, seashells, and an orange plastic container, the kind prescription medications came in. Even through the scratched plastic Tony could see several different colors and shapes of pills. There were no labels.

Leaning forward in his chair, Tony studied the contents. He was no expert, but the jewelry looked old, and if those large stones were real, very expensive. He thought it might match the reported items taken from a recent visitor's rental car and tried to remember if there was any mention of the items being in a plush toy. No, he was certain they had not been. The seashells were small and ordinary.

While Chris held the toy, Jamie's fingers were busy exploring more pockets in the hippopotamus. He pulled out a small packet of tissues, a tube of lipstick, some paper clips and a roll of money held together with a rubber band. The boy laughed as he pulled each item out of the pockets and waved it at his father and said, "It's got all kinds of hiding spots."

Thinking his son was paying no real attention to the contents, just the capacity, Tony took the hippopotamus and checked it for any form of identification or an address for its owner but found none. He counted the cash: over three thousand dollars. "Where was this? Exactly?"

Disappointment, Tony guessed from his own lack of enthusiasm, clouded Jamie's face. "It was over near the swings."

Chris leaned forward. "There wasn't anyone else in the park, Dad."

"I'm not accusing you boys of anything wrong. In fact, I'm sure someone will file a report about losing it." Tony grinned at the boys. "I'm proud of you for bringing it to me."

"Do we get a reward?" Jamie's blues eyes sparkled with delight. "Maybe a hundred dollars?"

"Or, maybe some ice cream." Tony had to admire the boy's enthusiasm. "After dinner."

"Sweet!" The boys abandoned their prize and headed back to the park.

With the boys outside, Tony took the time to explore the hippo more carefully. Wide awake now, he changed his mind about the type of owner it belonged to. There was something intriguing about a couple of the pieces of jewelry. But what? Had someone reported them lost or stolen? Was his imagination working overtime, or was this simply a child's toy left in the park? The large stones in the jewelry could be glass and not diamonds and emeralds.

He put the hippo and its contents in a box and wrote himself a couple of notes. He'd take the box with him when he went to work in the morning.

★ ★ ★ ★ ★

"Louise." The name was starting to haunt Tony. He and Wade had failed to find any information about the mysterious caller to teacher Jimmy Zink. So far they had turned up only two women anywhere in the county named Louise. A couple of citizens had relatives of that name, but no one who lived nearby or who was visiting. There were a couple of women named Lily. Nothing came to light during their search of similar phone numbers.

Still, there was something about the call that chewed on Tony's stomach. No number of antacid tablets was helping. In the middle of the night, Tony found himself wondering who Louise was. Unable to sleep, he got up and went to the basement in the Law Enforcement Center, where he expended some of his concern on the treadmill and weights.

His office had sent queries to all of their neighboring Tennessee counties and a few in Kentucky and North Carolina. So far, nothing about a Louise had been reported. If the call was a prank, it was a disturbing one. And why involve Jimmy? What could connect a third grade teacher and a mysterious and presumably missing, and possibly deceased woman?

Thinking perhaps it was from a case long grown cold, Tony decided to pay a quick visit, if there was such a thing, to former Sheriff Harvey Winston. In the past, the older man had been able to supply a bit of information on cold cases or simply old cases.

Surprisingly enough, Harvey didn't circle the question. The moment Tony said "Louise," Harvey's eyes widened and he leaned forward as he said, "Have you found her?"

"No." Tony explained everything he knew. That took about thirty seconds.

Harvey sat down, almost collapsing onto his favorite chair. "It's been so many years ago now."

"Why would someone call Jimmy?" Tony flipped through his meager papers. "He didn't even move to Silersville until, what? Maybe five years ago, now. How long ago did your Louise vanish?"

"Maybe fifteen or sixteen years." Harvey stared at the notebook in Tony's hands. "Look in the old files for Barnet. The case went cold but was never closed."

"A couple of years ago, I specifically asked and you told me all of your cold cases were solved."

"Did I?" Harvey's face hardened.

Tony wondered if the old sheriff was losing his memory or telling a lie. "Tell me what you remember."

Harvey stood up and ambled over to his desk, where a mess of unfiled papers surrounded a computer. He reached into a drawer and pulled out an old notebook before he went into the kitchen, where he poured himself a couple of fingers of whiskey and added two ice cubes. Without asking, he brought Tony a glass of water. After returning to his chair, Harvey simply held the notebook as he sipped his drink for a couple of minutes. He finally met Tony's eyes. "She vanished on Valentine's Day."

"So, the anniversary of the event is in a few days. At least there's some connection."

Harvey nodded. "Do you know your Jimmy's phone number?"

"Yes." Tony opened the current file. There was little in it besides the information supplied by Jimmy when he'd made his report. The phone number was written in several places.

Harvey opened his worn notebook. "Just so you know, I photocopied every last word in this notebook and put it in her file." Harvey read off Louise Barnet's phone number. It matched Jimmy's.

Tony felt a chill. "If that was her phone number, and she's dead, does the caller not know that?"

"We never found any evidence or a witness to tell us if she ran away or was taken. There was no ransom request, and she didn't take much but her car and some clothes. The car was just an ordinary dark green Chevy. And we think she wasn't alone. Another girl disappeared at the same time, Aurilla Dawes. The two girls just vanished into thin air like they'd been taken away by one of Orvan's flying saucer guys." Harvey stared at the notebook. "If someone did take her, who and why? If not, why didn't she ever call home? Are they hoping to reconnect? Is she living or dead?"

"It all comes back to what happened and where is either the living woman, or her remains." Tony could feel himself being pulled into the case. "How old would she be?"

"Thirty-three or thirty-four." Harvey shook his head. "Her folks paid for some private investigator when we couldn't learn anything. I guess they finally gave up. They moved away maybe ten years ago."

Theo worked her way through her quilt shop, occasionally pulling a bolt of fabric from its rack to move it to the sale bin. The bolts were arranged by color. Walking through the rainbow, it never ceased to surprise her how some fabrics practically flew off the shelves, all purchased within days of their arrival. Others sold more gradually but were still popular. A few sat unnoticed like wallflowers at a dance.

To get those fabrics out of the shop, the wallflowers were discounted enough to find homes. A good wallflower was often purchased in multi-yard cuts to be used to make the backs of quilts. Every quilt needed a front, batting for the center layer, and a back. The three layers were either stitched together by hand or machine—the actual quilting process. Theo noticed a small white paper heart flutter to the floor when she removed one of the less popular reds. She picked it up. Red ink proclaimed, "Don't miss the Valentine's Day party at the museum."

Theo waved the little paper heart at Gretchen standing behind the counter. "Is this yours?"

Gretchen glanced at it, shaking her head. She reached under the counter and retrieved a small stack of handmade paper hearts, large and small. Some were just white typing paper like the one Theo held. Some hearts were cut from red construction paper. A few were red paper hearts glued onto lace paper doilies. "I found all of these today."

"Where did they come from?" Theo glanced from the one she held to Gretchen's pile.

"I have no idea." Gretchen grinned. "I found the first ones yesterday. It was a really busy day with quilters and seniors and visitors. Anyone could have scattered them around."

"Was Jane in here?" Theo thought the hearts looked like something her mother-in-law might circulate to advertise the upcoming party and silent auction at the folk museum run by Jane and her younger sister, Martha.

"Not while I was here." Gretchen was distracted by a quilter needing some fabric cut.

Curious but not concerned by the appearance of paper hearts, Theo continued her selection process.

"Old man Rutherford is loose." Rex's voice came through the radio. "Last spotted in the park. In his underwear."

Tony groaned. The elderly gentleman was fond of roaming loose, and in spite of his dementia, he was sneaky. He might not remember his name, but he could watch someone punch in the number code for the locked door at the care home, and cleverly reproduce it. This might be the second time he'd vanished this week. His disappearances seemed to run in stages.

Tony had gone home for lunch. Since the Abernathy house

was directly across the street from the park, there was no valid reason he could come up with to keep him from collecting the old man and delivering him back to his residence. Tony headed out the front door and stopped on his porch in surprise. In the ten minutes he'd been at home, a snow shower had blown in. Huge fluffy flakes were drifting from the sky. It didn't look like real snow. It looked more like shredded foam rubber being dropped by a prankster.

The Silersville municipal park was fairly large for such a small community. The residents were lucky enough to have a pond, playground equipment, plenty of picnic tables and some ball fields. Separating the different sections were trees and shrubs. Tony didn't see the old man anywhere but he could see footprints in the new snow. Bare feet. Tony hurried, following the tracks. They led into an overgrown flowering quince, a shrub his mom usually called a japonica. They were well known for long, sharp thorns. The old man stared blankly at Tony with tear-filled eyes. He wore nothing but his underwear and was impaled on several of the shrub's vicious thorns. His thin skin was splotchy and turning blue.

"Mr. Rutherford." Tony spoke softly and began removing his jacket. "Let's get you out of there and into something warm."

"Snow." The old man looked pleased he had come up with the correct word. When Tony pulled away the branch holding him prisoner, he stepped out.

"Yes, sir. Now then, let's get you out of the park." He held the jacket open and the old man allowed him to wrap it about his skinny frame. Tony glanced down at the bare feet. "Shall we hurry?"

Thankfully, Mr. Rutherford had finished with his adventure and he hurried alongside Tony. When they reached the Blazer the old man's face lit up with delight.

"Car ride?" said Mr. Rutherford as he ran a gnarled hand

across the roof. The rack of lights on the top seemed to surprise him. "Mine?"

"Nope." Tony smiled and opened the door. Rutherford had ridden in the Blazer countless times, he simply didn't remember. Tony wouldn't mention that to him. "This is my work vehicle. Climb on in. I'll give you a ride in it."

"Siren?" Rutherford grinned like a two-year-old. "Please?"

Tony obliged. For one block.

Chapter Five

"Sheriff?" Ruth Ann's voice carried through the speaker on his desk. "Mr. Lundy has something he needs to tell you."

"Okay, you know the drill." Tony sighed. He wasn't sure whether to be pleased the old man was doing so well or aggravated that he was back to his confessions. A few months earlier the old man seemed to be on his last leg but now he looked as chipper as he ever had. Orvan Lundy was a spry eighty-something-year-old and as tough as a buffalo.

A few moments later, their regular small group gathered in the interrogation room known as the greenhouse. Orvan Lundy, the elderly star of this little melodrama, sat at the steel table with his gnarled fingers laced together. On one side of the little man sat Walter, Ruth Ann's husband and Orvan's community service contact. Wade carried in extra folding chairs for the audience and arranged them in a neat semicircle near the table.

"What can we do for you today, Orvan?" Tony thought he would get right to the point. "If you plan to confess, we need to get the prosecutor and your defense attorney in here as well."

"Weeel now, let's not be too hasty," said Orvan. "We ain't even said howdy to each other yet."

Reminded of his manners, Tony sat down. Orvan's confessions were as much social events for the old sinner as a meeting for coffee at Ruby's Café might be for ordinary folks. Understanding the situation and the protocol, Tony relaxed in his seat, and took a sip from a bottle of water. Across the table, Orvan sipped from his own bottle.

Tony took a deep breath and sighed. "So, how have you been?"

"C'ain't complain." Orvan accidently squeezed his plastic bottle, shooting a fair stream of water from the bottle and onto the floor, mostly because his rheumy eyes were focused on Ruth Ann. "Me and Walter have been getting along jest fine." The old man bobbed his head for emphasis.

Tony thought the movement, coupled with the contrast between his snowy sideburns and the ebony shoe polish enhancing the crown of his head, gave him the appearance of having a dancing skunk on his head. His overalls were neatly fastened and his threadbare plaid shirt had all of its buttons.

Tony preferred the neat appearance. Only a few months earlier, Orvan had been in bad shape and arrived to make his confession sloppily dressed. Not at all his style.

"We have indeed bonded." Walter nodded. "It helps that we both love the same irresistible woman." His broad smile displayed a lot of brilliant white teeth.

Ruth Ann, the irresistible woman in question, snorted indelicately. "You two deserve each other."

"Well, I'm happy everyone's having fun and getting along." Tony's patience was at an end. He ran a finger along the edge of his notebook. "Do you suppose we can get on with business now?"

All heads nodded but one. Orvan's shoe-polished head remained still.

"So, Orvan, what's new?" Tony was convinced the old man wasn't planning a confession. He wasn't wearing his guilty face and he hadn't requested an attorney.

The wizened little man squirmed on his seat. "I saw one of them flyin' saucer guys a-zoomin' around. There was this here trail of fire behind it shining like stardust."

Tony had to smile at the excitement on the old man's face. In spite of the cataracts, his eyes sparkled. Orvan looked like a kid on Christmas morning, albeit an elderly one. "Where was this?"

"I was on my way to see Miz Swift and make a delivery. Oops, I mean to say, I was goin' there to visit for a time." Orvan clamped one hand over his mouth.

Tony felt his eyebrows rise. He wouldn't have guessed that Mrs. Swift was one of the people who bought moonshine from Orvan. The old man's still probably couldn't produce much more than Orvan himself could drink. "Did you make a bigger batch than usual?"

Walter cleared his throat several times. He glanced at Tony and at Wade and then stared at Orvan.

Seeing Walter's expression, Orvan clammed up.

Tony sighed. "Let's go back to the subject of the flying saucer." In his own disjointed way, Orvan was often a great source of what was going on in the community. It usually took a fair amount of translation to get from one of Orvan's stories to the truth; in fact, he'd seen aliens before. "Where exactly did you see it?"

"The light come at me from nowhere." Orvan sipped his remaining water, taking his time telling the story. "I was in town, over toward the park. And suddenly the saucer come straight at me. There was a real bright light on it and one of them Martians what was all hunched up inside was boxing with something." Orvan's rheumy blue eyes were as wide as they could open. He seemed as mesmerized by the memory as he had been by the event.

He stopped to have more water. The bottle was empty but he gulped anyway.

"Only one light?" Wade spoke into the silence. There was a sparkle of mischief in his dark blue eyes. Tony could tell his deputy knew more than the rest of them about the vision.

Wade's expression made Tony really want to know what Orvan had seen. He tried to be patient, though, and let the story unfold in good time.

Orvan tilted his head, staring at the smile on the handsome deputy's face. Then Orvan cackled, "You seen it, too. Didn't ya?"

Wade nodded.

Intrigued, Tony glanced from man to man. "All right, I give up. Someone want to let me in on the secret?"

Clearly making an effort not to laugh, Wade said, "Jack Gates has a three-wheeler racing bike that he rides and propels with hand pedals in the front, hence the boxing Orvan saw. The bike has a headlight, but I've seen Jack wearing a headlamp as well. He says he likes to ride late at night when there's not much motor vehicle traffic on the streets."

Tony knew Jack had a damaged spine. He was able to walk, after a fashion, but often used a wheelchair. "Now that we solved the mystery of the mysterious biker and the Martians, maybe we can get back to work." He pushed his chair back and stood.

"Nossir, that's not what I come to tell you." Orvan's lower lip stuck out.

Tony sat, fighting back an irritated sigh.

"I come to say I've been bad. I ought not to, but I been makin' some hooch and keepin' it buried in a jug." Tears welled in his eyes and dripped onto the bib of his overalls. "Someone took it. Every last drop an' the jug with it."

Tony frowned. He couldn't imagine anyone sneaking up to Orvan's place and stealing a jug of moonshine. Orvan's mountain home was not on the beaten path. Who would know where it was kept? Besides Walter?

Theo stared past Tony. "I think that man is dangerous."

Tony turned enough to see who she was talking about. Jack

Gates. Surprised to see the man Orvan had mistaken for a Martian only a short time after his semi-confession, Tony studied him. Jack was a youngish man, maybe thirty five, maybe a match for his own forty. As described, Jack sat in a racing-style wheelchair. It was long and low, with hand operated pedals on the same plane as his chest. "Dangerous how?"

Theo shrugged but the expression on her face was undecipherable.

Tony thought his wife was often better at reading people than he was. He repeated, "Dangerous how?"

"Lock up your daughters kind of dangerous." Theo turned and smiled up at him. Her big green-gold hazel eyes sparkled behind the lenses of her glasses.

The laughter in her eyes made him realize she found the man attractive but had no real interest in him. Tony carefully studied what was going on in front of them. Sure enough, a small flock of women drew closer to the man on the bike. Moths to the proverbial flame.

Even in the fairly cold weather, Jack was dressed in a form-fitting, short-sleeved shirt exposing powerful arms and chest, bike shorts, and gloves. Beneath his helmet was a handsome, smiling face. His legs were surprisingly muscular in appearance.

"Do you know his aunt is Eunice Plover?" Tony doubted he was telling her anything she didn't know. He knew Eunice was a regular visitor in Theo's shop.

"Yes, they go to lots of places together." Theo rubbed the side of her nose. "Eunice was talking just the other day about a cruise the two of them are planning to take. It sounds like quite an adventure. I think it lasts about three weeks."

"Is it around the Caribbean?" Grateful for his jacket, Tony thought going somewhere with a little warmer weather had a certain appeal on this snowy day. Maybe it was because he'd had enough of a cold-weather adventure in the park with Mr.

Rutherford.

"No. They're headed for South America. Eunice said something about going up the Amazon River but I'm not sure about that part." Theo's eyes sparkled. "I do know that there will be a group of quilters on it, because she showed me pictures of two projects they are going to be working on during days at sea."

Her statement amused Tony because he had spent many weeks at sea in the Navy. There hadn't been any quilting though. He bent down so his eyes were level with hers. "You've talked in the past about teaching on one of those ships. Are you planning to sign up for one?"

"Are you worried I'll do it, or are you hoping I'll do it?" Theo's eyes sparkled. "You and the kids could eat at Ruby's every night. Just think of eating all that good food for a change."

Tony had to admit it was worry. He knew his wife enjoyed traveling and teaching, but he was not prepared to do his job and care for four children by himself except for short periods of time. Anything more than two days didn't qualify.

"Maybe your mom and Martha would stay with the kids and you could come along with me. I'd let you carry my sewing machine." Theo kissed his cheek while it was down at her level. "We could have a vacation."

"Now that certainly sounds better than having you desert your family." Tony was intrigued by the idea and started thinking about the possibility of taking some time off. Three weeks would be impossible, but maybe they could manage it for a week.

Theo waved at someone passing and Tony turned to look. A big man, part of the visiting star's entourage, saluted Theo. She laughed.

Recognizing Bear, Tony raised an eyebrow. "How do you know the bodyguard?"

"He saved at least a window and maybe both the glass and me." A frown crossed her face. "That nasty boy he works for started yelling at him for helping me."

Chapter Six

"Weems!" Tony shouted through the open doorway. "Bradley Weems!"

His voice startled Ruth Ann, sitting at her desk just past his door, and she swiveled to stare at him. "Sir?" When Bradley passed her desk and scuttled through the doorway, Ruth Ann turned back to her work.

Bradley didn't have enough good sense to remain standing, but plopped down on a visitor's chair like he'd been invited to tea.

"I was hoping that you would be J. B.'s replacement on the night shift when he retires." Tony tossed a paper from the stack on his desk onto another one on the floor. Tony had initially been impressed by the young man's resume. Bradley had graduated from the University of Tennessee. His degree was in chemistry, which seemed unusual for someone with an interest in law enforcement. Tony thought maybe Bradley would be better in a laboratory doing tests or maybe even working for the Tennessee Bureau of Investigation. Bradley was never going to be a good cop.

"Is there a problem?" Bradley looked shocked.

"Too many to count." Tony knew in the past few weeks he'd suggested some changes he'd like to have seen. Suggestions Bradley had totally ignored. "But I find the longer I work with you, the less I think you are capable of handling this job."

Bradley Weems was slightly related to Flavio, one of their

dispatchers. Flavio was a hard worker, who always had been a hard worker and who had greatly improved his abilities on the job. Although Bradley grew up in a neighboring county, it didn't take him long to find his way around Park County. Nothing negative had shown up in his background check. He was hired with their standard six-month probation. Now, only two months into his trial period, Tony was going to fire him.

Bradley looked real good in the chocolate brown shirt and khaki pants, which comprised the uniform of Park County's sheriff department. He was not tall, or at least not exceptionally so. He was about five-ten, well-built, and had attractive features and glossy auburn hair that only accentuated his deep green eyes. He looked like he could be a relative of Theo's best friend, Nina. It didn't take any time at all for the women of Park County to notice him. Although not as handsome as Wade, Bradley was *very available,* and he was taking advantage of the situation. It didn't take long before word reached Tony. Gossip in Silersville ran through avid listeners like water from an overflowing rain barrel. Tony didn't need a deputy who was in the center of a gossip firestorm.

"Stand up, Weems." Tony frowned. He didn't like having to do this. "There's no easy way to say this, but Park County doesn't need your services."

"Sir?" Bradley's normally smiling face turned serious. "I don't understand."

"It's simple. I don't want any of my deputies being the center of gossip or a love triangle." Tony held out his hand for the badge. "Frankly, I don't think you are cut out for law enforcement."

Weems stood motionless. After a few moments of silence he bobbed his head up and down and said, "I have to admit I really just wanted the uniform. Girls really like it, but the job's an awful lot of work and it cuts into my social life." He unfastened the badge and handed it to Tony.

Tony dropped the badge into a small drawer. "Then we are both agreed. I hope you find what you're looking for." As long as Bradley took his dream elsewhere, everything would be fine.

"Stand up and shut up!" A woman Theo had never seen before stomped into the quilt shop's workroom. She was almost as short as Theo and had a deep booming voice. Magenta hair stood straight out from her scalp in big, heavily glued spikes, exposing snow-white roots.

Without intending to, Theo rose to her feet. Several of the other ladies joined her. Theo managed to suppress the impulse to curtsey.

"As you were," Magenta Hair bellowed.

The women sat, except Theo. "I'm Theo Abernathy. Welcome to my shop."

"Excellent." The stranger waved an unseen wand of some nature, but Theo wasn't sure if she was blessing them or turning them into frogs. "I hope my staff informed you of my impending visit."

Theo wasn't sure if the woman was supposed to be royalty, a fairy godmother or merely an antique beauty queen. "Actually, no. Won't you introduce yourself?"

"I can't do that." The woman's eyes widened in apparent shock, and she looked from face to face.

Theo noticed the left eye was clouded with a cataract large enough to be seen across the room. Theo thought the visitor seemed taken aback by her request to say who she was. "Because?" Theo wondered if the woman even knew her name.

Clearly affronted, the magenta-haired woman stared at her. She seemed perturbed, not puzzled. "The herald ought to have announced me. It is, after all, his job."

Theo thought her accent sounded faintly like Katti Marmot's.

Maybe she was Russian, too.

"Where's the butterfly net?" Softly spoken, the words carried nonetheless. It might have been Eunice who spoke.

"How *do* they manage to find you, Theo?" Caro's voice held a hint of laughter, and her wide smile shoved all of her wrinkles closer together. "Some mystical force field?"

Theo had actually been wondering the same thing. Recently, she had talked to the other shop owners on Main Street, and none of them admitted to having a high proportion of nut cases as regular visitors. But Theo was pleased by this visitor, if for no other reason than Caro was smiling. After a long siege with Alzheimer's disease, her husband had died a few weeks earlier, and Caro was still coming to terms with this final loss. As if the woman hadn't suffered enough, now Caro was having balance issues. Theo was willing to deal with her goofy visitor if it would cheer up her friend.

"Everyone feels welcome in your place." Eloise from the souvenir and T-shirt shop had once told Theo. "Maybe because you let them wander about, assisted but not pushed to buy anything, and you give them coffee. For free."

The last comment had been a jab. Eloise sold gourmet coffee at her shop and several times had mentioned, in a not particularly friendly manner, that she didn't appreciate Theo giving coffee away. It was bad for her business.

Theo knew what she served wasn't great coffee, and it was good for *her* business. She decided to try again to learn more from the magenta-haired woman. "Is someone looking for you?" Even to Theo's ears, this was an ambiguous statement; what she had really wanted to ask was if the woman had escaped from her keeper.

"I can't imagine what became of my herald." The older woman studied the room. She didn't seem actually perturbed about the missing person.

"Won't you at least tell us your name?" Caro asked.

"I am the Grand Duchess Anna." It sounded like "Ah-nah," the way she pronounced it. Then she tipped her head at a regal angle, giving Theo and the other women somewhat disparaging looks as she moved her gaze from face to face. She frowned as if to express her continued surprise that everyone did not immediately recognize her.

The episode was starting to annoy Theo. She felt like she was reasonably easy to get along with, but she'd already had enough entertainment. Since Christmas, there had been at least three elaborate hoaxes or practical jokes played on her. She couldn't imagine anyone other than her husband and Wade wanting to do such a thing. Stepping away from the Grand Duchess, Theo dialed her husband's cell phone. When he picked up, she didn't give him a chance to say anything. "Was it you or Wade who decided to send the Grand Duchess into my shop?"

"The what?" Tony sounded confused.

Theo wasn't impressed by Tony's ignorant act. "You heard me just fine. Was it you or Wade who thought of the Grand Duchess?"

"I have no idea what you're talking about." Tony's voice reeked with sincerity, but it wasn't enough to convince her of his innocence.

"Anna, I presume short for Anastasia," Theo snapped. "You must know her. The Grand Duchess, as she likes to be called, showed up in my shop. She's a rather genteel loony." Theo massaged the back of her neck. "You must know her."

"A grand duchess?" Tony sounded impressed. "What country is she from?"

"I have no idea. How many countries have women with that title? But I do think, if you are truly not involved in this, we need to put a fence around the county. How are they getting in?"

"If she's Russian, maybe you could call Katti. She could translate." He paused. "Do you think she's dangerous?"

"No, not really dangerous. If she's not an actress, she is very convincing and really believes she is a Grand Duchess, and her English is better than mine, so no matter where she's from or thinks she's from, I don't think we need to bother Katti. The last I knew, the baby was sick and the Grand Duchess says she is waiting for her herald."

"Who is Harold?"

Theo didn't feel like getting into the whole scenario. It was already starting to sound like a vaudeville act. "I'll explain it later. Please just come and talk to her."

She felt like she had barely disconnected the phone call when Tony arrived. Wade, grinning like a fool, was with him. The deputy's happy expression triggered deep irritation mixed with suspicion. Theo frowned at him. Walking near him she hissed, "*No* more pranks."

Wade's expression instantly turned serious. "I swear, Theo, I had nothing to do with this."

Theo studied his handsome face and decided he was telling her the truth. "She's not hurting anything." She wasn't quite sure why she called for backup. She did know she was more interested to see whether her husband and/or Wade was involved with this woman's arrival than she was in having them ask her to leave.

The Grand Duchess Anna turned and smiled at the two men. "Courtiers, I presume?"

"My husband, the sheriff, and one of his deputies." Theo watched for any sign of recognition. There was none.

Tony whispered in her ear, "The Grand Duchess has purple hair."

"It's magenta," Theo corrected automatically.

Wade looked from one to the other. "Is there a difference?"

Theo nodded and Tony shook his head.

Wade suddenly excused himself, stepping away from the others, and listened to something on his radio. "Ah, it seems the Grand Duchess's entourage is awaiting her at the Law Enforcement Center. The call made it sound like we can leave her here, but it would be appreciated if we would go have a chat with them."

"Is one of them Harold?" Theo wondered if Anastasia was married.

Following Wade from the building, Tony whispered just before he left, just loudly enough for Theo to hear, "I think you're right."

Confused, Theo stared at him. "About what?"

"We do need a fence around the county."

"Sheriff?" A medium sized man with close-cropped silver hair waited in the visitors' area of the Law Enforcement Center. He wore a black suit with a white shirt and black tie. His sunglasses were pushed up onto his head. "I'm Richards. The Grand Duchess likes to call me her bodyguard. I'm really the chauffeur. My wife attends to her personal needs."

Tony's quick assessment of the man made him believe the Grand Duchess. If Richards was not a bodyguard, he was doing a bang-up job of imitating one. "I've met your employer."

"I'm glad to hear that." Richards's expression held curiosity and concern. "She slipped away while I was putting gas in the car. Is she all right?"

"We were told we could leave her where we found her. She seems to be happy over at the quilt shop, chatting with some other ladies." Tony glanced into the public parking lot and stared. A vintage black Rolls Royce gleamed in the sunlight, its highly polished chrome almost blinding him. "Holy smoke! What a car!"

Pure joy illuminated the older man's face. "I love my job. I'd do it for free just to get to drive that old baby around. The car, not the Grand Duchess, although she is actually quite sweet."

"And is that her actual title?"

"Absolutely." Richards pulled a card case from his suit-jacket pocket and handed a card to Tony. Embossed with a golden crown, the full name of the Grand Duchess took up two full lines. "She's the last of her family. They came over in the nineteen thirties, and she was the youngest of six daughters. Unfortunately, she has outlived all of her sisters."

"And the car?"

"Yep, they brought it along with them."

Chapter Seven

Theo heard an explosion. It had to be very loud for her to be able to hear it over the screams of the twins. The little girls were still teething, and not taking it in stride. Theo stuck her fingers in her ears as she hurried to her office window.

The window overlooked the main street of Silersville's small downtown area. She glanced down from her second-story view, half expecting there to be a hole blasted in the pavement, but the street below looked fine. Lifting her gaze to the nearest mountains, she couldn't help admiring their beauty. Snow gleamed on the higher elevations and the sky was a vivid blue, cloudless, without smog or even their customary "smoky" haze.

A plume of smoke rose into the sky.

Mere moments later, she heard the whine of sirens and saw the fire trucks belonging to their volunteer fire department headed out of Silersville, toward the smoke. The ambulance fell in line right behind it. As the vehicles made their way around the first curve, Theo saw Tony's Blazer join them. Following all the emergency vehicles, a veritable parade of local vehicles, cars and trucks, headed out of town.

Theo knew the curious citizens listening to the radio irritated Tony and the fire department, especially when the sightseers managed to arrive first at the scene.

It didn't take Tony long to make the short drive. Even so, by the time he arrived the fire was almost extinguished. He was happy it hadn't had a chance to spread. He wasn't happy about the source of the fire.

The culprit appeared to be Mr. Mayhew's still. A small shed smoldered in the woods maybe one hundred yards from the Mayhew house. It was easy enough to see inside the still. Tony focused on the copper kettle and the tubing. Knowing the answer before he asked Mayhew the question he said, "Are you licensed?"

Mr. Mayhew mumbled something Tony couldn't understand, but the answer was no. Tears welled in the old man's eyes. Tony wasn't sure what to do. He knew the law, but old man Mayhew had been making moonshine probably longer than Orvan Lundy. Tony also knew the old man never sold it. He drank it himself, or gave it to his relatives.

"What happened, Mayhew?"

Looking stunned, Mayhew blinked a couple of times and began, "Dunno, Sheriff." Before Tony could open his mouth, Mayhew continued. "Nothing about this batch was different. I cooked the mash same as always, and I made sure everything was all closed up good. Like always. It's important."

Tony had never made moonshine. He had seen a lot of stills, and most of them seemed to have looser construction than this one. Clean and tidy, at least by what they could tell by the unburnt bits. There seemed to be no reason for the fire.

Fire Chief Wendell Cox displayed the same puzzlement. "I've never seen a still explode like that." He mumbled just loudly enough for Tony to hear, "But I've seen some of them burn pretty hot."

Tony led Chief Cox farther away from the fire site. "Since it doesn't look like a normal—if there is such a thing—fire in a still, what do you think happened?"

"Arson. My first and best guess is someone doused the area with an accelerant like gasoline or charcoal lighter fluid and dropped a match on it. Smell's off for moonshine." The chief stared at the burnt-out shed. "Just off-the-cuff, the only motive I can think of for someone to torch a still is something personal. You know, like revenge or trying to put someone out of business. Maybe even some wacko militant teetotaler or a business rival."

Tony said, "Mayhew claims, and I've never heard anything to dispute this, that what he cooks stays with him and his family."

"Yeah," drawled the chief. "There are several small stills providing the homeowners with homemade alcohol. None of them are big enough to put a knot in anyone's knickers."

"I'll let you get on with your investigation." Tony moved closer to the burnt-out still. Fire investigation was not his strong suit, but he couldn't see obvious signs of foul play. What possible motive could be causing the rash of raids on stills and moonshine storage? Even more curious was how someone knew the locations of various stills and stashes. This one was invisible from the road.

The fire department was almost finished mopping up after Mayhew's fire when the next call came in. A citizen had spotted another fire burning in a different location, up on the Farquhar property. It was not even in the same general area. The firefighters all headed toward it.

Falling in line behind the engines, Tony was not expecting a good outcome. Angus Farquhar had a long and unpleasant and absolutely adversarial relationship with his department. The last Tony had heard, the man's sons were all off doing time at the penitentiary. Only luck, or possible coercion, had kept the patriarch from experiencing the same environment. It wouldn't shock Tony to learn Angus had framed one of his sons to take the fall for him.

Not unexpectedly, the fire department received an exceptionally unfriendly welcome from Angus Farquhar and his shotgun.

Tony climbed from his Blazer, serving as the escort for the volunteers. He made sure he stood to his full, and considerable, height and adopted a hard-as-nails attitude. He was not taking any static from this man. "Put the gun down, Angus."

"Go home."

"Are you going to extinguish that fire?" Interrupting the power play, the fire chief pointed to the blaze. It was visible from the road; no need to go onto Farquhar land to see it.

"Maybe." Angus narrowed his little piggy eyes. "I ain't impressed by your little red truck."

Tony turned to the chief and spoke softly. "It's Angus's property. As long as he doesn't let the fire travel off of his land, do you have the right to go on?"

"Why wouldn't he want the fire extinguished?"

Tony thought it was an excellent question. "Maybe he's trying to cover another crime?"

"Moonshine?" The chief snorted. "This would be the third still we've had to extinguish since the beginning of the week, and the second one today."

"As much as I hate to say this," Tony murmured, "I think for a change Angus is the victim."

"Angus the victim." Chief Cox rolled the words together as if they were all just one. "That is just so wrong." He ran a hand over his face leaving a great sooty smudge over most of it.

"I know. But what else would explain it?" Tony pulled up a map on his cell phone. "Look. The first fire was here. As I recall, we didn't think too much about it because it was an accident looking for a place to happen." He tapped a spot on the screen with his fingernail and then swore when instead of zooming in on the spot, an entirely different phone application opened. He groaned. "I thought I'd try something new, you know, twenty-first century and all."

The chief's laugh held a note of sympathy. "Yeah, I tried that one once, too. Let's use this instead." The chief pulled a paper map of the county from his truck and spread it across the hood of the Blazer. He tapped on a dot. "Here was the first one. Here's Mayhew's farm. And over here, Farquhar's still."

The most obvious similarity, at least to Tony's eyes, was the three fires were all about the same distance from downtown Silersville. They were not in line with each other but looked more like spokes from a wheel. "So why do you think someone is intentionally burning stills?"

"Well, they are illegal unless they have a permit, but unless you're keeping secrets from us, law enforcement is not the problem." The chief raised his eyes to the fire. "Only thing I can guess is maybe some holier-than-thou teetotaler is on a rampage and doesn't care if this whole end of the state goes up in flames."

Tony had to agree. "If someone wants to corner the moonshine market, why burn down those who aren't your competition?"

"And how does this person know where these stills are?"

Tony thought it wouldn't be a stretch for someone to know about Mayhew's still, because although hidden, it was not far from the road. But, who would have the nerve to go on Farquhar's land? The family had the reputation not only of shooting first and not bothering to ask questions, but also of shooting at people for the pleasure it gave them.

Chief Cox said, "Do you want to have some fun?"

Tony thought the chief's expression showed just how much the man enjoyed living on the edge. "After you." Although he'd said the words, Tony opted to march by the fire chief's side up the road next to, but not on, the Farquhar property. They paused to watch the flames now devouring a couple of trees next to the charred still.

Staring at his destroyed still, Angus looked defeated and

turned to the fire chief. A coating of soot over his normal dirt did nothing to improve the landowner's appearance. "Put it out."

"We'll do our best." The chief signaled for his team to go to work. They swarmed the area, clothed in heavy gear, attacking the flames with enthusiasm.

Tony had minimal training as a firefighter, but he could swing an ax. Staying out of the way, he chopped where the chief indicated. They managed to create a fire line to control the burn. As he stared at the burnt-out still, Tony assumed it had been arson, like the others. But why? And who? And where would the next one be?

Once the fire was under control, Tony returned to the landowner and dragged the chief along. "All right, Angus, tell us about the fire. How did it start?"

For a moment it looked like Angus would refuse to answer.

"I dunno." Angus paused, and then grudgingly he supplied a few facts. "There weren't any lightning." He wiped a soot-grimy hand on the already filthy shirt he habitually wore.

Tony thought it hadn't looked much worse the last time Angus wore it into town. "Did you see the fire start?"

"Nah. I was up there and comin' down from the house." Angus indicated a path worn into the underbrush. "The whole thing jest blew up. Fire everywhere. I ain't never saw nothin' like it."

Tony believed him. The stunned expression in his bloodshot eyes couldn't have been feigned. "How close to it were you when it started?"

"I was maybe about even with that shed." Angus indicated a pile of boards leaning against each other. "I, um, was on my way to check on somethin' in the shed, you understand."

"The somethin', I presume, is your stash of moonshine."

Angus seemed to find something on the bottom of his worn-out shoe very interesting.

The fire chief said, "You might want to check your shed and see if your stash is still in there."

Alarm widened Angus's piggy eyes and he scuttled away. A howl of rage told the rest of the story.

Tony wasn't going to admit his feelings to Angus, but he found more than two cases of arson more alarming than finding some homebrew. He hated the idea of having someone running around the county starting fires. The potential for disaster—major losses of property, or death—had him searching his pockets for his antacids.

Chapter Eight

Theo knew she was losing control. The shop phone rang incessantly, and a sales rep had lots of new fabrics to be decided upon—for or against her placing an order. She finally got rid of him and mumbled, "If one more person says to me, 'I don't know how you do it all,' I'll probably snap and zoom around like a runaway helium balloon."

"Now, Theo. Aren't you overreacting?" The shop's new part-time employee, Susan, stood in Theo's office/workroom doorway. Concern was written on her sweet face.

"Don't be silly. Of course I am." Theo breathed hard, like she had been running up and down the stairs in her shop. "I do not get it all done, and you know it."

Susan nodded. "But you try so hard."

"Yes, but look around this room." Theo gestured to one corner of the room, filled with toys and children's furniture, and on around past several different piles of fabrics, including the stack of juvenile flannels under a small black cat who was carefully grooming herself. Theo's cutting table was only visible because so many things had been shoved off of its surface and now were overflowing the plastic laundry basket beneath it. Her sewing machine was surrounded by a mountain of plastic boxes. "I can't keep up."

Susan stepped farther into the room. "Will you let me help?"

Theo felt silly and desperate. "I know I need all kinds of it. I just don't know what to tell you to do up here."

Susan reached for an empty box. "I'll just gather up the loose items, and you'll find a home for them later." Susan didn't wait for a response as she deposited a handful of pens and rubber bands into the box. "You grew up here, in Silersville?"

Theo nodded. "Like my parents and grandparents, I was born and raised in Park County. We learned to be careful of foreigners. As you've probably learned since moving here, that's anyone not born here and whose parents weren't either."

"And Tony? How did you meet him?" Susan carefully placed the rulers used with the rotary cutter into their wooden block with grooves cut into it, getting the rulers off of the table.

Theo stopped her frenzied movement and automatically fell in step with her new assistant, putting things away. "I remember when Tony and his family moved to town. I'd see him riding his bicycle or playing in the park across the street from my grandparents' house. It's our house now. Tony had so much freedom." Theo laughed. "He was big for his age and had three older siblings. Back then, I thought he was much older than I was, instead of just two years older."

"You didn't play in the park?" Susan seemed confused.

Theo gave a little shrug. "I was orphaned very young and my grandparents, who were old enough to be my great-grandparents, raised me. Even in our small community, they were often disturbed and anxious about 'foreigners' and 'meanness.' Both were equally not to be trusted." What she did not describe was the degree of their protective sheltering.

"But you married Tony?" Susan added more small items to the box, clearing off a section of the next table.

Theo began folding lengths of fabric she'd tossed into a basket. "Not until years after my college graduation. Tony had been in the Navy, went off to college and was working as a cop in Chicago when he returned here for his father's funeral. We reconnected. Not long after that we married and, of course, I went to Chicago as well."

"Now you live here again." Susan didn't ask it, but the question was obvious.

"Yes, we moved back several years ago so he could eventually run for sheriff." Theo took a deep breath and slowly exhaled. She didn't mention how badly injured Tony had been, shot while he was off duty. Distracted by old disturbing memories, she was surprised to see that in just a few concentrated minutes, Susan had cleared a path in the chaos. "Wow! You're a lifesaver!"

"I'm not quite that good, but I do have a lot of experience with less than ideal storage space." Susan laughed, even as she continued gathering and stacking.

Theo studied Susan's expression. "You look like you're developing a plan."

"I am." Susan waved at a space near Theo's children's nook. "I think we could put some shelves over there to hold some of these plastic project boxes. You'd still be able to see what's inside without having them spread out like this."

Surprised by the depth of her relief, Theo felt tears well in her eyes. "Of course. It's really so simple. I just couldn't see past the chaos."

"Psst," Gretchen murmured. "The Grand Duchess is back."

"Did her herald announce her?" Theo looked up and smiled. She felt friendlier than she had the first time the woman had arrived, probably because she wasn't feeling quite as overwhelmed and now was positive the woman's arrival wasn't a prank. "I didn't hear a trumpet, did you?"

Gretchen cocked her head to one side, listening. "Nope. No trumpet."

Theo stepped forward to greet the woman. The Grand Duchess wasn't exactly classified as a customer, but Theo felt no rancor, only simple curiosity. In spite of the woman's imperious manner, Theo had rather enjoyed her. She wasn't completely sure what title to use when addressing her so she mumbled, "Your Grace."

Wade's wife, Grace, heard the second word and popped up from behind a pile of flannel fabrics. "Yes?"

Theo grinned, thinking the conversation was starting to resemble a vaudeville act. "Who wants coffee?"

Jenny Swift and Eunice Plover had not been in the shop on the previous visitation by the royal. The two women, best friends since forever, were stitching on the charity quilt in the company of a couple of other women. They invited the Grand Duchess to sit with them. Moments later, five women were involved in an animated chat and much laughter.

"Excuse me." Theo tried to break into the conversation.

Grand Duchess Anna turned in her chair to face Theo. She lifted one finely arched eyebrow. "Is there a reason for the interruption?"

Theo managed a smile in spite of the disparaging expression. "Would you care for some coffee or tea?"

"Tea would be lovely. A touch of cream," the Grand Duchess stated, turned her back to Theo and, addressing the other women at the frame, said, "Isn't it nice to have staff?"

As Theo headed toward the kitchenette, she could swear she heard the sound of coffee blowing through someone's nose. She hoped it wasn't spraying onto the quilt.

As she was preparing the Grand Duchess's tea, Eunice came up behind Theo. She spoke softly. "I'm glad Jenny has so many cheerful people around her today. Thank you for the distraction."

"Why today?" Theo ran several possibilities through her brain but didn't come up with anything.

Eunice lowered her voice. "It's been twenty years today since Jenny's daughter died."

"Oh, my. I liked Shannon. We were in high school together." Theo felt both surprise and sadness. "It doesn't seem possible that twenty years have passed since her accident."

"I know," Eunice agreed. "Each year time seems to speed by faster than the previous one. Now it seems like I get the Christmas tree taken down only a few days before it's time to put it back up. Mine's artificial, so I'm thinking of just leaving the thing up all year long."

"If we weren't already so crowded in our house, I might consider it as well." Theo tried to imagine where they would leave a tree inside for an extended period of time. It was impossible. At Christmas, they had to rearrange all of the furniture in their living area, even relegating some of it to the garage. Not only was space a problem, but the whole family preferred the smell of a small, fresh tree. If they left the fresh tree in place, Theo guessed they wouldn't make it through January without having every needle fall onto the floor.

"Oh, waitress." The dulcet tones of the Grand Duchess carried across the room. "Where is my tea?"

Theo heard her speaking in a slightly softer tone, addressing Jenny. "She's not very efficient, is she?" A theatrical sigh followed. "Good staff is so hard to find these days."

Theo delivered the tea, with no apology, and was amused that the Grand Duchess gave her a coin for a tip. When she looked at it, though, she gasped. Gleaming in the palm of her hand was a United States one-dollar gold coin dated 1863. Theo was stunned. A coin from the middle of the Civil War? When she tried to return it to the older woman, her efforts were rebuffed. The coin felt warm in her hand. Since Theo actually knew nothing about the Grand Duchess, she thought she might ask Tony for his help getting the coin returned to some other member of the family.

If the woman was swimming in money, it wasn't apparent to

anyone looking at her. She was clean, but her poorly-dyed magenta hair needed touching up, and her clothing was straight from a discount store. On the other hand, Theo had seen the enormous antique Rolls Royce and suspected it would be worth more than their house and her car and the shop all put together.

Tony studied the small coin Theo had handed to him. She had been so curious about it, she'd walked over to the Law Enforcement Center, clutching the coin in her hand.

"Wouldn't you expect rubles or francs from the Grand Duchess instead of Civil War gold?" He was sure his grin wouldn't fool anyone. Tony was seriously interested in how and when and why their small county had acquired the woman and now her gold. The chauffeur who had stopped by Tony's office when he was searching for the woman had been only superficially informative. They did not know where she lived or where she was staying while visiting Park County.

Tony felt torn. He couldn't use simple curiosity as an excuse to ask people personal questions. He learned nothing except the Grand Duchess seemed quite pleased with the gentleman and, by extension, his ability to drive a car that looked as long as a school bus.

Neither of them had broken any law Tony knew of, and he left them to their privacy. He had never expected them, together or separately, to remain in Silersville for more than a day. It was quite a feat for them to arrive, apparently reside, interact with others and maintain close to total secrecy and anonymity for several days now. Maybe the royal family had local connections. If so, they were carefully staying off the radar and not in any of the local motels.

"I can't keep the gold." Theo frowned at him. "All I did was deliver a cup of hot water and a tea bag to her."

"I wouldn't think you could, at least not without our

determining she has ownership of it—as well as all her faculties." Tony didn't like the idea of the woman potentially becoming the victim of some ne'er do well who would fleece her out of her precious coins. "Did she mention where she lives, where they came from?"

Theo shook her head. "You know more about her than I do. She just appeared, with lots of attitude, in my shop the other day. She uses her title, not her name. As far as I know she hasn't told anyone where her home is, but we all know she has staff instead of family. The gentleman always escorts her to the shop and returns later for her. He doesn't share his own name."

"I know that much. His name is Tom Richards, and you're right. We met and had a short chat. Is the Grand Duchess still in your shop?" When Theo nodded, Tony decided to accompany his wife and have a little conversation with the older women who gathered in the classroom.

He knew most of the ladies. Some he'd known for about thirty years, and some were newer. He thought he'd start with Eunice and Jenny. The pair of women loved to flirt with him. That was just fine. He liked them, too. Once they made it through the "when are you going to leave your wife and take up with a real woman" business, they settled in to answer his questions away from the quilt in progress. It didn't take long to learn they knew no more than Theo did about the Grand Duchess.

Eunice frowned. "It's hard to imagine a non-quilter arriving in town and just happening to find the gathering at the shop. Someone must have suggested she join us."

"She's very dramatic," Jenny added. "But other than treating your wife like a serf, she doesn't talk much. She has lots of attitude and drinks tea, but she doesn't ask us about ourselves and she doesn't say anything about her personal life."

Theo joined in. She waved a hand to indicate the whole shop.

"The Grand Duchess doesn't even look around. The ladies who don't quilt and who come in for visiting usually at least admire the activity or the new quilts."

"Send Wade in to sit with them." Eunice laughed. "I'll bet she talks to him."

It was pretty much what Tony was thinking himself. He joined his deputy on the sidewalk and outlined the business with the coin and the woman's mysterious arrival and lack of sharing. "At least see if you can determine if she's in town voluntarily."

Tony watched as Wade found a seat at the quilt frame. It wasn't easy. Between the size of the group and the bulk of his duty belt, Wade finally managed to wedge himself between the two tiniest women. He picked up a freshly threaded needle someone had left behind. "You ladies don't mind if I add a few stitches?"

No one objected. Wade pushed the point of the needle into the fabric and pulled gently, popping the knot between the layers. The quilters nodded their approval of his technique. He took some more stitches, then paused and gave the Grand Duchess his best smile. "I don't believe I've met you."

The Grand Duchess agreed that they had not and favored him with a pleasant smile. She stared, evidently surprised to see a man at the frame. The group chatted for a while and Wade continued stitching. When he finished the length of thread he used, he excused himself and left.

Theo and Tony met him in the main room of the shop.

"Nothing, as I'm sure you heard." Wade hitched one shoulder and said to Tony, "Very pleasant. Very closemouthed about herself. The only thing I actually determined was a total lack of interest on her part in quilting. I don't think even your wife will be able to convert her."

"And you?" Tony knew Wade was an excellent quilter. Theo had shared that much information. "Did she convert you?"

"Nope. My grandmother always said I could run wild all day but needed something calming or I'd become unbalanced." Wade grinned. "I don't sew, but I do enjoy hand quilting from time to time."

"Let's lock up this little gem." Tony opened his hand to display the antique coin. "I'd really like to know where she got it."

Tony had been requested by Mrs. Violet Flowers Blake, the manager of their senior center, to drop by for a few moments. When he arrived, Violet was deep in conversation with one of four elderly men seated at a table near the window. The man listening to her words was shuffling cards. An unfamiliar red-haired boy about Chris's age, twelve, stood nearby watching all of them.

Tony thought the old man looked like an aging Caesar Romero with silver hair, his dark eyes sparkling with ageless mischief. His hair was quite thick and waved back away from his forehead. Using the sour grapes approach to life, Tony tried, but couldn't quite convince himself that the caring for such a coiffure would be worth the time it would necessitate. He was lying. He tried to imagine himself with hair. And failed.

A glance at the old man's hands made Tony regret his moment of envy. The fingers on the right hand were deformed as if a heavy weight had flattened them. The left hand had a thumb and pinkie finger only. Whatever had caused the problems with his hands did not prevent him from shuffling playing cards and dealing them to his companions. Standing next to the old man, the red-haired boy with freckles was wearing oversized work gloves and apparently studying the rules of the game. The boy nodded several times in response to something Violet was telling him.

The other three gentlemen seated at the table seemed much

frailer than the dealer, but they were all laughing as they played their cards. Scattered at nearby tables, Tony saw probably twenty older women watching the men. Like hungry predators, the women studied every move each man made and listened to every syllable they uttered.

Violet made her way to Tony's side. "As you can see, Sheriff, we have many more women than gentlemen. We welcome everyone, but sometimes the gentlemen have to be *encouraged* to come in. Rather firmly." Violet whispered, "As you go through the county, if you find any eligible men—of certain age, of course—would you please send them here?"

Tony promised to do what he could but no more than that. He wasn't going to deliver anyone to the senior center against his will. He'd seen sharks attack a bait fish. It hadn't been pretty. He doubted the women would rip a new man apart, but he wasn't totally sure. They looked hungry.

Chapter Nine

"Theo? This is Helen, down at the water department. I have you listed as the emergency contact for Nina Crisp."

"Oh, no. Has she been in an accident?" Theo had been thinking hard about something else and only really absorbed one word other than her best friend's name. "Emergency." It made her almost stop breathing. The idea of something happening to her best friend was difficult to process. Then her brain caught up. Why on earth would someone from the water department contact her about an accident?

Helen's voice held a note of asperity. "How would I know? I assume she's fine. What I'm calling about is she has you listed as the person I'm supposed to call if there's a problem with the utilities at her house."

Theo was relieved that nothing had happened to her friend. "Wait a minute. What's the problem at her house?"

"Water."

Helen, Theo knew, had never been notable for her long-winded conversations. But even for her this was ridiculous. "What about the water at Nina's house?"

"Oh, I didn't explain, did I? Well, it seems there is water running from under the front door and down the sidewalk. The mail carrier noticed it and notified us. I've been trying to call Nina. I couldn't get hold of her, so now I'm telling you."

Theo guessed that was the longest string of words Helen had ever put together. Theo tried to visualize the situation. "Nina's out of town. I'll go over there and see what's going on."

"Call me when you get there and let me know what you need." Helen coughed. "If you can't find the valve to turn off the water, I'll send someone out to help. At least she's using water from our system and not a well."

The statement didn't make any sense at all to Theo but she said, "Thank you," automatically. Helen disconnected and Theo picked up her purse and looked over at the twins in their play area. Maybelle wasn't expected for another hour. They would have to go with her. Thinking it would just be a quick trip out to Nina's house to check things out, Theo picked up the toddlers and staggered down the stairs, carrying both of them. She vowed the girls needed to learn to do stairs a bit faster on their own. They could do it crawling, but even snails could beat them in a race. As Theo left the shop, she told Gretchen where she was going.

Nina's much newer and more modern home than Theo's own sat on a several-acre wooded lot outside of town. It was part of the land that had been in her family for generations. Impossible to farm, it was a beautiful residential area now. Nina's house, unlike Theo's simple two-story home, was built in tiers, involving several short staircases.

It was designed to capture the beautiful mountain views and it did. Huge windows framed the Smoky Mountains on one side and the woods on another. Although there were other homes in the subdivision, they were not near neighbors.

When Theo reached Nina's house, she released the twins from their car seats and, carrying them, headed for the front steps. Although she'd been warned, the amount of water she saw was shocking. Water cascaded under the front door, down the steps and poured into a flowerbed. The narrow flowerbed resembled a lake. The overflow continued onto the lawn, moving downhill. It hit a few rocks and turned into a small waterfall.

Theo stared in disbelief. There was so much water. Where could it be coming from?

Almost blinded by tiny fingerprints on her lenses that she couldn't wipe away with her arms full, Theo headed toward the back door. She set the twins down on the large flagstone patio. Thankfully, there was no water out here. Hoping that was a good sign, Theo felt slightly relieved. Using her key, she let herself into the mudroom. The burglar alarm near the door beeped its warning and Theo punched in the alarm code to disarm it. It worked and she sighed.

Seconds later, all sense of relief vanished as she paused just inside the mudroom door. In the silence of the empty house, Theo could hear the sound of water splashing on the kitchen floor on the other side of the second door. She gathered her girls up again and, juggling them, she turned the knob and opening the door a little, she peeked into the kitchen.

Even half expecting what she'd find, she gasped. The throw rug in front of the sink was covered by at least two inches of water. It wasn't exactly floating, but it was shifting back and forth, pushed by the current. Water cascaded from the kitchen ceiling, pouring out of recessed light fixtures, and then, like a slow moving river, it moved toward the front of the house. More water dripped through the seams between pieces of the sheetrock ceiling. A strip of drywall tape dangled in the center of the room. The pendent lamp that should hang near the ceiling sagged so low it nearly touched the island. More, normally hidden, electric wires hung from a hole in the ceiling and were dangling into the water on the floor. A giant water-filled bubble was trapped under the surface of the paint on one wall.

Theo recognized a small blue and white teacup bobbing on the surface of the water next to a plastic bag containing twist ties. The teacup was Nina's souvenir from a trip to England. The last time Theo had seen it, the cup had been on a small shelf over the kitchen sink. The shelf was empty now and although some water was vanishing down the sink, most was pouring from the ceiling directly onto the floor.

Lizzie, the busier of the two girls, struggled to get down. She pulled hard on Theo's hair. Even Kara had had enough arm time and was ready to roll. They began to protest in earnest.

Concerned about the little girls' safety and not willing to step into the water and possibly electrocute her own self, Theo was cautious as she tried to determine what might have happened. She carried the girls back to her car, fastened them into their seats, and pulled out her phone. She lowered the SUV's windows enough to supply them with fresh air.

Theo tried to envision the location of the shut-off valve in her head. She had spent lots of time at Nina's house. Why couldn't she remember where the water shut-off valve might be? Standing outside and leaning against the car, Theo stared at the house even as she called Helen. "I'm not sure where the valve is. How can I shut the water off?"

Helen said, "I'll send someone out. Can you tell what happened?"

"Not really. The water seems to be coming from upstairs. With the power on, I can't get up there but I do know there's a second hot-water heater just for the master bedroom. Nina has one of those big whirlpool tubs and it holds gallons." Theo had been jealous. The idea of lounging in a whirlpool after a long day of work and motherhood had sounded exotic. It wasn't as appealing at this moment.

Chapter Ten

The water department guys, as Theo thought of them, arrived in short order. They uncovered a valve near the road and turned off all the water to the property. Once the water stopped pouring over the porch, they came over to talk to Theo. They even managed to look cheerful.

"Wow! What happened?" The taller member of the crew, whose name escaped Theo at the moment, stared at the house.

Since Theo didn't have an answer, she merely shrugged and shook her head. "Now what do I do?" She hadn't meant to speak out loud so she was startled to hear an answer.

"That water had better be sucked out pronto or she's going to have a mold and mildew farm." Casey, the senior member of the water crew, ran a hand over his crewcut brown hair.

Now that he mentioned it, Theo remembered hearing an advertisement for a company that did just that. "You think I should call in the professionals?"

"Yeah, I would." Casey made a sweeping motion with his arm. "Insurance companies would rather pay for water removal than deal with long-term problems. You know how mold is: once it starts growing, it's hard to stop." The words were barely out of his mouth when his pager went off. "Oops, come on, Frank, got another call."

Wondering how she had ever lived without one, Theo pulled her cell phone out of her purse and dialed Nina's number. Her call went right to voicemail. Theo hung up without speaking. It didn't seem like the kind of event you should hear on a recorded message.

In the backseat, the twins suddenly seemed as upset as Theo herself and started howling. Theo felt like joining them. "Calm down, girls, we're going back to town."

Theo hurried back into her shop and gave thanks when she found Maybelle there waiting to take charge of the twins. Theo wasn't sure when she had been so happy to see the babysitting angel. Theo handed off the babies and hurried upstairs to her office.

Theo tried again to get hold of Nina. She failed. Desperate, she looked up the number for the flood abatement company and called for help.

After she went through the entire explanation of what she knew and who she was and who she wasn't, a voice assured her a crew would arrive in just a couple of hours and would call her when they were approaching Silersville.

Theo promised to meet them at Nina's house with the keys. While she waited, she worked on her paperwork for a while and then looked for inspiration about what special thing she could do for the shop-hopping people who would arrive in a few days. In comparison to the damage to her friend's house, the event sounded trivial. Although, in all honesty, it wasn't. Theo needed the additional business the shop hop would bring.

Every few minutes, she paused to redial Nina's number. Still no answer.

Buried in the paperwork she had forced herself to concentrate on, it seemed like only moments had passed and she had barely gotten back to the office when she received the call from the restoration crew. She imagined they must have broken some speed limits along the way. Theo promised she would pay their fine if they received a speeding ticket.

On her way out the door, she told Gretchen and Maybelle where she was going and that she had no idea when she would be back. She promised Maybelle a nice bonus if she would stay with the little girls, pick up the boys from school and keep all the children in order until she could return. Theo left a message for Tony letting him know about the same things.

Upon her return to Nina's home, Theo was relieved to see that now with the water shut off, not only was water no longer pouring down the front steps, but the steps themselves were drying in the sunlight. It wasn't much but it was some improvement. She sat on the top step to wait.

From her perch, Theo glanced down into the flowerbed on her right and noticed a large wooden square. It was almost the same color as the dirt around it. After a moment's puzzlement, she remembered the old storm shelter. The door, actually more of a hatch, covered the ladder down into it. It had been right in the path the water had taken. There was no lock and no need for one, because it did not open into the house. Theo trotted down the steps and over to it. Grasping the iron ring, she pulled, hoping she'd be able to lift the cover far enough for her to check for water. As heavy as the wooden cover was, the hinges were in good shape, and it was surprisingly easy for her to open.

The old storm shelter was completely filled with water. She couldn't see past the surface of the water because of the darkness, but she could smell water and something more disturbing. Something vile. She expected to see the bloated body of some small animal floating on the surface.

Theo released the door, letting the cover fall away from her and lean against the wall, exposing the water. Hearing a vehicle, she turned to see two members of the restoration crew had arrived. They climbed out of a truck with a large tank instead of a bed. Two more people got out of a heavy-duty pickup. In all, there were four workers. The crew boss, a young woman carrying a clipboard, met Theo at the porch. "I'm Kathy. Have you been able to reach your friend?"

"No. I'm still trying."

"Well, I'm sorry, but my boss doesn't usually let us start a job without the homeowner's signature, you know, unless we can at least talk with them."

After trying to contact Nina once more on her cell phone, Theo was undeterred. "I'll pay for it if her insurance won't."

Kathy spoke to her boss on the phone, relaying Theo's determination. When permission had been granted, she handed Theo a sheaf of papers to sign and asked for her to write a deposit check. Theo did everything she was asked to do, hoping Nina's insurance would pay. Even as Theo was dealing with the woman and the paperwork, two young men headed around the side of the house, toward the back door and into the flooded kitchen. By the time Theo reached them, they had already started a vacuum with large hoses connected to the tank on the truck and begun sucking the water from the floor. Obviously seeing her confusion, one of the young men explained, "We will pull the water out and put it into the tank instead of sending it into the sewer. We show them how much water did not go through the system. That way, if there is a charge for sewage, it will save your friend a lot of money."

Theo considered it a brilliant idea.

While those two were vacuuming up water, the third man began hauling furniture and every manner of household items found in the wet zone out of the house. Soggy things that had been on the floor or under the cascade were placed on the grass. If they were dry, he moved them into the empty garage.

They cranked up the heat in the house to the warmest temperature and left the doors open.

Understanding the need to dry everything as quickly as possible, Theo still couldn't help but wonder if it would save Nina enough to pay for heating a goodly portion of a snow-covered mountain.

Feeling absolutely helpless, Theo watched the steady parade of things belonging to Nina and her children leaving the house. Even Nina's fuzzy pink slippers dripped as they were carried outside. A couple of cardboard boxes, wet from the bottom up, caught her eye. She recognized treasure.

"Leave those with me. I can work on them and maybe save a few things." Framed photographs and loose pictures, as well as drawings and school projects made by Nina's children, filled the boxes that had been neatly stored on a closet floor. They should have been safe but were soaking up water like a sponge. Theo felt like crying but there wasn't time. Even as she began carefully separating the papers so they could dry, one of the crew members was asking if there was electricity in the old storm shelter by the front steps.

"I don't think so. But I've never actually been down there." Theo ran through her memories. "Before this house was built, a ramshackle old house sat on this spot. When this house was built, Nina wanted the view and thought the old storm cellar would be useful in case of a tornado, so it was left as part of the flowerbed."

"Okay, we'll start removing the water from it. It looks like that's where most of it headed once it got outside. Only after it was full did water overflow and head downhill."

Theo nodded, agreeing that was her thought, and then was distracted by the big blue dehumidifier machine on wheels that was being set up in the living room. There was another one in the kitchen. An array of heavy duty fans had already been turned on. The sound level was intense with all of the machines running at once. Theo was tempted to look at the electricity dial on the outside of the house to see if it was spinning like something in a cartoon.

Kathy, the crew's supervisor, was busy drawing diagrams of the rooms and making detailed notes, writing down the identification number and location of each piece of equipment. Also on the notes were notations of the moisture level in baseboards and walls. One of the tools Kathy used looked like an odd-shaped barbecue fork, but it was not for food or fun. As the technician punched it into the wall to check the moisture level, she wrote down the location and a number.

Theo was fascinated by the process and looked to see what Kathy was writing. Most of the numbers ranged from forty to eighty. "What's normal?"

"Ten."

"Oh, no, that sounds terrible." From the little spot where Theo sat, picked because it appeared to be out of the way of the workers and yet near enough to allow her to answer their questions, Theo could see the light fixtures and parts of the ceiling being taken down in the kitchen and family room. The soggy drywall crumbled as they handled it. In seconds there was a pile of wet rubble on a plastic sheet spread over Nina's beautiful wooden floor. Trying to remind herself that these were only things and Nina and her children were safe, Theo carefully peeled another wet photograph off the glass in a frame and found it a place where she could leave it to dry. She tried to contact Nina for maybe the nine hundredth time. Still nothing.

A couple of minutes later, the technician working outside in the storm shelter trotted back into the house, looking pale beneath his beard. "We've got a real problem. There's something terrible down there."

Theo didn't doubt that. She would be surprised if a storm shelter filled with water wasn't terrible, especially the way it had smelled. Her thoughts were confused and disorganized and she was momentarily distracted by seeing Nina's carpet and rugs being pulled off the floors and hauled outside and placed on the lawn. Water ran from them, headed downhill, crossing the driveway. She couldn't imagine how many gallons of water cascaded away. Even the dog's bed was a soggy mess.

Kathy was fussing about what they were going to have to do to save the hardwood floors. Evidently it required a different treatment than the carpeted areas.

"A real problem?" Theo's question was for the bearded technician. She was getting a headache, probably from having her teeth clenched for so long. Like the rest of this mess was not a real problem? In whose world? "Okay, what's the real problem? Is more water coming in from somewhere else? I thought it was all shut off."

"No, ma'am." The technician swallowed hard and waved his long-fingered hands as if he were warding off something terrible. "There's a dead man down there."

"Like a burglar?" Theo's brain wasn't taking in the whole scenario. Maybe if she could turn off a couple of the fans, she'd be able to think.

The technician looked at Theo. His expression said that she was the nuttiest person he had ever talked to, and he wasn't sure if she was crazier than she was stupid. "What do they look like?"

"Who?" Theo couldn't seem to follow the conversation. She was still thinking about the disaster inside the house. "Who looks like what?"

"Burglars." The technician snapped.

Something clicked in her head. "Uh, oh. I think you better show me." Now Theo's brain was paying complete attention. She followed him outside and reached for her cell phone even as the technician pointed down into the water exposed by the lifted hatch. Sunlight illuminated the interior. Theo was impressed. The powerful pumps had already removed at least a foot of water from the hole since the first time she'd looked in there. Now she could clearly see the body of a man, face up in muddy water. Very dead.

Worse than just dead. She knew this man, and hadn't liked him. Nina's ex-husband, Daniel.

Theo called Tony.

In some previous episodes, Tony had congratulated himself on being able to find some amusement, although not much, in situations involving his wife. This was not one of them. As he approached Nina's house, his breath was not taken away by the magnificent view, as it normally was. Instead, he was struck by Theo's strained expression and great rolling tears dripping from her chin. His wife rarely cried. He wasn't even sure she realized she was crying now. Jaw clenched, he parked the Blazer.

Wade parked his vehicle right next to his. It was unlikely any evidence that might exist on the lawn had not already been trampled by the cleanup crew. But they carefully watched the ground they traveled anyway.

He could hear the cleanup crew fussing at Theo because she had told them to stop what they were doing and to wait for him. Easily the smallest of the five people standing on the front porch, Theo held her ground.

Tony called out. "Leave her alone. She's right." Five heads turned in his direction, surprised expressions on four of them.

Theo started trotting toward him, wiping her streaming eyes with her bare hand. She held her glasses in her left hand and mopped with the right. Before she reached him, she veered and went back toward the open hatch, clearly expecting him to follow her. She did not look down into the hole.

Quickly reaching her side, Tony did look down. Even more unpleasant dead than he had been alive, there was no question of the man's identity. Daniel had been a handsome man. He was not now. "Wade, call Doc Nash."

A few seconds later he heard Wade begin talking to the doctor, and then Wade's normal reaction to a dead body, the sound of his lunch coming up and landing in a shrub. From Wade's small phone, Tony could also hear sounds indicating their coroner was not a happy man.

Tony led his wife away from the site and handed her his handkerchief. He stood facing the house, forcing her to stand with her back to it. "Have you been able to reach Nina?"

"No. I've called about a hundred thousand times." Theo's curls bounced as she shook her head and wiped the tears from her cheeks. "Just a few minutes ago I finally left a message for her to call me right away. And that was *seconds before* the technician found *him.*"

Tony needed to know if Nina had expected her ex-husband to be at the house or not. Since abandoning his family for an Internet cutie, the man had shown up from time to time, mostly to visit his children. The cutie had been replaced several times. Tony knew the children were with Nina. He looked away from the bobbing corpse and back to his wife. "When was the last time you saw him?"

"You mean alive?" Theo returned the handkerchief.

Knowing that Theo's sassy attitude was a shield to cover her distress, he nodded and shoved the soggy piece of fabric into his pocket.

Theo took a deep breath and held it for a moment. She exhaled sharply. "Last week. From my office window, I saw him parked in front of the Coffee Bean. There was a curvy blond woman with him. She seemed overly affectionate and underdressed for the weather. It was snowing."

Tony didn't ask if she knew the woman. He could tell from her expression that she did not. "Did he see you?"

"Oh, yes." Theo's eyes flashed. "He waved up at me and leaned over to kiss his new girlfriend, almost like he'd been waiting for me to look out the window. I didn't mention it to Nina."

"Do you know where he's living now?" As soon as the words were out, Tony realized the stupidity of the question. "I mean until now."

Theo did smile at his statement. "Well, the last I knew, and believe me, it's not a subject Nina and I discuss very often, he was living somewhere in the Chattanooga area."

"Doing what?" Tony stared over Theo's shoulder at the corpse's exposed head. Not a pretty sight.

"I think he was selling television satellite dishes or something like that." Theo shrugged.

Tony had not liked Nina's ex-husband any more than Theo had. The man was a classic snake-oil salesman. He could sell ice in Antarctica. Mostly, though, Tony didn't like him because of Theo's descriptions of his bad behavior and treatment of Nina.

Their conversation was curtailed by the arrival of Doc Nash. The unhappy physician, also the county coroner, trudged across the lawn carrying his case. He'd arrived in record time. Tony was relieved they at least hadn't rushed him away from a patient. The doctor's eyes narrowed as he glanced from face to face, settling on Tony's. "Where is he?"

Tony tipped his head toward the open hatch. Wade stood above it, his camera clicking steadily.

"Tell me you're kidding." The doctor started complaining the moment his shoes got wet on the soggy, dead winter grass. His diatribe got worse as he got closer to the hatch and encountered some slippery mud. "Someone could have told me I would need hip waders."

No one made a comment.

Doc Nash finally stopped and stared down into the water. "Well there's certainly no question about his being dead." After putting on his gloves, he reached down and touched the body, moving it slightly. He ignored the sound of cameras. It wasn't the first time he'd been called out to examine a suspiciously located dead body. "I can't tell you anything else until we fish him out of here."

Tony glanced at the faces surrounding the hatch. No one was making eye contact with him. No one, himself included, wanted anything to do with this. Wrestling a lifeless body out of a fairly narrow, water-filled hole was not going to be easy. "Maybe we could have more water sucked out before we try to move him."

Wade studied the business end of the vacuum tubing. "Maybe we could fasten a screen of some kind over the nozzle so only water would travel down the tube."

"A brilliant idea." Tony thought the plan would allow them to lower the water level and perhaps keep any potential evidence from vanishing into the tank. Without the water, they would be able to simply lift the body out. As it turned out, the vacuum's operator had the perfect attachment. It was already in use.

The powerful vacuum lowered the water level amazingly fast. The storm cellar itself was maybe six feet deep and the corners were roundish like it was shaped by the curve of a shovel. The hole was wider than the opening, beginning up against the house's foundation and extending out about six feet. As the water level lowered, Tony could see that, other than the body and a wooden ladder, there was not much inside. It was crudely constructed, as was the wooden frame that supported it. Above the hole, the flowerbed was shallow and muddy water dripped through the spaces between boards in the wooden ceiling. A narrow bench ran along the longest wall. It was not designed to be the party room. Safety in a storm.

The door, really more of a hatch cover, was a solid wooden square. The outside surface was made of six-inch-wide boards. They were at least two inches thick. The interior cross boards were two-by-fours. The cover was heavy for its size. A large iron ring on top was for lifting it open. Inside, there was a heavy iron bolt so it could be latched from the inside only. The heavy-duty hinges were oiled, and appeared fairly new. Although awkward, he knew from Theo's description how easy it was to open.

If Daniel had been alive when the hatch closed, there should have been no problem with his opening it, or climbing out.

The restoration crew was busy complaining about the door's construction and the probability of wood swelling because of the dampness. Salvaging it might be difficult. Eventually the water level dropped far enough so Tony and Wade decided they'd be able to lift the remains out of the hole. The corpse smelled worse than vile and Wade threw up again. Tony fought hard not to join in.

By the time Tony and Wade managed to pull Nina's ex-husband from his watery location, Tony was not only soaked to the skin but thoroughly confused. He had no idea if the man had been dead or alive when he hit the water, or if indeed there had been water in the hole at that time. Doc Nash, however, had seemed confident that he would be able to perform the autopsy. Tony considered this good news. It would mean a shorter wait before they leaned about the cause of death. The doctor was a busy man, but now with Dr. Grace Claybough involved in his practice, at least he was less frazzled.

According to Theo, one time when the subject of her friend's ex-husband had come up in a conversation with Nina, she had confided that Daniel had always believed that Nina and her family had a cache of money hidden from him. There was none. Or, if there was one, it was hidden from her as well. Tony wondered if Daniel had been searching for imaginary money down in the shelter.

Not only was Nina Ledbetter Crisp his wife's dearest friend, but Tony knew the two women and Daniel from high school. Nina had married her high-school sweetheart. Daniel Crisp had been in Tony's graduating class, two years ahead of their wives. The problem was that Daniel had never been a good man. He was what Tony thought of as a "sort of" guy. Not vicious. Not stupid. Not smart. Sort of pleasant and more than sort of lazy. Tony guessed the marriage had failed, several years and two children into it, because Daniel just "sort of" lost interest in Nina. And about the same time, he sort of discovered other women more appealing.

Daniel's job history was sprinkled with a variety of fairly short-term employments. He'd worked in retail at both the Food City and at the hardware store. He'd gotten his insurance license, but hadn't put enough effort into it to earn a living wage. Daniel didn't like jobs where his hands might get dirty, which ruled out farming, construction, mechanics and a host of other job opportunities, especially in Silersville. Shiftless, but charming. If he applied himself, Tony guessed the recent job resume of selling television dishes to farmers might be right up the dead man's alley. So to speak.

"Not the freshest body you've invited me to examine." The statement might have sounded as if the doctor intended to insert a little levity into the grim proceeding. It wasn't. Doc Nash wasn't smiling, and he was busy dictating notes into his phone.

They finally wrestled Daniel onto an open body bag and zipped him in. "Whew," Tony exhaled sharply. "I wonder how long he's been down there."

No one said anything. The ambulance had arrived during the extraction, and the paramedics had wheeled a stretcher close to them.

"Okay, Doctor, do you still want to do the autopsy?" Tony studied the man's face and guessed he knew the answer.

"Hell, no." Doc Nash peeled the latex gloves from his hands. "I changed my mind. Send him to Knoxville. I'll let the more professional professionals determine the cause and time of death. Even if I wanted to, I don't have the necessary equipment to delve into the truth of this matter."

"Fair enough." Tony made a couple of calls. Then he placed a seal on the body bag. After he signed for it, the ambulance crew carted Daniel away. "The TBI will be here as soon as they can. I should have called before we removed the body, but my first thought was it had to be an accident. Now, I'm not so sure."

Soaked from the extraction and wallowing in icy mud, Tony stayed outside. He stank to high heaven and didn't feel like adding more dirt to the mess in Nina's home, much less add in the smell of rotting flesh. Seeing Theo shiver outside near the porch even though it was much warmer in the house, he frowned. Her big, green-gold hazel eyes looked empty staring at the hole. "Go home, sweetheart."

Theo looked up, meeting his eyes. "No."

Tony would have guessed she would jump at the chance to leave. This was not a good place to be. "Why not?"

"I have to stay here." Theo flapped her hands indicating the restoration team. "Either until Nina gets here or until these people go home. I'm responsible."

Tony recognized her implacable expression and nodded. "Will you at least go inside where the heat's turned up to bake? Your shivering is making me cold."

She did smile then. "Good advice." She left him, and trotted around the side of the house, clearly headed back to the kitchen.

With Theo and the body gone, Tony couldn't help but notice some of the things that weren't nearby that he would expect to see. Most outstanding was the lack of any kind of vehicle. How had Daniel gotten out here? It wouldn't be impossible to walk out to Nina's house from town, but why would he? And if he came out with his girlfriend or another driver, where was this person now? Was the girlfriend involved with Daniel's death? Tony was anxious to know the cause of death. Did he drown?

Was he already dead when the hatch was closed?

"Sheriff?" said Wade. "What do you think could have happened?"

Tony shook his head and tried to push away his thoughts but failed. Most importantly, Tony needed to know if Daniel was already dead when Nina left for Washington, D.C. He called Ruth Ann. "I need the phone number for the school principal."

Tony contacted the school principal. "Sheriff Abernathy here. I'm calling to see if you have a contact number for Nina Crisp?"

"Just her cell phone." Surprise and curiosity threaded through the answer.

"I've tried that. It's been turned off."

"Well, I expect them to be getting back to the school at any time now. She called earlier to let us know she, Mrs. Clubb, and the field trip kids were on their way back. They're supposed to be here in time for dinner with their families, and no one has called to change that." A tinge of distress crept into the man's voice, replacing the curiosity. "Is there something I should know? Should I have her call you?"

"Thank you, but I'd appreciate it if you would call me. It has nothing to do with your students, but I have some news best given in person. Call the main number, not nine-one-one, and give them the message."

When Tony finished his call, he saw Doc Nash still standing at the front of the house, staring down into the storm shelter. The man looked like he was working on a puzzle. "Do we know when the water filled the hole?" Doc looked at Tony. "Until the autopsy, we have no way of knowing if he drowned or fell in and broke his neck, or if he was dead before he got wet."

Tony thanked the doctor for giving them an easy answer to solving at least part of the timing mystery. Any information would help him decide if he needed to close the area as a crime scene or not. Carrying a small bag containing an emergency change of clothes and hoping to remove some of the stench, he walked around the outside to the kitchen. There he found Theo sitting on her perch, spreading personal papers and pictures out to dry on the counters. "Did you call the plumber?"

Theo shook her head. "The county came out and turned off the water. The postman knew there was flooding. I didn't even think about calling in a plumber. I was interested in having less water, at least until now. No water means no plumbing, and I really need a bathroom. I do know Nina has used DuWayne's plumbing services in the past." She grabbed her keys. "I'm going down to Kwik Kirk's before I embarrass all of us. Keep an eye on things."

Tony nodded his understanding and called DuWayne Cozzens on the phone. "Would you come out to Nina Crisp's home and see if you can tell what caused the water to destroy so much and about how long ago it might have started?"

DuWayne agreed to make it his first priority. Well, second. He'd drive up right after he reassembled Mrs. Purdy's toilet. "First things first, you know."

"I believe we can wait that long." As he unbuttoned his shirt, Tony was impatient but realistic. He'd lived around women most of his life. There wasn't a single one of them who was forgiving of a non-functioning toilet.

Chapter Eleven

Vince from the Tennessee Bureau of Investigation took Tony's call. "Don't tell me, Sheriff, but let me guess. Someone has perished in your fair county, and other than wringing your pasty little hands together; you can't decide what to do next."

Tony admired Vince for his ability to find minute evidence and his ability to inject a bit of humor into an otherwise grim situation. "True, so true. You up for a little evidence collection, on a case that's maybe an accident and maybe something more serious?"

"Body still there?"

"No." Tony knew he couldn't shove it back into the hole and refill it with the water from the tanker. "It's headed to Knoxville, but I've got all of the water neatly packaged in a tanker truck."

"No way."

"Oh, yeah." Tony laughed. "You'll love it. The body was found in a storm shelter during a flooding situation. We think the water problem was caused by a water heater leak. The body is definitely the ex-husband of the homeowner. She's out of town, and our body is not super fresh. After hauling him out, I had to change my clothes."

"Okay. I'm hooked." Vince began humming the tune for a game show finale. "I'll be there with some guys in maybe a couple of hours. Can you keep that tanker? It might be interesting to do some tests, even though I'm sure the water wasn't spotless to begin with."

"Sure. How about the home's interior cleanup? You want me to stop it?"

"You have any reason to believe he was killed in the house?"

"Nope." Tony felt confident now. "The ex-wife had every lock changed and an alarm system installed when she threw him and his stuff out a couple of years ago. The alarm was not triggered, but frankly, I'm not sure the death wasn't an accident."

Vince sounded positively jovial. "Unless, the ex-wife killed him."

"I suppose it is possible." Tony leaned his forehead against the door frame. "Okay, I'll stop them doing anything besides running their fans."

"Maybe your handsome sidekick can check the alarm keypad for fingerprints and save some time, laddie." Vince mangled his attempt at a British accent.

"Laddie?" Tony waited until he'd disconnected to groan. As far as Tony knew, Sherlock Holmes never called Inspector Lestrade anything resembling "laddie." If Vince was having one of his Sherlock Holmes–impression days, this investigation could go on for a long, long time. Tony warned Wade and sent him on the fingerprint hunt.

When he explained the situation to the cleanup crew and gave permission for them to continue drying, but only the interior of the house, they were less than pleased. They had a procedure and he was messing with it.

Curious about the extent of the flooding, Tony climbed the stairs to the bedroom level of the house. The carpeted stairs crinkled under his feet because a type of plastic wrap had been spread across them to protect the carpet from messy foot traffic. In the small utility closet, water spread out from the upstairs water heater. He guessed the kitchen was directly below. Nothing else upstairs seemed wet.

He sat down on Theo's abandoned perch to wait. The sight of soggy pictures, coupled with the sound of a host of fans, dehydration machines and the pounding of dampness meters, gave him a headache in record time. He decided being wet and cold worked better for him and headed toward the front door, avoiding stepping on the hoses.

He arrived at the front of the house at the same time as the plumber. To Tony's limited knowledge, formed by the few plumbers he'd actually met, they came in tall and stocky, and small and muscular. DuWayne Cozzens was one of the second category. When DuWayne had installed a new hot-water heater in the Abernathy home, it had been like watching an ant carrying a hot-dog bun up the steps and into its tiny closet. Amazing.

"Sheriff?" DuWayne extended a hand. "How can I help?"

Tony gave the plumber a quick tour, including the water-damaged ceiling in the kitchen. He explained what DuWayne could and couldn't do before the TBI arrived. They stayed away from the storm shelter and Tony suggested the plumber use the kitchen door from now on. "There's a hot-water heater in there." Tony pointed to the utility area. "The one upstairs has to be the cause of the flooding."

"Thanks, Sheriff, but I know my way around the plumbing in this house." DuWayne led the way. "The one upstairs is a brand spanking new hot-water heater." All traces of humor vanished from his face. "It can't be over two months since I installed it." He grabbed his tool box and headed up the stairs at close to a dead run.

Feeling large and clumsy, like Frankenstein's monster, Tony followed, lumbering behind the more agile man. Much more slowly.

In the manner of all experts, what was hidden to an amateur was glaringly obvious to the professional. "This is a piece of trash. I've never had a problem with this brand before." Du-

Wayne tapped the cylinder with a fingertip. "There's no way this should have happened." He pulled a notebook from his tool box and wrote down the manufacturer and the model and a series of other numbers. Pulling out a wrench, he stopped water from flowing into the broken tank. "With this turned off, we can turn the rest of the water in the house back on."

Tony started to say something but heard light footsteps behind him. Theo was back.

"Miz Theo." DuWayne's eyes gleamed and he smiled. "Always a pleasure."

"Hi, DuWayne." Theo greeted the man warmly. "I'm glad you were able to come so quickly. What should I tell Nina?"

DuWayne's expression clouded. "You kin tell her this piece of junk was what has caused the flood."

"Any way to tell how long it's been leaking?" Tony rolled his shoulders, trying not to visualize the bobbing body.

"Nope. I did see a fair amount of runoff as I was driving up." DuWayne looked like he wanted to ask a question but held off. "The water department might be able to tell when she started using more water than usual. They should at least be able to narrow it down to their last reading. Wouldn't hurt to ask."

Tony looked at Wade, remembering the blond Theo had described. "While we're waiting for Vince and the gang, let's go find the girlfriend."

"Cherchez la femme!" Wade grinned. "I finally get to say it."

The blond bombshell was easy to spot. Almost as if she enjoyed being onstage, she sat at a table in the center of Ruby's Café, calmly reading a magazine and sipping a cup of coffee. When Tony and Wade approached her, she gave them a wide smile and leaned slightly forward, making it easier for them to enjoy her assets.

Not being particularly interested in her bosom, Tony kept his eyes on hers. "May we join you?"

The woman looked surprised, then waved them toward the empty chairs. "Sure, why not?" She stared openly at Wade.

Over the years, Tony had used Wade's exceptional good looks to his advantage. Women usually, but not always, and some men, stared openly at his deputy. Wade knowingly aided and abetted Tony's interview plans by drawing the focus away from questions. All it ever took was a smile to get someone's attention. Tony said, "I believe you came to Silersville with Daniel Crisp."

"Oh, yeah, sure." She kept her eyes trained on Wade.

Wade smiled again. "Would you please tell me your name and address?"

Staring back at him, she looked like she was going to melt. "Nancy Crisp. I live in Chattanooga."

"Do you know where we might find Daniel?" Tony asked, making himself a mental note of her answer. He wondered if she was a cousin. He knew Daniel had no sisters.

Her eyes flickered to Tony's face and back to her perusal of his deputy. "I kinda thought he would meet me here."

Tony believed she was telling the truth. She didn't seem to be aware of her Daniel's passing. He wasn't sure what to tell her. "Did you have plans to meet today?"

"Sorta." She looked bewildered. "He says Ruby's is the only place in this town with decent food so I figured he'd come here for lunch. He didn't, so I came back for pie and coffee."

There were a few other dining options in Silersville, but Tony had to admit preferring Ruby's Café to other restaurants like the Riverview. He thought he would try a different tactic. "Did you go out to his ex-wife's house with him?"

Nancy straightened and looked directly at him. "Oh, sure, a couple of days ago. He said he wanted to get something from his ex." She ran a finger over the handle on her coffee cup. An assortment of inexpensive rings sparkled on her hands, but none on her left ring finger. "I thought he was talking about getting money to buy a nice ring for me. You know, since we're married and all."

"Married?" Tony hadn't heard Daniel had remarried.

"Yes." Her wide smile creased her face into some unflattering wrinkles.

Thinking the woman was older than she looked at first, Tony delayed delivering the bad news until he learned a bit more. "He thought his ex-wife would give him money so he could buy *you* a ring?"

"I know. I told him it wouldn't work."

Wade was busy taking notes, but looked up frequently and smiled just to keep her focused on him. "What happened with the ring?"

"His ex-wife wasn't home. Then he started talking about the house and how nice it was and all, and how he'd like to look around for a while for old times' sake." Nancy's face took on a decidedly unhappy expression. "I got bored so I said for him to just walk back to town if he wanted to stay, and he could look around the place all he wanted. And then, he said he knew where he could get ahold of some money and would I wait for him while he went inside."

"And did he?" Amazed by her ability to deliver the whole jumbled statement while pausing for breath only once, Tony was jotting down more questions to ask Nina. Since Nancy claimed Daniel didn't have a key or the alarm code, what reason might Daniel have to think he could enter her house? Could he have been given the code to get inside, maybe by one of the children? Tony knew Nina's sophisticated alarm system had not gone off.

"No. He didn't get into the house, at least not while I was there. I sat on the porch until I got tired of waiting for him. He opened the lid to some dark hole by the front door and climbed down into it. I was not going in some place like that for nobody, so I left." With one bejeweled hand, she flipped her curly blond hair out of her face. The expression in her heavily mascaraed blue eyes reinforced her irritation. "I thought he was fun or I wouldn't have married him, but it was always promises, promises and no action."

"You weren't concerned when he didn't return to town?" Tony sighed. "Where were you staying?"

"Well, you see, I didn't have a room. When I left, I drove back to our place in Chattanooga. I figured he'd stay with one of his old friends. He does that a lot because of his travels. We hadn't planned on an overnight trip, and I needed to get home and feed my little angel." A genuine, delighted smile erased years from her face. "Here's her picture." She whipped out a spiffy new cell phone and started pushing buttons until a photograph of a black, white and brown teacup-sized dog smiled at them. "Taffy."

"Very nice." Wade spoke softly and smiled at Nancy. "I'll bet she was happy to see you. What time did you get there?"

Nancy laughed and showed them another picture of the dog. "Taffy was dancing and barking, running in circles, she was so excited. It was just exactly six o'clock. That's what time she eats."

"As Daniel's wife—" Tony paused and exhaled sharply. He rearranged his expression to one more somber than pleasant. "I'm afraid we need to give you some sad news."

Nancy's head tilted and she stared into his eyes. "Me?"

Tony thought they should break the news outside. The interior of a busy café was not his preferred location for a death notification. "Would you step outside with us for a moment?"

Reluctantly she led the way into the parking area and stopped by her car. "What's the matter?"

"It is our sad duty to notify you that your husband, Daniel Crisp, has died."

"No!" Nancy shook her head. "That's not possible."

Tony didn't have any particular reason to believe she wasn't surprised. He was sure she was lying about something. "Did you talk to him after you got home? You know, check in and let him know you got there safely?"

"No."

"Did you come back the next day to pick him up?"

"No."

"But you're here now, waiting for him?" Wade managed an expression verging on disappointment.

"Sort of."

"You drove away and left him with no transportation and no plan to return for him?" Tony was seeing a less than perfect marriage. He'd guess Daniel either had alternate travel plans or she really didn't care if he ever got home. "Was he already dead when you drove away?"

"Of course not."

Tony and Wade simply stood near her and waited.

Her lips turned down into a pout. "He was acting all funny ever since we drove into this one-horse town. Sometimes it was like he didn't want anybody to recognize him or he didn't want to be seen with me. Next thing, he'd act all different. I'd thought he'd be proud to introduce me to his friends." Real tears pooled in her eyes. "It hurt my feelings, so I left him alone up there so he'd miss me. He was standing on the front step looking in that hole instead of chasing me or even waving good-bye. Like he didn't care I was gone." She sniffed and wiped her streaming eyes with her fingers.

Theo sat alone in Nina's house. The restoration squad had departed for the night, leaving the heat cranked up warm enough to bake cookies on the counter and the fans and dehumidifying equipment running. Blocking out the noise as best as she could, Theo started writing a note of explanation to Nina, detailing everything she had seen and heard. A thud and a thump preceded her best friend and her children stepping through the utility room doorway carrying their travel bags.

"Oh, Nina, I'm so sorry." Theo jumped up, hugged her best friend and said, "I'd hoped to get some of this cleaned up for you."

Nina looked like she'd been slapped. Her eyes went kind of jiggly and out of focus. "I talked to Tony. He came and met me at the school when we got back." Her voice cracked. "It looks even worse than I expected."

Theo hugged the kids. "Your bedrooms are fine if you want to go upstairs."

They needed no further encouragement. After a few amazed exclamations about the mess, they charged up the stairs.

"Do they know about their father?" Theo hadn't like Daniel's treatment of Nina, but he'd at least tried to be a good father.

Shaking her head, Nina sank down on a kitchen chair, staring at the drywall tape hanging from the ceiling. Water dripped from it into a plastic tub. "I'll tell them in a little bit. I'd like to be able to explain what happened. Why was Daniel out here? And alone? No car?" She buried her hands in her auburn hair, pulling it away from her face. "It doesn't make any sense at all."

Boiling water to make tea, Theo had nothing to add. Like Nina, Theo would be surprised if Daniel ever even bothered to walk across the street. He was, or had been, happiest when someone was waiting on him hand and foot. "So you didn't expect him to come out here?"

Taking the mug of hot water and adding a tea bag, Nina frowned. "No. I haven't heard from him in several weeks. Not since he hinted he'd like me to give him some cash so he could take the kids to the movies and I told him I wouldn't ever give him money. He's supposed to give *us* money but he's months behind in the support payments. He swore at me and said he'd find a way to turn the kids against me."

Theo hoped her friend wouldn't tell Tony that. It sounded like motive for murder. Until they knew when Daniel arrived, hopefully long after Nina left for D.C., Theo herself probably had the next best motive. A good alibi for Nina would move Theo up in the suspect list.

Sipping their tea, Theo and Nina stood to one side watching the fans drying the house, and then went out onto the porch and stared down at the open storm cellar, still surrounded by yellow tape. Theo found it disturbing and tried not to think about the body that had been down there. It was futile. Theo tried to pull Nina back into the house but her friend resisted. "I'll bet you were surprised to see Tony."

"I couldn't believe he was standing there waiting for us as we got back to the school. I barely parked the school's van when he and Wade came up and opened the door for me. I was afraid something had happened to you."

Theo gave her a hug. "I'm sorry about all of this."

"My father never liked him," Nina whispered.

Theo hadn't liked him either. But she didn't say so. "Why?" Theo dropped the one-word question she never asked directly before. It was both a question about her father's attitude and Nina's own decision. There was often no apparent reason that two people married, surprising family members on both sides.

Nina stared unseeingly at the hole. "He was handsome, and he had a devil's smile, but he was well mannered." She shrugged. "By the time I realized what I had gotten myself for life, we were married and I was pregnant."

"And you thought he'd change?"

"Yes." Nina sighed deeply. "I believed that fantasy for years."

"What will you tell the kids?" Theo could imagine very little more difficult than Nina having to tell her children about their father's death.

"The truth. We don't know what happened. Or why." Nina began to shiver. Now the shivers were getting worse. Nina didn't protest when Theo took a lap quilt from the sofa and wrapped it around her shoulders. Theo pushed Nina toward the door. "Let's go inside and get some overnight bags packed."

"Why was he down in there? It doesn't make any sense."

"You know you can't stay here." Theo had arranged for a reservation at the Riverview motel for Nina and her family. Theo looked up to see the children on the stairs. "You kiddos ought to go up and pack some clothes and stuff."

"Wait." Pale and shaking, Nina kept moving her head from side to side, but her eyes were trained on her children. "I have to give you some bad news. Some really bad news. About your dad."

Theo watched as Nina gathered her children together until the three of them formed a small knot wrapped together in one small quilt. They stood together for a long time whispering to each other. Theo left them to themselves and, without a plan, returned to the front window, the one overlooking the boxlike shelter. The porch light reflected from the yellow crime-scene tape. It had become dark outside, and the box had disappeared.

Echoing her thoughts, Nina's voice came from just behind her. "You remember how we always called it 'The Box.' " Nina took Theo's arm like a blind woman might.

"Yes." Theo smiled at the memory. "Your dad told wonderful stories about it, but they never contained any of the same facts."

Theo remembered some of the stories about The Box told to them as children. At that time, Nina's grandparents, Sib and Freddie Ledbetter, still lived in this spot, in a ramshackle frame house that had a major sag in the roof. The sag had made an impression on Theo. She was always a little afraid the whole building would collapse inward while they were visiting. The Ledbetters were friends of Theo's grandparents, and Nina and her parents lived in a still smaller, even more ancient house, not far away on the same piece of poor land.

The story most often told was of a high-ranking officer of the Confederacy who hid on the property during "the War of Northern Aggression." He had paid handsomely for his makeshift chamber. Confederate money. Worth little in the old days, especially in this area that contained mostly union sympathies, the present family had hoped the bills could be sold to collectors. Ruined by the damp and mildew, they had received a pittance.

Other stories, for Nina's grandfather was a grand teller of tales, suggested the soldier had brought gold. A few stories implied that the old officer had joined the family and was related to Nina. Others insisted no officer had ever existed at all. Coins? No coins. Jewels? No jewels. The truth would most likely never be known.

When the old house was dismantled and the newer one constructed, there had been no sign of money in paper or coin, jewels, or even a brass belt buckle.

The Gift Quilt—Mystery Quilt
The Second Body of Clues

Begin with the 48 squares 3-7/8″ of fabrics (A) and fabric (B).

Mark a diagonal line on the wrong side of the lighter of the two fabrics.

Sew a line, a scant 1/4″ from both sides of the line. Cut on the line. Open and press to darker fabric, making 96 half-square triangle blocks. Trim off "ears." If needed, trim to 3-1/2″.

Divide the squares into two stacks of 48 block units (A+B), placing corner of fabric (A) on the far right. To the right of one of these stacks, place 48 squares 3-1/2″ of fabric (B). Being careful not to rotate the half-square triangle, flip a square of (B) right side down onto triangle block and sew together with 1/4″ seam along the right edge. Make 48. Press to solid square (B).

Repeat the process using the remaining 48 half-square triangle units (A+B) and the 48 squares of fabric (C). Press to square (C).

Place the (A+B) segments with square of (B) on the right edge. Rotate the (A+C) segments and stack above the (A+B) segments. The center points of triangle (A)'s should touch each other and form a butterfly. Sew all. Press to (A)+(B)+(C)'s. Block should measure 6 1/2″ square. Make 48.

Set aside.

Chapter Twelve

Tony's morning activity of reading through some of his endless paperwork was interrupted by a call from Mayor Cashdollar, not requesting but actually commanding him to hotfoot it over to the funeral home. And the mayor insisted Tony should bring at least one deputy with him. No other details were given, and the call had been disconnected before Tony could ask for an explanation. The funeral home was only a few blocks away from his office and he was sure anything was better than reading the detailed reports from the jail staff.

Daniel Crisp's autopsy had not yet been completed so at least Tony didn't have to read that cheerful document. Yet. He had delivered the unpleasant news of Daniel's death, not only to Nina, but to the man's parents, and his new wife, Nancy. The elder Crisps were devastated by the death and blindsided by the mention of Daniel's new wife. Surprised the parents knew nothing of the marriage, Tony managed to stifle any comment.

Now Tony stood in the funeral home office, the workplace of Mayor Calvin Cashdollar, and if Tony concentrated, he could hear, coming from the chapel, the sound of someone playing the piano. The sound was faint and he tried to focus on the music and block out the sounds around him. The pianist was not just banging out the notes of a hymn, practicing for a service, but played beautifully, the sound rippling through the building. The sheer beauty of it distracted him momentarily. He wondered who the musician was.

In this small room, three female voices and one male were speaking at once. Tony wanted to silence all of the voices screeching around him so he could hear the music. It was as good an excuse for begging for silence as he could produce in the circumstances. The urge to stuff old dirty socks into the four voices plaguing him was powerful. Luckily, or maybe not, he had no supply of used socks except for the ones on his feet. He finally couldn't take it any longer. "Quiet!" He spoke more loudly than he intended.

The chatter around him ceased. Into the silence, the heavenly music swept through the room. No one but him seemed to notice it. Maybe his wishful thinking produced audible hallucinations.

"Why are we here?" Tony looked at Calvin for an explanation since he was the one who had demanded Tony come. Wade stood silent at his back. Although they were not partners, whenever Tony went out on a call, Wade was often the deputy to accompany him.

"Um, well, um." Calvin swallowed hard. "I thought you might need to meet the wives. That is, Daniel Crisp's wives."

"Wade and I have met his wife." Tony saw the blond standing near two other young women. He nodded in her direction. "Nancy."

Calvin turned back to Tony. His blue eyes flickered nervously. His lanky frame trembled and his huge hands flapped as he whispered, "You don't understand. She's only one of the wives."

"Wives?" Tony listened to the word bounce around in his brain. The piano music continued but was suddenly upstaged. His full attention now turned to the three women. The two women facing Nancy were totally unfamiliar. Without names, he mentally categorized the women as Small, Medium and Blondie. "Did I understand that all of you claim to be married to Daniel?"

"Claim?" The smallest of the three women spoke. Her voice was barely audible. "I don't know these other women. I'm his wife, Nannette." Her brown eyes filled with tears.

"No. I am." Three words spoken in unison by the two other women. They each took a step toward the small woman, fingers tensed into talons.

"Oh, no, no, no." Tony and Wade inserted themselves into the situation. "No fighting, ladies." Tony assigned each of the women a chair to sit on. No one was within arm's reach of another. He wanted to turn the chairs to face away from each other but there wasn't enough space. "Sit. Stay."

Once the women were seated, Tony spoke softly to Calvin. "Could you fill me in? What is going on?"

Calvin's eyes were wide, exposing the white surrounding the blue irises. He didn't blink. His Adam's apple moved up and down as he gulped air. "The last of them showed up about ten minutes ago. I don't know where they came from or how they got here."

"Do you have Daniel's body?" Tony couldn't believe the pathologist in Knoxville would release the man's remains to a funeral home without first notifying his own office of the results of the autopsy.

"No. It's still in Knoxville." Calvin finally blinked and turned to Tony. "The curvy blond woman showed up first. She dropped by yesterday after you broke the news to her. I explained the process and the fact that we cannot make any plans until the body is released. She told me that since she's the widow, she wants his remains cremated as soon as possible. She bought one of my finest urns. Paid cash."

The music stopped.

While the words were spoken softly, the message carried in the silence. Small wife shot to her feet, glanced at the frown on Tony's face, and sat again. "As his wife . . ." Nannette yelled the last word. Her voice was surprisingly deep for such a small woman. "I want him embalmed, placed in a nice casket and I want to take him home to bury him in our home-town cemetery."

"Don't be so quick to steal my husband's body," the third voice joined in. Medium wife, a dishwater blond with enormous gray eyes, pounded on the lamp table next to her. The lamp wobbled and threatened to fall. She ignored it and the quick action taken by Calvin to protect his property. "No one even bothered to call and tell me of his passing. What kind of people don't notify the next of kin?" Her glare was aimed directly at Tony. "I had to read it on the internet."

The blond twisted around, trying to see the other women. "As his *wife,*" she snarled, "I have the right to have him buried wherever I want to or have him dipped, battered and fried if I damn well please."

The commotion following that inflammatory statement must have been heard in space.

Tony felt like Calvin looked. He hoped not to be caught in the crossfire.

Wade whispered just loud enough for Tony to hear, "As much as I love Grace, I cannot begin to imagine juggling three wives like baseballs."

"It looks more like juggling chainsaws." Tony thought his mouth might have fallen open during the revelation. "Who do you suppose is legally the widow?"

"I think it's the one he married first, unless they're divorced. Can you get divorced without the other person signing something?" Wade coughed before whispering, "He isn't still married to Nina, is he?"

"No, no." Tony was certain of the end of that marriage. Nina had shown him and Theo the final divorce papers. In fact, she had thrown an impromptu party with champagne and chocolate cake. But if Daniel had married any of these women before the divorce was final, it could change everything about *her* legal status.

Hearing movement in the hallway, Tony looked up. He held his breath, hoping another wife wasn't headed their way. The office door had been left open to accommodate the number of people inside. An older couple slowly approached the doorway. Tony recognized Daniel's parents and thought he should somehow warn them of the current discussion but didn't find a way before Calvin stepped forward. Whatever disagreements Tony had with the mayor from time to time, the man was good with people. Especially grief-stricken people.

Calvin managed to intercept the couple. Tony heard Calvin's diplomatic statement about the wife being in the room without giving any indication of which woman he referred to.

"Isn't Nina here?" the deceased's mother asked. Her eyes searched the crowded room. She looked lost and bewildered. "Nina should be here."

"Now, now, dear." Her husband patted her hand, with the one of his not already clutched in hers. "Nina's not married to our Daniel any longer. There's no reason for her to be part of the funeral planning."

"I want her and the children to sit with us at the service. He was my baby and I loved him." Mrs. Crisp wiped the tears from her cheeks. "Still, as much as I hate to say it, she was better than he deserved."

Tony wondered what Mrs. Crisp might think about this new set of wives. He was not about to introduce them. It was not his job.

Calvin suggested the couple return home until the body was released and then arrangements could be made. He mumbled something about needing to clear up a few things for some other people.

Tony was relieved when the couple followed Calvin's excellent advice and turned to leave. He wished he could leave, too. Pulling out his notebook and pen, he turned toward the still seated wives. This was not his first case of dealing with extra spouses. "I do need to ask each of you a few questions."

Medium wife frowned. "Can't we do this another time?" Her gray eyes were bloodshot and filled with tears.

As much as Tony would have enjoyed just letting them scatter, he couldn't imagine a group more likely to have a vengeful wife among them. "Please, humor me. It will take less time for all of us in the long run. We can certainly begin with you."

Small wife and Blondie crossed their arms over their chests and glared at him. If he wasn't bald, their expressions might have lit his hair on fire. He stepped away but didn't turn his back on them.

He moved closer to Medium wife. Wade stood next to him. "What is your full name and where do you live?"

Medium's voice was subdued. "Nora Douglas. I kept my maiden name." She wiped her eyes on a tissue. "We live in Cleveland."

"Ohio?"

"Tennessee."

That put her home southwest of them. "When did you marry Daniel?"

"Three and a half years ago."

Tony didn't say anything but he knew Nina's divorce hadn't become final until two years prior. His fingers tightened on his pen and he wrote down her answers. "How did you meet?"

"I happened to be visiting my folks, and he was selling them a television dish."

"Any children?" Tony had to ask.

"A boy, Daniel, Jr." Her smile made her look younger than she had. "He's two."

"Thank you."

Tony sent her back to her seat and signaled for Small to join them. Clearly reluctant to cooperate, she finally came forward, but the first time he asked for her name and home town, she simply stared at him and Wade. "I can stand here as long as it takes," Tony said and asked again.

She exhaled sharply. "My name is Nannette Crisp, and I live in Dalton, Georgia."

"When did you two marry?"

Nannette's head moved from side to side like she was listening to music from a game show. After about thirty seconds she gave in. "A year and a half ago."

"Any children?"

"A little girl. Danielle."

"How did you meet?"

"It was at church. He was visiting." Calmer now, Nannette closed her eyes but it did not stop the tears leaking under the lids. "He tries to be a good father, but he has to travel so much it's difficult for all of us."

When Tony signaled for Blondie, she flounced over like a teenager and draped herself on the chair and crossed her legs, letting the top one swing. "This is so lame."

"A few things have changed since we first talked." Tony held up his notebook. "What is your name and where do you live?"

"I'm Nancy Crisp." Blondie flipped her golden curls. "Chattanooga's where my dear departed husband and I live. Lived."

"How did you meet?"

"We met in a bar." She heaved her mighty bosom. "He was staying at a nearby hotel. You know him, always traveling for work."

"And when did you get married?" Tony flipped to a new page in his notebook. After their previous conversation about rings, he expected it to be only a matter of weeks. He was wrong.

"Hmm, a year and a few months ago, maybe six." She winked at Wade. "Numbers aren't what I do best."

"Children?"

"A precious little girl. Her name is Danielle."

Tony didn't ask more but sent her back to her chair. He looked at Wade. "What do you think?"

"I can't believe it." Wade blinked as if he'd just awakened from a deep trance. "What if these are not his only wives?"

"You're right, of course." Tony stood. "We can't assume anything. There could be a charter busload of them headed here now."

At that comment, Wade's eyes rolled. "What a guy! Do you suppose it's intentional they all have names that start with the letter N? Nora, Nannette and Nancy."

"Don't forget ex-wife Nina."

Tony watched the angry wives head down the sidewalk. He had collected all of their phone numbers, home addresses, email addresses and work contacts. They might all be in the same boat, but they were not rowing as a team.

Of the threesome, the center wife was the only one who walked like a normal person. He'd dubbed her Medium, now she was Nora. The one on the left, Nannette, moved in a precise line, placing one foot directly in front of the other, like a tightrope walker.

The third wife, Nancy, rotated her upper body from side to side with each change of leading foot. It struck him that it looked like she was giving a full display of her assets to a cheering crowd she imagined on each side of the street. There was no crowd on a blustery February day to appreciate her performance.

Tony and Wade had each filled a notebook with the information. Tony looked at Wade. "What do you think? Who's his widow?"

Wade's deep-blue eyes were somber as he tilted his face down and looked at him over the top of his sunglasses. "Honestly?"

Tony nodded, deeply curious if the deputy had the same opinion as his own.

"I don't think any of them are legally married to him." Wade turned his gaze to the women. "I think he deluded them into believing him. If there was a private exchange of vows, I'd say it was officiated by one of his friends."

"Sadly, I agree. We'll know more after the marriage certificates are presented. I'll give Ruth Ann the job of tracking down the paperwork. She'll love it." Tony sighed. "On the other hand, if none of them is married to the man, at least she won't be inheriting his unpaid bills. If any company was dumb enough to give him a card, I'd guess he's got massive credit-card debt."

"Speaking of credit cards." Wade looked back at Tony. "He did have three different cards in his wallet, all from the same company but different banks. I was surprised when Mike and I did the inventory. I didn't think anyone would extend him credit. Not with his past history."

"Let's see if we can find a co-signer, or if the account is in a different name and he was given a card by the owner. Maybe one or more of his wives." Tony felt a flash of hope. "If he ran up big numbers on a credit card, and especially if he was buying things for another wife, that could be some serious motivation for someone to dispose of him."

Wade nodded. "If he's in debt to a loan shark, it could have been serious, too. Maybe someone tracked him down and scared him, and he dived into the hole, committing suicide to get away from them."

"Killing wouldn't clear up a debt unless there was insurance.

A broken man can pay. A dead one, not so much." For some reason, Tony didn't believe money was the issue.

Theo looked at Nina. Her friend's beautiful green eyes looked glassy and bloodshot. Clearly shock and fatigue were taking a toll on her.

Nina released a half sob and collapsed onto a chair near Theo's cutting table. Nina was taking the day off from teaching. "My house is in shambles. Not only from the flood and Daniel's death, but the steady parade of wives coming out to *my* house to 'see where my love died' is creepy and annoying."

Theo couldn't imagine dealing with the wives. The scenario sounded like something from a really bad daytime television melodrama. "What's happening inside your house? Is it dry now?"

"The kitchen is useless. The refrigerator is in the garage. The stove's in the den. The washer and dryer don't work for some weird reason but can't be fixed or replaced until the insurance company says so. The same with the kitchen flooring, which had to be ripped up to reach the water soaking the plywood underneath it." Nina tried a smile but it failed. "I don't mind not cooking, but those kids of mine need access to food twenty-four hours a day. The insurance company will pay for our motel a bit longer, but none of us is enjoying the stay at the Riverview Motel."

Theo leaned closer, almost afraid to ask. "And since *you* don't actually own your house?"

"The insurance, you mean?" Nina guessed.

Theo nodded.

Nina did smile then, a huge sunny smile accompanied with a soft laugh. "You know my dad. He's a hardheaded, tightfisted old coot. He insured the house to the maximum with replacement values, not original cost, for everything. I pay him back for the premiums on the house insurance and then I also pay rental insurance because he told me I had to."

"Really?" Theo had never thought of the details of the unusual house ownership arrangement.

"Oh, yeah, my dad's insurance agent thinks I'm a gold mine. Who else but my family has to pay twice on the same house?"

Theo had known Lead Ledbetter since her childhood. Diligent and hardworking, he was always surrounded by laughter. He loved to have a good time and played all kinds of pranks on friends and family. The only times Theo had seen him truly angry, Daniel Crisp was involved. Daniel's treatment of Nina was a continuous issue, and once Daniel was caught stealing some of Lead's moonshine. She sincerely hoped Lead was not involved in Daniel's death.

Tony left his office and wandered down the hall to Wade's tiny fingerprint cubicle. It looked like the deputy was taking inventory of his assorted powders and brushes.

"I'm looking for ideas of how we can find out if there are more than three wives." Tony rested his back against the door frame. "I'd sure hate to stop collecting them before we have *the wife.*"

"If there actually is a legal one." Wade looked up and spun a brush between his fingers. "Speaking ill of the dead isn't the same thing as telling lies. He could have gone through a marriage service without it being legal."

"What do you mean?" Tony felt grateful for Wade's intelligence and insight.

"It's been a while since you got married. Grace and I still haven't found room for some of our wedding presents."

"And?"

"Well, first you have to get a license. For that you need a picture ID, birth certificate, social security number and cash.

Then after it's issued, you have a month to use it and file it with the state. When you do that, you get your wedding certificate. Proof you are married."

Tony listened carefully, wondering where Wade was headed. "So?"

"If you don't use the license in a timely manner, it expires. If you still want to marry, you'll have to shell out more money to get a new one. Not only that, it has to be a license for the county you'll be married in."

A zing of understanding pierced Tony's brain. "So, if you never file proof there was a wedding, you are not married?"

"I think that's the case. If Daniel had a ceremony in Park County, but never filed the paperwork, he'd be single as far as the state is concerned. He could 'marry' in another county pretty easily because no one in the marriage license office would recognize him as a recent customer."

"Wow." Tony was impressed by Wade's theory and Daniel's underhandedness. "Why bother?"

"Make the women happy. They think they're married. They don't know the truth." Wade's handsome face frowned.

Tony was still looking for the hidden flaw. "But to have the name changed on the driver's license, wouldn't it have to be filed?"

"I would think so, but, maybe somewhere there's a clerk who will accept the license as proof. If you're not married, why would you bother with the paperwork?"

Tony felt sorry for all the women in Daniel's life. "Or your new husband says for you to keep your maiden name on the bank accounts and such, but you can call yourself Mrs. Crisp everywhere there isn't a legal document involved."

"Oh, man, no wonder he's dead." Wade shook his head. "Any one of them, or several acting together, could have had enough with the secrecy and pushed him, or maybe he dived into the hole to get out of the jam and broke his neck. Just because they say they didn't know, can we absolutely believe none of them had an inkling about the others?"

Tony had no sympathy for Daniel Crisp. Only for the wives, and especially for the children. As far as Tony could tell so far, none of them were likely to inherit anything. "I guess I'll put out a press release all over the state and Georgia, maybe North Carolina, about his death and our department looking for next of kin."

Wade frowned. "I certainly hope there are not any more families."

"Me, too."

Chapter Thirteen

"Sheriff?" Flavio Weems's voice came through the intercom on Tony's desk.

It wasn't the word itself, but the intonation giving Tony the chills. "What's happened now?"

Flavio spoke carefully. His training for the dispatch desk meant he had to maintain his calm no matter what the emergency entailed. "Mrs. Eunice Plover has died."

Tony's first reaction was sorrow. He enjoyed the feisty older woman. "Please tell me it's from natural causes."

"Doc Nash said I should call you. He said something about it didn't seem right and asked that you come to her house." Flavio sounded like he was reading it from a note.

"Did he say why?" Even as he asked the question Tony stood, preparing to leave.

"No, sir."

"Find Wade, and have him meet me there." Pulling his jacket from its hook, Tony headed to his parking bay.

Tony had known Mrs. Plover almost from the first day his family had moved to Silersville when he was a boy. On her most recent birthday, the spry older woman turned seventy-five and had invited a multitude to her party. Eunice and Jane, Tony's mother, had been great friends for a while and then suddenly they were not. Neither of them had ever mentioned the problem in his presence.

Eunice Plover's lovely home was a short distance out of town.

As he approached, Tony stared at the large, white, brick home. The green roof slanted down to cover a wide porch, which extended across the front of the house. A curved driveway edged with a neatly trimmed small hedge connected with a straight driveway leading to a double garage with a green door. Window boxes filled with artificial greenery accented every window not shaded by the porch roof. Even from the driveway, he could see tiny, live green sprouts of some early bulb interspersed among some fake ferns. Whatever grew there had not started blooming, but he wouldn't be surprised if they were ready in a couple of weeks. Spring would arrive in a flurry. From the outside, the home looked perfectly normal.

Tony climbed from the Blazer and joined Wade in his vehicle. "You got here first. Do you know who found the body?"

"According to Flavio," said Wade, glancing at his notebook, as if double-checking his information. "It was her next door neighbor, a Mrs. Johnson. I guess Eunice Plover watched the neighbor's daughter most mornings until the school bus picked her up. Evidently Mrs. Plover simply did it as a favor because she, that is the mother, works the early shift at Food City. Mrs. Johnson told Flavio she called the doctor first and then nine-one-one."

"Any idea what she actually saw?" Tony continued his study of the home's exterior, looking for any sign it had been broken into.

"Yes. She told Flavio that she opened the door after a brief knock. I gather it was not unusual for them to knock and then just enter so she and her daughter went inside. Mrs. Johnson saw Mrs. Plover stretched out on the couch in the living room, and the neighbor started making calls when she couldn't wake her up."

Tony saw no one in the area. "Where is Mrs. Johnson now?"

"She took her daughter to another neighbor's home and

explained the situation. Once her daughter had a place to wait for the bus, Mrs. Johnson left for work." Wade glanced up. "I called the manager at Food City. He said Mrs. Johnson arrived on time and is at her register like she's supposed to be."

Tony couldn't fault the woman for her behavior. An elderly neighbor passing away was a tragedy, but the mother couldn't afford to miss work. Tony happened to know the manager at the grocery store. The man ran a tight ship, and not showing up could cost the woman her job.

Like Nina's home, the Plover house perched on a hill with a beautiful view of the Smoky Mountains from the front porch. It was valuable land, and the house was fairly new and in good condition. Her husband had died only a few years earlier. Without any recent information, Tony assumed he wasn't missed by his widow. It was well known that Mr. Plover had been a bully at home even though he'd been a popular man in the business community.

The double-faceted Mr. Plover had been a local man who made good. He was raised in poverty but he'd been ambitious, so he married into money and beauty and used both to further his career. He had commuted from Silersville to Knoxville.

There had been rumors over the years that his former business partner and Mrs. Plover had been lovers quite a few years prior. No one knew for sure. There had also been rumors that some of his business deals had been shady. If something had happened to her, could it be that after all this time, someone thought she could link them to something personally damaging? It seemed unlikely.

Tony glanced at the front porch again and saw Doc Nash waiting there for him in the open doorway. Wade and Tony climbed out of the car and walked up to meet the habitually cranky doctor. "You called. What do you know?"

Doc Nash massaged the back of his neck and gave Tony the

"I'm not sure of anything" look. "She wasn't my patient but as far as I can tell, Mrs. Plover had no particular illnesses, or chronic conditions or any other reason I'm aware of that she should be dead today."

Tony listened carefully to the doctor's words and what he wasn't saying. "People, especially not young ones, die all the time of no particular reason. Seventy-five isn't quite young, but it's not as old as it used to sound." Tony didn't doubt the doctor's instincts for an instant. He wanted to, though. He didn't want this to be a homicide, and he couldn't abide the idea of suicide. "So, what do you think killed her?"

"I'm guessing some form of poisoning." Doc Nash frowned, clearly unwilling to make an educated guess.

Tony could count on one hand the number of times the doctor had appeared so uncertain about his statements. "Poisoning? That's not very specific. Drinking too much moonshine can poison you."

Doc Nash did smile at that comment. "That's true. I didn't see anything like a container, though."

"Okay, so what do you want us to do?" Tony would follow the doctor's lead. Doc Nash was irritable, overworked and absolutely without imagination. Facts were his friends, and he wouldn't be having this discussion with Tony if he wasn't convinced it was necessary.

"We need to send the body out for a more in-depth autopsy than I can do. I especially want a specialized toxicology report." Doc Nash waved one skinny arm toward the body. "Look at her. She looks like she's been very sick for a long time, but she hasn't been, at least not to my knowledge anyway. Yesterday I saw her out and about, walking down the sidewalk, and she seemed fine. Her color was good and healthy, and I couldn't help but notice she still moved like a much younger woman. Now look at her. I'd say her skin's gone a bit yellow."

"What poisons do you want them to check for?" Tony knew enough about toxicology to know that one test would not find every possible poison. He also knew that the more tests they did, the more expensive it would be. He didn't want to waste the department's money if the test wasn't necessary, and he didn't want to save money if it would let a killer run loose.

"That's an excellent question." Doc rubbed the side of his nose again. "I'm hoping when you and Wade search the house, you'll be able to find some suggestion of how poison was administered, if indeed she was poisoned."

"If you truly believe she died of foul play, we need to leave her in place while we do an investigation."

"Yes, yes. I'll go back to my office. There's nothing for me to do here." The doctor scuttled away. "She's as dead now as she will be later."

Tony watched Wade carrying his camera and fingerprint case across the yard. In response to Wade's questioning expression, he said, "I'll take the pictures while you do your fingerprint thing."

The serious expression on Wade's handsome face grew sterner. "Who would kill such a nice old lady? And why?"

Tony wondered the same thing. "I have no idea. I'm hoping the doctor is wrong."

As Tony and Wade made their way into the house, Tony saw nothing out of place or obviously disturbed. The well-maintained Mrs. Plover was stretched out on the sofa, but she did not look like she was sleeping, or had died in her sleep. Moments later, Wade vanished and Tony heard him being sick. Tony thought Eunice didn't look over sixty-five. Her hair was carefully colored a soft brown and her skin was firm for a woman of her age. As the doctor had observed, now her skin did have a yellow undertone.

Minor twisting of her fingers indicated some arthritis but not a severe case. The eyeglasses still perched on her nose looked like simple magnification glasses and not prescription.

A book open to almost its middle rested on the coffee table next to a half empty cup of tea. Tony could see the tea bag in the bottom of the cup. He saw no obvious signs of violence. Only the body itself did not look restful. He understood why the doctor was concerned about the cause of death. "Wade, we need to find out if she's complained to her friends about feeling ill."

"That should be easy enough." Wade had returned and was busy with his brush and powders. He looked up from his fingerprint kit. "They should all be gathering together soon. It's almost lunchtime at the senior center."

Tony very carefully placed the cup and its contents into a bag and filled out the required details for evidence. He sealed the bag. He'd make sure to keep it sitting upright in a box on its way to the laboratory for analysis. He went outside to see if there was a clear view to any of the neighbors' homes.

Standing at the top of Mrs. Plover's driveway, Tony could easily see the front doors of four houses, and six to some degree. He wondered how she got along with her neighbors. He also wondered if he should have called in the TBI. They'd barely left the county after the scene they'd worked at Nina's home. The TBI had spent a lot of time in his county in recent months, supplying the equipment, manpower and the expertise his small department lacked.

Rightly or wrongly, Tony decided his department could handle this case without outside assistance, except for the autopsy. While Wade was continuing with his fingerprint search, Tony decided to visit the neighbors. He called for Deputy Mike Ott to join him, and it took only a few minutes for him to arrive.

They found no one at home at the first two houses, but at

the third house his knock was answered by a thirtyish woman holding a small girl. A boy, maybe three years old, had both arms wrapped tightly around her leg. Tony smiled at the children and the woman. "Do you know Mrs. Plover?"

"Yes, of course. I talk to her frequently in the summertime but not so much in the winter. We share an interest in gardens, particularly flowers." She tried to peer around him. "Mrs. Johnson came by the house this morning. She was all upset, something about Mrs. Plover having died, and asked me to keep her little girl this morning until the school bus came by. She was in such a state I really didn't get much information. Did Eunice really die?"

"I'm afraid it is true." Tony wondered how much to tell her. He preferred to gather information rather than give it out, but since he knew Mrs. Johnson had already mentioned the babysitter having died there was no valid reason for him to pretend otherwise.

"No way! It just doesn't seem possible." The young woman's eyes widened. "She's the healthiest person I know. Even though she's an older lady, she's always outside walking or riding her bicycle or gardening. I'm sure I couldn't keep up with her."

Tony held up his notebook. "And your name is?"

"Christi." She shifted the child in her arms. "Christi Fuller."

Tony wrote it down, wondering why the woman had feigned surprise about hearing of the neighbor's death. With such bad acting, Christi was not destined for the stage. He said, "I have heard she was always very active, but nevertheless, I need to ask you a few questions."

She interrupted him. "Have you told her family?" With her free hand, Christi gripped the edge of her front door hard enough to whiten her knuckles.

There was an edge to her avid expression and questions Tony found disturbing. "I'm hoping that you have contact information for them."

"I guess I do in a way." Christi frowned. "Not too long ago, Mrs. Plover gave me a list of her relatives because she's afraid of them. She told me they've been trying to steal her house and asked me to let her know if I ever saw any of them creeping around while she was away."

"Steal her house?" Tony felt his eyebrows rise. "How did she think they could do that?"

Christi abandoned her hold on the door and opened it wide but didn't invite him inside. The little boy eased out onto the porch and began studying the equipment attached to Mike's duty belt.

Christi settled one shoulder against the frame like she was expecting to be there for a while. "Well, what she told me was that it is actually her late husband's brother's children who want to take her house away from her. According to her, the two nephews and a niece spent their own family inheritance and now think her property should belong to them. They offered to move her into town, into a dumpy little place, and said they would take care of her property, but she knows that means they plan to sell it out from under her. She told them time after time to leave her and her house alone."

Surprised by the sudden onslaught of information, Tony said, "Do you know who inherits now that she has died?" He didn't like to think this story could be true, but he knew people had been murdered for less.

"No." Christi shook her head vigorously. "I just know she made a will because she and Carl Lee Cashdollar came over and asked if I would sign as a witness. My understanding is because she had no children of her own, her late husband's kin think it should be theirs. That doesn't mean she had no friends or relatives she planned to leave it to."

Tony didn't disagree with her statement. "Did you see anyone at all near her house last night or this morning?"

"Well, no." The young woman looked thoughtful. "There could have been though. After dark it's impossible to see much. We don't have streetlights out here, like in town."

It was a valid point. A few homes had yard lights, but Eunice Plover's home did not. "Thank you." Tony and Mike headed toward the next house. No one was home. No one was home at the next several houses either. At the sixth house, the one with the most obscured view, Tony knocked on the door and was greeted with the business end of shotgun.

It felt like a scene from the movies. A very bad movie showing nothing but badly dressed villains with stills and shotguns, and in which everyone acted stupid and nobody had teeth. There were only a few people that completely fit that description living in his county, and this man was not one of them. This man wore silk shirts, had all of his teeth, all of his hair and enough money to buy and sell most of the people in the county. The front door didn't sag on its hinges but was a beautiful dark wood with beveled glass panels. He was not a bootlegger. Tony did not like his welcome. "Mr. O'Grady, put down the gun."

Complying, Mr. O'Grady growled like a dog before saying, "You got business here?"

"Your pretending to be ignorant is annoying." Tony waved a hand in the general direction of the house further up on the hill. "How well do you know Eunice Plover?"

"Why don't you ask her if it's so important to you?"

"I'm asking you." Tony didn't understand why some people went out of their way to be difficult. "Is there some reason you don't want to answer?"

"I can't see it's any of your business if I spend time with my neighbors or not." Mr. O'Grady's lower jaw jutted forward and his eyes narrowed. "Why don't you go on back to town?"

The last thing Tony wanted to do was to get into an argument with anyone. Mr. O'Grady might have money and a shotgun, but from Tony's point of view, the man wasn't totally rational. If he had "mental issues," Tony didn't want to disturb him more than necessary. "Mrs. Plover has passed away."

"Oh, no. No." Suddenly the man seemed to crumple as if his bones had dissolved, and he slid down until he was sitting on the porch. "That can't be true."

Shocked by O'Grady's reaction, Tony softened his voice and reached out to steady the man's shoulder. "Did you notice any vehicles or people visiting her yesterday?"

"Just the same ones as usual." Unchecked tears streamed down the creases in his face, splashing on his hands. "I can't believe it. I loved that woman all my life."

"Did you two have a personal relationship?" Tony wasn't quite sure how else to phrase it.

"Oh, no. I always worshipped her from afar." O'Grady rolled over and rested his head on the bottom step like it was a pillow, pressing a fist against his lips. The tears continued.

Tony quickly realized there was nothing else the broken-hearted man could tell him, and he and Mike returned to the house. Mike muttered something about never knowing what people will do or think.

There was little else for Tony to do at the house. At least for now. Wade would be busy using his fingerprint powder for a bit longer. The ambulance had been requested, and the deceased Mrs. Plover would soon be on the way to Knoxville for an in-depth autopsy.

As Tony collected the tea cup and the tea box on the counter, he stared at the mess they'd created and considered the problem left behind. He sent Mike on his way and picked up the camera again.

Once the evidence was collected and the body on its way to Knoxville, Tony, guessing they might need to renew their search for answers, placed seals on the doors before heading to the doctor's office to follow up on his report. "Now that you've had some time to think about it, have you changed your mind about what happened?"

"No. That was not a natural death. There had to be a poison." Doc Nash spoke with confidence. "I haven't got much experience with the various categories, but unless she was suffocated, what else could have been responsible?" He sighed. "You know, it doesn't have to be exotic. Someone else's prescription medication can fall into the lethal category—along with certain foods, allergens and about anything else she could ingest. However, from what I could tell, this one apparently worked quickly. A lot of poisons are just not that strong."

"Fabulous." Tony's voice reeked with disgust as he considered the implications. If there was a person in his county he believed was less likely than Eunice Plover to have an enemy prepared to kill her, he couldn't guess who it would be. His own mother had more enemies, and she was well loved by most of the locals. Just not all of them.

He needed to find out more about the relatives who might be trying to get her house. It could be nothing. But he liked to think he was bright enough to think "fire" when he saw smoke.

Theo stepped back to admire the overall effect of their work. The gaily decorated walker was a gift from all the quilters for their recently physically less stable friend Caro. This was not the standard cage of aluminum pipes they had started with. Now it had been spray painted neon green and reflective tape glistened where someone had applied it generously to the legs.

Jenny Swift, between attempts to call Eunice Plover who was unexpectedly absent, had attached a bike light on the front and tail lights on the backs of the hand rails. The lights flashed in different modes according to how many times the on/off button was pressed. Nina had contributed a bell to warn others of her approach; that is, if Caro wanted to warn them. Caro might prefer to sneak up behind people and just scare the wits out of the unwary. Theo had sewn a shopping bag/purse holder using scrap patchwork blocks. It could be attached to the front, or removed, using hook and loop straps.

Caro had been down in the dumps recently because of her falls. To Theo's knowledge, Caro had fallen no fewer than three times, just in Theo's own quilt shop, in the past week. The older lady prized her independence, and had many unpleasant comments about the standard walker some of her friends were forced to deal with. She hadn't been more complimentary about the snazzy newer models with a built-in seat and hand brakes. The bottom line was Caro did not want to be losing her balance. The quilters refused to be cast aside.

Some of her friends from the Thursday Night Bowling League, a social gathering that had nothing to do with bowling and everything to do with quilting and laughter, decided to take action. There had been several suggestions about how to help Caro, but the decorative walker was the only one that seemed as though it might work.

Holding another handful of the homemade valentines she'd found scattered in the shop, Theo was keeping an eye on the cash register as well as helping decorate the walker. Like Jenny, Theo was surprised and concerned when Eunice had not answered either her home phone or her cell phone. There was little Eunice enjoyed more than an impromptu party.

Theo considered calling Tony to ask if the older woman had been in an accident or pulled over for speeding but decided against it. Eunice did have a tendency to ignore her speedometer.

★ ★ ★ ★ ★

Tony had his hand on the Blazer's door handle, and Wade was already inside his vehicle preparing to leave the Plover residence, when Tony saw Jenny Swift turn into the driveway and head toward the house. Jenny was definitely exceeding the speed limit when she made the turn. The brakes squealed when she stopped abruptly. Jenny waved both arms to attract Tony's attention. Since she already had it, the motion was unnecessary.

"Sheriff! Oh, Sheriff." Jenny hurried out of her car and jogged toward the house.

If the situation were not so serious Tony might have found it amusing to watch the middle-aged woman jogging up the driveway flapping her arms like a giant bird. "What's the problem, Jenny?"

"I was hoping you could tell me. I can't think your being here is good news, but I've been calling Eunice's phones all morning and she hasn't answered." Jenny stopped, bending over and resting her hands on her knees as she gasped for air. "Is she all right? Why are you and Wade here?"

Tony wasn't quite sure what he should tell her. He knew the two women were close. It was rare to see one without the other. The woman before him looked to be on the edge of collapse, and hearing that her dear friend was deceased would not improve her condition. He thought he'd ease into the sad news. "Were you supposed to meet her this morning?"

"Not exactly. She wasn't at Theo's shop this morning, so I did try calling her, often. When she didn't show up at the senior center either, I headed here. It's not like Eunice. She's almost always there for lunch. And when she isn't going to come, she always tells me ahead of time. She didn't call, not all morning." Jenny released a shuddering breath. "We were all concerned."

Knowing the large number of their seniors who gathered every day for lunch was divided into several close-knit groups, the news was hardly surprising to Tony. He glanced over Jenny's shoulder, avoiding the anguish on her face. "I hate to have to tell you this, particularly under the circumstances, but Eunice Plover has died."

"No. That can't be right. We're supposed to leave this afternoon for Paducah. We're taking a fun trip for a few days to see the quilt museum." Jenny shook her head and waved her hands in front of her face as if pushing away the news. "There has to be a mistake. Eunice is in perfect health. I'm fifteen years younger than she is, and I take three times the medications she does."

"I'm afraid that it is true. We aren't quite sure what has happened but there's no question that it is Eunice and she is deceased." Tony led the woman back toward her car and opened the door for her. She collapsed onto the seat. "Do you need someone to drive you home?"

"I–I'm not sure." Tears began sliding down her cheeks, her pallor alarming. "I just can't believe it. She's gone?"

She began shaking so hard that Tony was afraid she would crash her car. "I want you to sit here in your car until I can find someone to drive you home. Will you do that?"

"Yes."

Thinking the woman appeared on the brink of collapse, Tony made sure the window was rolled down to give her air. Wade stood nearby, so Tony instructed him to drive Jenny Swift home in her car and catch a ride back to collect his own.

Tony called for Sheila to meet him at Jack Gates's home. At the very least, they could try to notify Eunice's nephew before he heard the news on the Park County gossip grapevine.

Jack Gates was in his garage, the big door open. He had his back turned to the driveway and was using a small wrench to adjust something on his hand-powered cycle. It might have three wheels, like a child's tricycle, but that was where the resemblance ended. This was a very high-tech set of wheels. A green sedan was parked in the driveway.

Tony knocked on the wall. There was no response. So Tony and Sheila entered the garage together, calling out to attract his attention. They were only a few feet away when Jack realized he had company.

Straightening with a jerk, Jack turned to face them. He pulled ear buds from his ears and the music was loud enough for Tony to hear it.

"I'm sorry we startled you," Tony began.

"That's fine, Sheriff. I was off in another dimension, I guess." Jack's expression as he studied Tony and Sheila was curiosity. "Can I help you?"

"I'm afraid we have come to deliver some bad news." Tony hated, absolutely hated, having to tell people they lost a loved one.

Jack shook his head even as he asked, "What? Who?"

"Your Aunt Eunice." Tony paused for a breath. "Has died."

"No way." Jack's voice was strong and certain. "Eunice might be quite a bit older than I am, and even though she's overweight, she's healthier than anyone I know."

"I'm sorry." Tony spoke softly but firmly.

The reality of what Tony was saying finally sank in. "I don't understand. What happened? Was she in an accident?" Jack walked toward them, his awkward dragging gait even more pronounced than usual.

Tony saw no reason to lie. "Honestly? We're not sure what did happen."

"Have you already told the predators?" Grief and anger filled his voice. His hands trembled.

"Who?" Sheila's voice held a note of surprise. "The predators?"

Jack hesitated a moment. "That's what Eunice calls that pack of thieves, also known as her late husband's relatives."

"Not yet." Tony wrote himself a note about Jack's reaction. "We're headed to talk to them next."

"If they already know, they're probably busy stripping everything out of the house. They probably weren't told it isn't hers anymore. She gifted the house to a charity. Along with all of the contents. She's merely the caretaker now." Jack's expression held satisfaction mixed with grief.

Tony saw no reason to mention the house being sealed, off limits. "We'll keep that in mind." He nodded for Sheila to leave and he followed.

"Shall we pay a visit to the predators?" Sheila wasn't smiling when she asked. "I think it's a pretty apt description of the Plover clan."

Although Tony wasn't thrilled by the idea, he knew it was what they needed to do. "Do you have any idea where to find them at this time of day?"

"Oh, yeah, they'll either be drinking at the Spa or they'll be having a nap in an old beater they park overlooking Kwik Kirk's."

Tony voted to start at the popular parking spot. Sure enough, they found the nephews sleeping in the sun, resting up for their upcoming evening in the bar. Grateful they wouldn't have to go to the bar, he pounded on the car roof to rouse the pair.

Snarling, the pair of men jumped out of the car, fists raised, eyes blinking in the bright light. "What's the matter, Sheriff? We can park up here if we want to. It's not illegal."

"That's true." Tony often enjoyed the view from the same location. "I'm afraid I have to inform you of your aunt's death."

"No kidding?" The nephews spoke in almost perfect unison.

The taller one continued blinking. "How much money do we get?"

"That's not my department." Tony was reminded of Jack Gates's comment about the house and contents going to charity. "I thought I'd better let you know that your aunt's house has been sealed. Photos have been taken of the contents, and if you try stealing anything from her property, or even pick one of her flowers, it won't go well for you. And tell your sister, too."

Chapter Fourteen

"Sheriff?" Rex was now on the dispatch desk.

Tony wasn't sure if Rex sounded amused, concerned or if he was suppressing laughter. The day had been arduous so far, and Tony would appreciate some relief. "Yes?"

"Blossom Flowers Baines is on her way back to your office."

Tony was a little shocked to hear that Blossom was headed his way. Since her marriage several months ago, she had not been delivering as many baked goods to him. He had lost a couple of pounds. Tony hated to admit how much he missed her visits. It wasn't just the baked goods, although that certainly was the largest reason, but Blossom was sweet and entertaining and often as not had information about things going on in the county that he was unaware of.

Sitting just outside his door, Ruth Ann spotted her and said to him, "She looks serious."

When Blossom waddled into his office, Tony saw how true Ruth Ann's observation was. Physically, Blossom looked much the same as ever. Her overweight body was encased in an amazing, flamboyant, pink and purple ensemble. He thought it resembled flamingos in a flower garden. However, her thin, shocking orange hair did not appear to have been combed. Not typical Blossom. Instead, she looked like she had gotten dressed and left the house in a hurry.

Tony checked her hands and noticed she did not arrive empty-handed. Normally Blossom would deposit her baked goods, given as gifts, on his desk and greet him. Now that she was a married lady, her normal expression around him was no longer one of adoration, but even so, Blossom appeared totally distracted. Instead of speaking to him, she managed to wedge her oversized bottom onto the visitor's chair while balancing an apple pie in one hand and clutching the handle of a paper shopping bag in the other. Her tote bag–sized purse hung over one chubby forearm. After releasing a giant sigh, she sat in silence.

Concerned by her appearance and attitude, Tony said, "Is there something I can do for you, Blossom?"

Blossom didn't immediately answer. She just stared at the floor in front of his desk. Then she heaved a great sigh and tears flowed over her cheeks, dripping onto her bright blouse.

The moment she started crying, Tony reached for the box of tissues always on the corner of his desk and, as he offered it to her, he asked, "What's happened?"

They both realized at the same time that she could not take a tissue and hold onto the pie as well as the bag. A flicker of amusement crossed Blossom's face as she seemed to notice she had not even given him his pie. She held it up to him. With a smile, Tony moved the pie onto his desk and returned to offer the tissues. Blossom grabbed a tissue from the box he held and at the same time handed over the shopping bag.

"A pie? And a bag of . . . ?" he asked but Blossom was occupied with the tissues and didn't answer. Tony thought the shopping bag had to weigh about ten pounds. He waited patiently while Blossom blew her nose using a succession of tissues and lined them up in a neat row across her lap. He smiled. At least *this* was normal behavior for Blossom.

Suddenly, like a switch had been thrown, Blossom seemed to recover from her unhappiness. Her chubby cheeks lifted, almost obscuring her bulbous blue eyes, and she managed a smile. "There are cookies in the bag, the kind you like with the big chunks of chocolate, caramel and extra pecans." She blinked back a few errant tears and wiped her face. "I made them just for you."

Tony felt his stomach growl, and his mouth began to water. Through the open doorway, he saw Ruth Ann watching them from her desk. Evidently seeing Blossom making a recovery, Ruth Ann relaxed in her chair and extended a hand, palm up, begging. Tony spoke to Blossom. "Cookies and a pie? This looks like a serious case of bribery to me."

Blossom's answering laugh was quite musical.

When Blossom began to laugh, Tony was able to relax a bit. "We haven't seen you for a while."

"Well, what with the little girls and being a married lady now, I've been rather busy." The mention of her stepdaughters and her husband brought a wide smile to her face. Finally done with her meltdown, Blossom rose to her feet and disposed of the tissue collection in his trash can.

Tony felt sure whatever her problem was, it did not involve her stepdaughters or husband. So far, so good. "I guess you woke up this morning and decided I needed fattening?"

"No, not that." Blossom pressed her finger against her chin, thinking. She seemed to be taking his question seriously. "Mostly everything's okay, you know with Kenny and the girls. It's my sister Dahlia."

"Dahlia?" Tony thought he had met all of Blossom's flower garden of sisters but he didn't immediately recall Dahlia. "Does she live around here?"

"Oh, no, she moved off to the city years ago." Blossom waved a clean tissue for emphasis.

"What city are you talking about, Blossom?" Tony was still recovering from his surprise that a member of the Flowers clan had left not only the county, but the eastern end of the state.

Blossom glanced up like she expected to find the answer to

his question written on the ceiling. "Well, first Dahlia moved to Atlanta, but then when she got married, she and her husband moved to Nashville. He's a musician." Clearly satisfied with her statement, Blossom rummaged in her bag and found a miniature candy bar she unwrapped and popped into her mouth. She chewed contentedly.

"Is she your oldest sister?" Tony knew Blossom was the youngest of the Flowers sisters.

"No, she's the second oldest." Blossom pasted on her well-rehearsed "thoughtful" look even as she continued chewing. "Let's see . . . Dahlia was older than Chrysanthemum and Marigold."

Tony was afraid Blossom was about to launch into the recitation of the entire family tree and interrupted before she could say another word. "That's okay. Let's just go back a step. Tell me about Dahlia and why you are so concerned about her."

"She's gone missing, of course." Blossom squinted at him as if wondering why he didn't already know the information and, since he was ill-informed, she might have to reconsider involving him. Maybe she'd even repossess the pie.

Tony persisted. "Since she doesn't live around here, how do you know she's missing?"

Blossom ran her fingers through the thin, orange hair, fluffing it up a bit. "Because she left a message on my cell phone."

"Is the message still on your phone?" Tony thought maybe listening to the exact message would be more effective than getting it thirdhand.

The light of understanding illuminated Blossom's eyes and she reached into the tote bag still dangling from her elbow, just the way it had been when she had carried it into the room. She started digging in her bag and eventually held up a very modern, and expensive, cell phone. Her chubby fingers flew over the screen, making Tony jealous. Nothing made him feel larger and more awkward than trying to push the buttons on his own cell phone.

"Okay, listen to this." Blossom held the phone to face him.

Tony leaned forward, listening to the call on speaker setting. At first he couldn't make any sense out of what he was hearing, and then he was able to separate the words in his mind. According to the phone message, Dahlia was in trouble. The type of trouble was unclear. It sounded like she had been involved in a car collision, and whether she was injured or someone else was seemed to be the topic. What didn't make sense to him was why she called her sister instead of emergency services.

"You know your sister. Does this sound like one of her normal messages?" Tony was thinking specifically about his own mother's telephone calls when, to her, every event seemed to be an emergency. The woman who raised him had a gift for melodrama and for getting herself in tight places.

Blossom stared at him for just a moment and then suddenly smiled as she realized what he was asking. "Dahlia does have frequent, um, emergencies. Uh-huh, yes she does. Usually though, she calls Marigold, who is much better at dealing with her."

Tony thought they were finally on track. "Have you checked with Marigold to see if she has heard from Dahlia?"

"No, Marigold is off on a Caribbean cruise. Everyone knows all about it." Blossom leaned forward as if telling a secret. "Marigold said she wasn't even taking her telephone with her. I know Dahlia knew all about Marigold's trip, because she's been going on and on about it for weeks."

In most cases like this, Tony knew the family simply hadn't been given all of the information. But certainly not in all cases. It was true something serious could have happened to Dahlia. "I'll need some information from you and then I'll see what I can find out. Okay?"

Blossom nodded and wiped her eyes again.

"Where does Dahlia live now?"

"Nashville." Blossom pressed a finger against her chin, her preferred thinking position.

Tony thought if Dahlia was living in Nashville and decided to visit her family, it was just over a two-and-a-half-hour drive, maybe three, unless she decided to do some sightseeing along the way or had car trouble. With information about the car and the license plate, he would check first to learn if the vehicle had been involved in an accident. It could be as simple as her running out of gas in one of the few areas where there was no cellular service. "Can you give me her address, and do you know what kind of car she drives?"

Blossom's fingers flew across the cell phone's screen, retrieved her address book in the device and read off her sister's home address. "She drives a dark red Cadillac. A brand new one."

"Dahlia's still married?" Tony seemed to recall there had been talk about some brother-in-law who was not getting along with Blossom's laundry list of sisters.

"Sort of." Blossom wiggled on her chair. "The last time I talked to her, she said she told that no good sack of dirt he could live under the bridge but not in her house."

"And how long ago was that?" Tony considered the statement to indicate a less than idyllic relationship. It added both a greater reason for her to come visit her relatives and, unfortunately, perhaps another reason to be disturbed by her disappearance.

"It was just a few days ago." Blossom hesitated. "She was mad. 'Course she's usually mad at somebody most of the time."

"I'll see what I can learn, Blossom." He handed her a notepad and pen. "If you will write your new cell-phone number down for me, I'll get back to you as soon as I learn anything."

Nodding and chewing on another chunk of chocolate, Blossom painstakingly wrote her new phone number in nice large numbers. Once done, she drew a flower face around it and then handed it to him.

"You be sure to call the department number and let us know if you hear anything from her." Tony waited for her to respond.

Finally, Blossom agreed, and heaving herself to her feet, left his office.

The moment she was gone Ruth Ann and Wade showed up in his office carrying a stack of plates, a knife and three forks. Tony laughed. At least he was not the only one who had been missing Blossom's pies.

A quick check with other agencies did not show Dahlia's Cadillac to have been involved in any accident, nor had it been reported abandoned in a parking lot. Even if Dahlia left her husband and drove to Los Angeles, there was nothing illegal about it. Officially, she wouldn't even be listed as missing. If she remained missing without checking in with her family, or if the Cadillac was located under suspicious circumstances—something like being left in a ditch with the driver's door open—then they would be able to pursue her disappearance.

Tony placed a call to a friend of his in the Nashville police department. After the initial greetings and questions about family, Tony got to the point. "It's not an official investigation at this stage, but I would consider it a favor if someone could check her house to see if her car is parked there or if she is there herself, or if there is some reason to believe she is in any danger."

"What's going on?" Sergeant Byrd asked. "You don't usually deal with us citified folk."

Tony ignored the jibe. "The woman's sister, the best-of-the-best baker of pies in East Tennessee, is concerned. She's one of those people who believe everything shown on TV, even if it's science fiction. She thinks we can find her sister's car anywhere on the planet, pretty much at the touch of a button."

"Does she have reason to believe that something has happened to her sister?"

"Only that the sister's recently told her husband to leave." Tony sighed. "In my experience, we would be just as likely to find them in the local motel, kissing and making up, as finding her deceased."

"I hear that." Byrd heaved a heavy sigh. "Just last week, I found myself in the middle of an intense marital spat. As far as I could tell, the only thing the couple agreed upon was they didn't like me interfering with their argument."

"No kidding." Tony could sympathize. The same thing had happened to him, too, more than once. "I think only one time in recent memory was I greeted with 'Yes, I called you and now I absolutely want you to lock this sack of manure up and throw away the key.' "

Byrd chuckled. "Okay. Give me the address and I'll swing by and check on the house. With any luck, she will be there and everything will be fine."

"Sounds great." Tony read off the address.

"I'll be in touch."

Tony was in the middle of some paperwork when Byrd called back. "What did you learn?"

"Well, I learned she's not in the house. He is not in the house. The neighbors haven't seen him for about a week now, and they saw her drive off at maybe ten this morning."

Tony checked his watch. It was almost three o'clock in the afternoon. "There's no way she's been driving for five hours and hasn't reached here yet."

Sergeant Byrd said, "She could still be in Nashville. She could be at the mall having a little shopping therapy, or she could be at the bank closing the account, or she's having her hair done."

He mumbled, "The best thing about being an adult is not having to account for every single action."

Tony knew he was right. "Well, thanks for checking. I'll let you know if she shows up here."

Tony had barely gotten off the phone when his radio crackled with a new call. Rex's voice said, "There's another fire in a still." Dispatch controlled all emergency calls, whether for an ambulance, a fire or the sheriff's department.

"Where is this one?" What Tony really wanted to ask was, how many stills existed in the county? And how did someone know where they all were? A memory of a fairly recent conversation he'd had with Quentin about bootlegging was triggered. Maybe these were only high-school boys looking for free alcohol? Was there a chance they had known the location of several stills and had crept in and stolen some and set them on fire to cover their tracks? Was he trying to make the case too complicated by turning bad behavior into a tidal wave of arson?

"Orvan Lundy's place." Rex's voice held its normal calm intonation.

"Is the old man okay?" Tony hadn't heard of anyone with a still being targeted twice.

"As far as we can tell. Ruth Ann's husband, Walter, called it in."

Why Tony was so relieved that Orvan was safe, he couldn't have explained to himself or anyone. He liked the old man, in spite of, or possibly because of, his contrariness. Orvan lived life on his terms. "I'll go up there, too."

He pulled Wade away from his fingerprint project.

Driving the Blazer up the twisting road, he was glad he didn't have to drive the fire truck. The road barely qualified as one. Up here, it was actually two strips of bare earth carved into the stony ground. Wade bounced around in the passenger seat, even with his seatbelt strapping him down.

"Thank goodness for the invention of seatbelts." Wade grinned like a kid on a roller coaster.

"Certainly saves a lot of wear and tear on the head." Tony had actually bumped his head on the ceiling of the Blazer on a couple of particularly rough bounces. "I do believe this road is getting worse."

"Maybe we should tell Not Bob to work up here." Wade's voice sounded like he was gargling underwater when they thumped through the deepest pothole.

Tony was amused. Not Bob actually had a very nice name but he'd never heard anyone in his department use it. The first time they'd heard of him he'd used the name Not Bob to identify himself. It stuck. "I'll let Sheila tell Not Bob. My guess is he would be more likely to mention the condition of this road to his boss if it would make his sweetheart happy."

"Speaking of Not Bob, I thought he would give Sheila an engagement ring for Christmas." Wade sounded displeased.

Tony made it his policy to try to stay out of his employees' personal lives as much as possible. However, in this case, he was as curious as the rest of the citizens about the romance between Sheila and the man known as Not Bob. Besides being the victim of a vicious attack, the man was known to everyone who drove in Park County as the well-built young man who filled potholes during the day and attended college at night. "Well, as I recall, you kept your courtship of the lovely Mrs. Wade Claybough pretty quiet."

"Yes." Wade laughed. "It wasn't easy, though. Having Grace living in Georgia at the time helped a lot."

Their conversation ended the moment they made the last curve and Tony saw Orvan's home. Orvan Lundy owned very little. The land was his, but it had belonged to his family forever. Orvan lived in a tiny cabin almost as old as the mountain it sat on. Behind the cabin was a shed or barn, or something in between the two. It was there Orvan did his work of building and repairing ladder-backed chairs. He made each of them by hand, using tools even older than the cabin. He was particularly well-known for fine quality cane seats that he wove in his own distinctive pattern.

The Lundy clan had practically died out. The ones who remained were either extremely old or, as Orvan liked to say about some of the younger ones, "They were picked before they were ripe." A few of the younger Lundy men had passed through the Park County jail, but they had mostly given up crime, which was a good thing because they weren't very good at being bad. Tony recalled the time one of them had purchased a stocking cap ski mask, then asked the sales clerk for assistance in putting it on, and then, garbed in what he perceived to be the correct costume, tried to rob the store. The same store, the same clerk, without even going outside for a minute. The arrest had taken fifteen minutes. The first thirteen of the minutes were used up waiting for the clerk to stop laughing long enough to report the event. "I swear, Sheriff. I thought it was a joke. I mean, who is that stupid?"

By the time Tony and Wade arrived at Orvan's home, the fire in the small still had already been extinguished. Old Orvan sat on a stump watching the firemen taking care of the last of the hot spots. Tears ran down his face and dripped on the bib of his threadbare overalls.

Tony did not approve of stills. He wasn't fond of drunks. He enjoyed a good beer and occasionally a little whiskey, but even if he wanted to over imbibe, he couldn't because he was always on call. Orvan, on the other hand, didn't drive, didn't sell what he made and could barely afford the ingredients. If he'd delivered some to another person, it couldn't have been much. He'd been making his own, and drinking it, for decades. Tony guessed it was the only pleasure left to him.

Ruth Ann's husband, Walter, stood near Orvan. Anger tightened his usually jolly chocolate-brown face. He stared at Tony. "First they steal his stash, and now they come back and burn the still? Who would do this?"

"I don't know." Tony looked from the firefighters into Orvan's face. "I swear everyone in my office is trying to catch the arsonist. The destruction of private property, and the very real danger of forest fires, put them high on our list of priorities."

Orvan snuffled, wiping his nose on the frayed cuff of his long-sleeved shirt. "It's just pure meanness."

Tony couldn't disagree.

Chapter Fifteen

Frustrated by the arsonist, Tony was not amused when he returned to his office and found information on his desk supplying the names and addresses of two more Mrs. Daniel Crisps. The Crisp bride count was now up to five. Of the two new ones, one lived in nearby Knox County and another in equally close Blount County. According to the notes, written in Ruth Ann's clear handwriting, the newest widows had heard about the death on the news and contacted his office. Geographically, these two lived the closest to Silersville.

Even though it would take more time to drive to each of them for a visit than to make phone calls, Tony wanted to meet them in person.

Nikki, now in Tony's notebook as "wife number four," lived in Knox County. After a brief telephone call to verify her location, Tony drove to her home in Knoxville.

Wade accompanied him, but the two of them spoke little on the drive. Along with the continuing melodrama after the discovery of Daniel Crisp's body, Tony had stills burning all over the place, Mrs. Plover's death and Blossom's missing sister moving in a continuous loop in his brain. He found it confusing and tiresome. At least, the bar-fight victim, in spite of losing most of an ear, had refused to cooperate or press charges. Tony wasn't sure if he was more irritated or intrigued. Clearly the man felt he'd deserved to lose an ear. It left them with a ton of paperwork, but they could scratch one investigation off their list.

Nikki opened the door to their knock.

"We're sorry for the circumstances," Tony began.

Nikki said nothing but waved them into the apartment. The room was small but tidy and its most striking feature, as far as Tony was concerned, was the large color photograph of the couple in wedding regalia. As she stood near the photograph, almost like she was posing, Tony noticed that Nikki's hair—short, brown curls—looked the same as it did in the picture.

"How long have you been married?" Tony thought he'd jump in. He'd offered brief condolences when he called to make the appointment.

"A year." Nikki's red-rimmed eyes met his. "Our anniversary was just last week."

"I'm sorry," Tony murmured. And he was. "How did you two meet?"

"I'm a nurse at the hospital, and I usually work in the emergency room." She dabbed her overflowing eyes with a tissue. "Daniel came in one evening with an infected wound on his hand. We talked. He was nice and he told me his wife had recently passed away, and even though I shouldn't have, I agreed to have dinner with him. He was lonely."

Tony sincerely hoped the widower story was one Daniel told for the sympathy factor and there wasn't a deceased wife somewhere.

"And you married him." Other than the photograph, Tony saw nothing in the apartment that he thought might have belonged to Daniel.

"Yes." A sob shook her. "I hardly ever saw him. I work shifts at the hospital, and he traveled for work. And now he's dead."

"I wish there was a better way to tell you this, but, well . . ." Tony wondered if it was easier when the wives had learned about Daniel's death from someone else and all he had to report was the duplicitous nature of the marriage. "As it turns out, Daniel has several wives, er, widows."

"What do you mean?" Nikki straightened quickly, as if he had slapped her.

There was simply no way to sugarcoat his explanation. "As unpleasant as this is, you are the fourth wife I've talked with, and I'm going to see another after I leave here."

"Four?" The word hung in the air.

Tony and Wade simply nodded, waiting for the meaning of the words to truly sink in.

"That's not possible." Finally Nikki blinked as if she'd stepped from a dark room outside into bright sunlight. "He's married to me."

"I'm afraid that isn't necessarily true." Tony gave her the condensed version of Daniel's marital deception. When she had nothing to add, he decided he'd learned everything here that he could. He and Wade left her to her misery.

Wade had been silent through their drive and the entire conversation with Nikki. He had carefully not interrupted Tony's thoughts. At least not until they were back inside the Blazer.

"Daniel Crisp was lower than the lowest." Wade squeezed both hands into tight fists. "Why would he treat all of these women so poorly? They have cooked for him, loved him and probably even done his laundry. Some have given birth to his children, and now they are all dropped by the side of the road with no insurance, no claim to any property or money, and aren't even legally considered the widows."

"I believe the word you are looking for is 'bastard.' " Tony felt the same rage.

"We didn't ask her if she'd ever been in Silersville."

Tony realized Wade was correct. He stared at the apartment building. "We can ask her at another time."

Their next stop was actually not far from the hospital. Wife number five, the second Nancy, worked at a car dealership between Knoxville and Maryville. Tony decided he would refer to her as Nancy2 in his notes. He'd use the correct name when he wrote his report.

A name plate reading "Nancy Crisp" was prominently displayed on a modern laminate desk between the entry door and a wall decorated with a calendar and a small quilt. The woman sitting in the chair behind the desk had dark red hair and green eyes. In appearance, she could have been Nina's sister.

"May I help you, gentlemen?" Nancy2 smiled up at them. Her smile lingered a bit longer on Wade, but not much.

Tony studied her ring finger. Maybe he was just cynical, or maybe with all his recent practice he was learning the difference between high quality and fake, but he'd bet the diamonds in her wedding and engagement rings were paste. These didn't have any fire. "Mrs. Crisp?"

"Yes." She pointed to the name plate. "That's me."

"I just wanted to make sure you were sitting in the correct desk." Tony nodded to the pair of chairs facing her. "Do you mind if we sit?"

Nancy2 looked confused but waved for them to join her. Tony and Wade pulled the chairs closer to the desk before sitting.

"We have come with bad news." Tony thought about suggesting they leave her desk area and go outside into the fresh air where there would be relative privacy, but there were no clients or salesmen immediately near them.

Some of the perky expression on her face faded. "Daniel? Is this about Daniel?" The words were spoken quickly, fearfully.

"Yes, I'm afraid it is." Tony said. The news of the man's death had been on television before they learned of the additional wives. He thought the nurse could have been working at the hospital when the story aired, but this one? "Did you happen to watch the news last night?"

She nodded. "I assumed it was a different Daniel Crisp. The news said his wife's name was Nita, no, Nina."

"His ex-wife is Nina." Tony emphasized the "ex."

Nancy2 made a sound like a cross between relief and anger. "So why are you just now notifying me? Shouldn't you have been here before anything was said on television?"

"We would have, or certainly would have tried, had we known of your existence." Tony wasn't in the mood to fight with a widow. "As it turns out, your husband has an extensive number of wives." He hurried into his explanation of their discovery.

Her eyes widened and her mouth opened. Then closed. "Well, that no good, dirty, two-faced cheater."

"Pardon me?" Tony wasn't sure he'd heard correctly.

"So, I guess we aren't really married, are we?" Her eyes flashed with more anger than grief.

"Most likely not." Tony added a shake of his head for emphasis. There was always the chance Daniel had a legally married wife in the harem. "You don't seem as surprised as the others. Did you suspect he was already married?"

"I suspected something. I think he could sell ice to Eskimos. Isn't that the phrase?" She didn't wait for an answer. Her anger level rose quickly. "He came in here and found me and swept me off my feet. I believed him when he told me it was love at first sight."

"Have you been to Silersville lately?" Wade finally managed to speak.

Nancy2 stared at him.

Wade threw in his second-best smile.

She melted a bit. "No. I never go there."

Tony was sure she was lying. But why would she? Silersville

was a popular place for day trips from the nearby counties. People enjoyed picnics, hiking, shopping. He spoke softly. "Do you quilt?"

Nancy2's spine straightened so quickly, it should have made a snapping sound. "Why yes, I do." She pointed to the small wall quilt hanging above a calendar. "I made that."

The odds were good she'd at least visited Theo's shop. He could ask his wife if she recognized Nancy2. It wasn't crucial, but Tony felt certain he was correct about the lie.

It was late afternoon by the time he and Wade returned to the Law Enforcement Center. Tony spread a large map of the state on a table in the conference area. He found it interesting that all of the wives lived in a line running from northern Georgia and traveling northeast. It made him wonder if Daniel had a regular pattern, like Mondays he was in Chattanooga and Tuesday was Cleveland.

If so, maybe the pattern would help the investigation. Somehow.

He studied the list of wives. All of the first names began with N. Now they had two Nancys, a Nikki, a Nannette and a Nora. If he threw in the first wife, Nina, there were six Ns.

Wade said, "All those wives."

"And why all Ns? Do you suppose they were cataloged in his head as N-one, N-two and on up to five?"

Mike stood in the open doorway. "How many did you say?" He looked like he hadn't quite understood Tony's comment.

"You heard right. We are up to five current wives now. That we know about." Tony gestured to his map. "All along this line." He guessed Daniel Crisp's marital adventures were going to become a continuing melodrama. It was going to take lots of man hours and more than a single jumbo jar of antacid tablets. He considered buying them by the case. "And one ex-N."

Mike came into the room and sat down, watching Tony and Wade making notations on the white board. "How do you suppose he kept them straight? You know, like birthdays and anniversaries."

"I can't believe any of this." Tony lifted a box already filled with documents and files. "He could have a wife in every county."

"Only one out of state?" Mike's fascination was obviously growing.

"Just the one we know of in Georgia." Tony simply couldn't get inside Daniel's head. "I've dealt with some truly bad people from time to time, and I'd swear they made more sense. Kill a man because he's wearing a T-shirt celebrating some team that beat one of your favorites? That's bad, stupid, crazy and displays really poor impulse control." He exhaled sharply. "But serial marriage? That's planned."

"And why only Ns? Coincidence or a fetish?" Wade shuffled the files. "Do you suppose he called them each by name or were they all 'Honey'?"

"We're going to number them according to the sequence of our encountering them." Tony pulled out some sticky notes. "Number One is the buxom blond." He looked at Wade and Mike for their opinions.

Wade began. "I think that's as good a plan as any. So, then Number Two is Nannette, the small woman from Georgia and Number Three is Nora, the Cleveland bride." Wade developed a frog in his throat and stopped to clear it.

Mike leaned forward. "Who'd you learn about this morning?"

"Number Four is Nikki from Knox County." Tony watched as Mike's expression went from curiosity to amazement and, still holding a handkerchief over his mouth, Wade bobbed his head, agreeing. "And Number Five lives in Blount County.

That's our second Nancy."

"Those two are practically in our backyard." Mike looked stunned.

Tony wanted to meet with the rest of the day shift. He pushed the intercom button to talk with Rex on the dispatch desk. "I know where Wade and Mike are; what's Sheila up to?"

"It's pretty quiet. She's just driving around."

"At the risk of jinxing that, would you ask her to come join us for a quick meeting?"

By the time Tony gathered a few files and notes, the three deputies stood in the meeting room, staring at the white board. "I'll make this brief."

He handed each of his deputies a copy of wife Number One's driver's license. "She was here, visiting from Chattanooga. Did anyone see her in the past few days?"

They all nodded.

"How about numbers two or three?" He had taken a photograph of the next two wives standing together and had printed it out.

"I saw this one," Sheila pointed to the wife from Georgia. "She and a child were downtown, at the coffee place next to Theo's shop."

"When?"

Sheila closed her eyes and was silent for a moment. Her eyes opened abruptly. "It was at least two days ago. I saw them, and then Rex sent me to check on some vandalism. We can check the call log."

Then Tony pulled out the newest two pictures, Nikki and Nancy2. Everyone said they looked familiar. They had been in Silersville, if not in the past two days, frequently enough to be remembered. No one could remember seeing them together.

"I'll check with the others at shift change." Tony's stomach protested with a gurgle of acid. No one smiled. "Keep an eye out for these ladies. I don't know whether they're friends, foes, or unknown to each other. Is their being here coincidence? A family reunion? Or a plot among the wives to do away with a problem husband?"

He decided to go visit Nina. With the chaos created by the water damage, she might welcome his questions about her ex-husband as a diversion. "Wade, Mike, you two go and do your usual thing. Sheila, I want you to meet me at Nina Crisp's home."

Tony thought Nina's past few days must have felt like a nightmare. The stress showed on her face, which looked tired and pale instead of her usual pretty and perky. There was no sparkle of mischief in her brilliant green eyes. Just a combination of fatigue, sorrow and confusion.

Tony hated to bother her with more questions. He knew without a shadow of doubt that Nina played no part in Daniel's death. The pathologist hadn't relayed all of his findings yet, but had shared his decision about the window of time during which Daniel's death could have occurred. Nina was gone during all of it.

"I'm sorry to have to ask you such personal questions." Tony led Nina away from the deconstruction at the house toward a quieter, more private location. "Unfortunately, I'm guessing you know things that could help clear up some of the confusion."

Sheila caught up with them near the woods.

Nina didn't try to smile. "Go ahead. Ask me anything."

"Do you know where Daniel actually lived?" Tony thought he'd start with something easy and totally impersonal. "Did he ever give you his address?"

"No."

"What if you needed to get in touch with him? Or forward papers to him?"

"For all I knew, or cared, he lived in a cardboard box. If I needed to talk to him, I'd call his cell phone." Nina blinked. "If anything came in the mail for him, I forwarded it to his post office box. It's here in town."

"And the kids? I know he visited them. Did they ever go stay at his home?"

"He *was* good with the kids," Nina said. Her hands trembled as she pulled her sweater tighter around her. "I'm sorry my children have lost their dad. Whenever he came to visit them, he'd take them to his folks' house, or sometimes they'd go over to Pigeon Forge and stay in a motel and have a fun weekend. The kids never mentioned Daniel taking them to a house or an apartment, or wherever he actually lived."

Tony wondered how the man had been able to afford it all. "Was Daniel paying you alimony and child support?"

"Money?" Nina looked confused by the sudden switch in topics. "Now you want to know about money?"

"Yes. We know you didn't kill him, but there are loose threads everywhere." Tony didn't have a choice. He needed answers, and some of them only Nina would have.

"He pays—paid—four hundred-eighty dollars a month in child support." Nina's tired expression deepened. "I guess that's gone, too."

Tony knew the amount was based on Daniel's net income. The man had a college degree and was bright enough to be very successful. "That's not much."

"Tell me about it." A spark of anger flashed in her eyes. "He claimed he made less than twenty thousand dollars a year."

Either Daniel was lying, or he wasn't declaring his full income. Nina absolutely needed the money for her children. But if he wasn't lying, there was a good chunk of his modest income not available for his own living expenses. "Did he pay on time?"

"Yes. Well, most of the time until recently."

"Do you think his parents helped pay, either for the kids' sake or to help Daniel?"

"No." Nina wiped a tear from her cheek with the back of her hand. "They are wonderful people, and I love them dearly. The kids love them. They spend a fair amount of time together." She stopped.

"But?" Tony waited.

"Unless they have a stash of money none of us knows about, they live on their savings and social security. Daniel's dad always worked two jobs and his mom cleaned houses, just to make ends meet. It seems unlikely they're sitting on a golden nest egg or could afford to give any money to Daniel."

Tony nodded. He knew a few people who had a golden nest egg, but they were mostly people you'd expect to have socked away money other people might have spent on extras like movie tickets or a new jacket every ten years.

He made himself a note to check into the details of Daniel's finances.

"Speaking of gold—" Tony got no further before Nina jumped in.

"There is *no* gold. There has never been any gold."

"Easy, easy. Take a breath, Nina." Tony laughed. "I'm actually not interested in the reality. I want to know if Daniel believed the old stories."

"Probably. It would have suited him just fine to find a buried treasure. You know, Civil War gold, or money from a train robbery, or anything that would supply him with big bucks without his having to put out any work."

"If you guessed—based on conversations—would you say Daniel actually made more money than he declared or enough to provide for his six families?"

"Not even close."

One of the house reconstruction workers came looking for Nina.

"Go ahead. I think I've asked enough questions for one day," Tony said. "Oh, and Theo wants you and your crew to come for dinner tonight."

Nina did smile then. "Yes. I suppose we need feeding, maybe even badly enough to eat your wife's cooking." With a wave of farewell, she headed for her house.

After Nina left, Sheila stepped forward. She had silently listened to the questions and answers, making copious notes. "He's lucky no one killed him before this."

Tony couldn't deny it. "What do you think?"

"I think with five wives, one ex-wife and, what, five children, he would need to make a lot of money somehow." Sheila grinned. "A man with zero money and lots of kids is *not* a hot commodity in the dating market."

"He has lots of living expenses, besides paying Nina child support. Each wife must have expected that he would contribute to the household funds." Tony pulled out his cell phone and accessed the calculator application, but wasn't sure what to enter after Nina's child support payment. He started making wild guesses, giving each family the same amount as Nina received. "What else?"

Sheila said, "He's on the road almost constantly, so gasoline, food, hotels for nights he's not with one of the wives. He drove a new car. Nice clothes."

"If he was as generous with all of his children as he was with Nina's brood, they spent a lot of money on entertainment." Tony looked up from his phone. "That's a lot of satellite dish installations."

"Even if the man *could* sell milk to a cow, I don't see how he could afford everything." Sheila waved at Nina's home. "Do *you* believe he was hunting for gold in the storm cellar?"

Tony didn't know what he thought anymore. He felt like the center in a gathering storm. The idea that Daniel merely fell into the hole and broke his neck was one he liked. However, it was a stupid one. Still, stupid was easy to find. The world was full of it.

Tony stood in front of the erasable white board with a full package of new color markers. Six wives. Each was assigned a color.

Blondie was appropriately yellow. He wrote her name at the top of the board and added columns to detail all of the information he knew about her underneath. Name. Age. When married. Where they met. Where she lived. Children's ages. When and where did they last see each other? Where was she when Daniel Crisp died, his neck broken?

He had barely begun filling in the information when Wade joined him. Together they sorted through reports and notebooks, and created a detailed accounting. As detailed as they could make it.

Using a second white board, they decided to rearrange the wives list to a chronological one according to their wedding dates. Number one was Nina.

Number two, Nannette, married Daniel a couple of years before the Crisps' divorce.

Nikki, the nurse, was immediately after the divorce. Tony thought she might have the best chance of being legally married. Except no papers were filed.

Nancy1, Nancy 2 and Nora were each married to Daniel six weeks apart. It was long enough for the previous marriage license to expire and for the next quick marriage to take place. From what he'd been able to gather, Daniel was a whiz at encouraging short courtships and engagements. And he'd used the exact same sales pitch. Tony had heard it from all of the wives but Nina. "I knew the day we met that you are my destiny, my only love, my future."

It had taken all of Tony's self-control to keep from expressing his personal opinions. Seriously, the man had a script for marriage proposals? No wonder he was dead.

"Let's look at this a different way." Tony stared at the columns. "Excluding Nina, who discovered his wedding addiction? We need different information. We need to know what they *really* knew about his finances and his other wives."

"You mean you don't think he was smart enough to keep all his wives secret from the others. Were they all as dull as sheep?" Wade grinned. "I can give you Grace's opinion."

"Theo's, too. If I was dumb enough to try to juggle wives, I'd expect to have my throat slit in the night."

"No, that's just it." Wade stepped closer to the white board. "If you were that dumb, you'd expect everyone around you to be just as dumb. What if the wives worked together?"

"It couldn't be all of them, but maybe a couple of them decided to fix the problem. Maybe they hoped if it looked like an accident, no one would ever know they had been tricked by a spineless man with a penchant for marriage." Tony put check marks by the names of the women seen in Silersville. "They might have hoped their unfortunate decisions to marry would not be exposed."

"Ah, but just because no one has said they saw the others, it does not mean they weren't here."

"True, so true." Tony studied the list. "From what I've seen, Nancy1 is the strongest personality."

Wade said, "Because she was able to talk him into bringing her on a weeklong trip? That would seriously mess with his usual visitation schedule."

"No kidding." Tony shook his head. "What if she called a meeting of the Wives of Daniel Crisp Club? They could have all been here at the same time."

"And if they all pushed at the same time, who would be the guilty party?"

"Their acting is pretty good." Tony stared at his notebook. "Do you suppose we could arrest them all for conspiracy?"

"Not without proof."

Chapter Sixteen

Doc Nash arrived in Tony's office, at Tony's request. Tony handed him a written report regarding Eunice Plover's autopsy results that had been faxed to his department. The doctor gave it his undivided attention, studying it carefully. Page after page.

Tony understood the information well enough to understand that, according to the tests, Eunice Plover's system contained enough arsenic to kill off every rat in the Eastern United States. The doctor finished reading, then sighed heavily and looked up at Tony.

Tony thought as a change of direction from the adventures of the Crisp wives, it was sad and disheartening. He took possession of the report again. "Tell me what you know about arsenic. How does it work?"

Doc Nash settled onto the chair. "Well, it's found in many places. I wouldn't be surprised to find that you had arsenic in your system right now."

"What do you mean?" Tony leaned closer, listening intently.

"Well, it hasn't been very long since I read a report that showed many foods and beverages we eat or drink all of the time contain traces of arsenic, everything from baby food to rice." The doctor looked angry and a little queasy.

"So, if Eunice ate too many of whatever foods from the arsenic-loaded list she could have poisoned herself?"

"Doubtful, extremely doubtful." Doc Nash steepled his fingers and put on his professorial expression. "The amount of arsenic found in foods like vegetables, meat, beer and wine is comparatively minute. If she ate a lot of contaminated foods every day, she might have consumed enough on her own to eventually feel somewhat ill. But, for her to die as she did, Mrs. Plover had to have eaten a very high dose of arsenic or have been given a fatal dose of poison in another manner and all at once."

"So this was not an accident?" Tony felt his hope of semi-natural causes slipping away.

"It could have been suicide." The doctor's face twisted with either anger or disgust. "You might want to check and see what her mental condition was. She wasn't one of my patients, at least not recently, because several years ago she did not care for a diagnosis I gave her, and she swore she would never let me treat her again."

Trying not to form any premature theories, Tony asked, "Where would she be able to find enough arsenic to commit suicide?"

"That part is fairly easy." Doc Nash shook his head. "It's just not a good way to kill yourself. There are many more dependable, less uncomfortable ways." He fell silent and stared at Tony.

Tony understood. "What you really think is someone killed her with malice aforethought, as the saying goes."

"I do. She could be an irritating woman but still, I can't imagine anyone going to the trouble of poisoning her. I would expect her killer to be someone under great pressure or intense exasperation, snapping and strangling her with their bare hands." The doctor shrugged. "For the most part she was a nice, generous, caring woman. I am truly sorry that she is dead."

"You just contradicted yourself. You think someone killed her with arsenic but don't think anyone would poison her. You read the autopsy notes. Did you notice anything I need to know about?" Tony's mind was flying in circles. "Do they even sell arsenic anymore?"

"Truthfully, I don't know." Doc Nash's shoulders rose and fell. "Historically, I've heard some people intentionally ingested increasing dosages of the poison and developed a form of immunity. They were called arsenic eaters. So, two people could have eaten the same thing and only one died, if the other was immune."

"That's interesting but it hardly suits this situation."

"Well, not as far as we know." The doctor was reading something on his cell phone. "It used to be sold for rat poison. And years ago, it was in many products, even wallpaper. There was even a time when people applied it to their skin to achieve a certain type of complexion."

Tony frowned. "I doubt she was trying to do anything about her complexion."

"I doubt that, too. But, people do the strangest things."

"I suppose the first thing to find out is where to get arsenic these days and if she purchased it, or if someone we can connect her with recently purchased arsenic." Tony opened his notebook. "I know besides rat poison, it's used in a lot of ceramics."

"Ceramics?" The doctor's evident surprise made him blink several times.

"In the glazes." In spite of the seriousness of their conversation, Tony had to grin. It wasn't often he could surprise the doctor. "I took a pottery class when I was in college and we used arsenic and white lead in some of the glazes. We often joked at the number of people we could do away with, with our poorly made pottery."

"Ceramics?" Doc Nash seemed to be stuck on the one word.

Tony actually laughed at his doctor's expression. The doctor didn't seem to have been expecting this comment. "Is there a problem?"

"No. This is the first time you've mentioned it in all the years I've known you." The doctor stared at Tony's hands as if trying to visualize them working with clay. He raised his eyes and blinked again.

"I'll bet you took at least one class in college just so you could be in the same classroom with a certain good-looking girl." Tony gave a slight shrug. "Not only that, it satisfied a requirement that I had some sort of life-improving class like art or music or literature in order to graduate."

"So, what did you learn about arsenic?" The doctor had finally come to terms with the concept of Tony creating ceramics. "How was it stored?"

"It was kept locked in a special cabinet. It was not something we could access without restrictions. There was also white lead and the possibility of other poisonous chemicals involved in the glazes."

"In other words, are you saying Mrs. Plover could have been taking a pottery class and accidently ingested stuff she was mixing up?"

Tony shook his head. "I think we'd have heard about a class. Plus, I don't know how much arsenic it takes to kill someone, but I do remember a little about the amount used in ceramics. I doubt she would have had access to enough in a community class to kill a mouse. From my experience, everyone is very careful to keep track of exactly how much arsenic is being used and how."

"Well, you might be on to something with the mouse part of the story. Lots of people used to keep arsenic in their homes. It was the main ingredient in rat poison." The doctor scratched his head and looked thoughtful. "Do you think this poisoning was intentional, or some sort of bizarre accident?"

"I have no idea. I've known Eunice Plover since we moved here when I was in the third grade. I don't believe I've ever heard anyone say anything bad or threatening about her at all. And, except for your personal squabble with the woman, I've heard pleasant descriptions of her." Tony stared at the doctor. "Who feeds poison to an innocuous woman?"

"I'd say you've got your work cut out for you." Doc Nash looked sympathetic.

The Gift Quilt—Mystery Quilt
The Third Body of Clues

Using the remaining 3-1/2″ squares of fabrics (A) and (B): Sew right sides together on one edge to form a two-patch rectangle (A+B). Press seam to (A). Make 48.

Using the 3-1/2″ squares of fabric (D) as center, sew two (A+B) rectangles on opposite sides with fabric (B) touching (D). Press to (B). Make 12 A+B+D+B+A. Set aside.

Form a stack of 24 of the four-patch butterfly blocks from Clue Two in a single pile with Fabric (C) in the upper right-hand corner. Stack the remaining 24 butterfly blocks to the right of them, leaving a small space. Rotate the right-hand side blocks until squares of fabric (C) are in upper left corner. Into the center space, place stack of remaining (A+B) two-patch blocks with fabric (B) separating the squares of (C). Sew together. Make 24 rectangles.

Lay out the strips (A)+(B)+(D)+(B)+(A). Place on each long side of it the sections of butterfly blocks. Corners of fabric (C) should touch the corners of center square (D). Sew together. Press to center. Make 12 blocks.

Chapter Seventeen

At a loss about his next step with the Plover case, Tony added the names of the various counties where Daniel Crisp had gotten a license and had a wedding to the white board detailing Daniel's complicated marital history.

"Sheriff." Rex's voice held a note of tension. This unusual occurrence brought Tony's full attention to his words. "Deputy Holt isn't responding to my radio calls."

"Your last contact?" Abandoning his project, Tony headed toward his office. "When and where?"

"Ten minutes. A wellness check on Molly Burleson."

"At whose request?" Tony knew Molly. The elderly woman lived alone and was quite independent. In the summer her garden was magnificent. She probably worked ten hours a day in it. Tony couldn't imagine the old lady would have set a trap and Holt fell into it, but Tony heard unimaginable things every day, saw them on the Internet and heard them on the news.

"Her son called from Atlanta. He told me he'd tried calling his mother and kept getting a busy signal. Hang on." Rex paused to handle another call. "Okay, I'm back. Anyway, Holt said he'd stop by and see what was happening over at her house, and I've heard nothing from him since."

Tony glanced at their list of citizens they checked regularly. Mrs. Burleson wasn't on it. "Should she be on the list or is this something new?"

"As far as I know, she's never needed us, except to rescue

that cat of hers."

Tony had dealt with the cat in question. Mrs. Burleson's cat was perfectly capable of getting out of the tree on his own four paws. The only reason Tony's department ever got involved with it was the next door neighbor's complaints about the cat chasing birds. The rescue was actually to prevent the neighbor from shooting at the cat with a BB gun.

"What about Wade, Mike or Sheila?"

"No, sir, they're all tied up. Wade said he'd get there as fast as he could."

"I'm on my way." Tony was still talking to Rex as he climbed into the Blazer.

Rex spoke crisply. "You better not stop talking to me. Er, sir."

Mrs. Burleson's house wasn't far from Tony's boyhood home. He'd played in her front yard often as a boy. Her son had been on many of the same sports teams as he had, but after college he'd decided city life was more his style. As Tony sped down the road, lights flashing, he was alert, looking for anything out of place. He saw Holt's vehicle parked near the curb in front of the Burleson house. "Rex? Anything?"

"Sir, still nothing from Holt."

Tony saw Wade driving toward the house from the other end of the street. "Wade's arriving here, too."

Even with their quick examination of the yard, it was easy to see that neither Holt nor Mrs. Burleson was anywhere in it, front or back. The shrubs were neatly trimmed, although not many plants were brave enough to grow at the moment. Spring would arrive soon.

Tony considered their options. He could walk up and ring the doorbell or he and Wade could creep around the house and try to see in the windows. Neither option sounded great. A moment later the decision was made for him.

"Help." A woman's voice called softly. "Help."

If Tony hadn't been standing where he was, close to the window on the side of the house, he would probably not have been able to hear it. "Mrs. Burleson?"

"Help," was the faint response.

Tony carefully peered through the window closest to the sound. It was hard to distinguish much through the sheer curtain so he leaned forward. Suddenly he realized what he was seeing. He spoke to Wade. "Holt's flat on the floor and it looks like Mrs. Burleson's trying to move him."

Tony heard Wade talking to Rex, relaying the message.

Everything he saw and heard made Tony confident they could enter the house without jeopardizing anyone. "We're coming in, Mrs. Burleson."

Silence. Tony turned the knob on the door and the door swung inward. "Help." The voice came from the left. Two steps took them to the doorway. Darren Holt was unconscious on the floor and Mrs. Burleson was pinned to the floor by the weight of the much larger man. "What happened?"

Wade relayed the scene on his radio. "We need the ambulance."

Tony hurried forward to see what he might be able to do to help either or both of them. "Mrs. Burleson. Are you injured?"

"Not bad." She smiled up at him from the floor. "He's heavier than he looks."

Relieved she could smile, he looked at Holt. The deputy was moving. "How long's he been unconscious?"

"I'm not sure. It feels like a long time."

As if realizing they were talking about him, Holt's eyelids fluttered and lifted. His eyes seemed unfocused, though. "Sir?"

Tony considered it both good and bad. Good that Holt was regaining consciousness and bad that he'd been knocked out. "The ambulance will be here soon."

Wade gently helped Mrs. Burleson to her feet. She wobbled

and gripped his forearm with both hands.

Tony watched Holt and Mrs. Burleson with concern. "What happened? We came because Holt wasn't reporting in or answering his radio."

"I heard it." The elderly woman pointed toward the blue and tan, striped curtains. "When the radio call came, he had both arms full, helping me get Snowflake off the top of the curtains. All at once, that darn cat leaped right at his face and knocked him over, and as he fell into me and started to knock me down, he tried to twist around. He was trying not to land on me, but he landed on me anyway and his poor head just slammed into the floor. She patted Holt's shoulder tenderly. "I couldn't get up and I didn't know what to do."

Just then, Snowflake strolled near, leaped onto the sofa, sat down and proceeded to lick one small orange paw. As befitted her status as royalty, she didn't make eye contact with any of them.

"Is your telephone off the hook?" Tony didn't see one. "When we tried calling, we kept getting a busy signal."

"Really?" Mrs. Burleson's shocked expression was priceless. She pointed to a small table behind Tony. "It should be right there."

A glance showed the receiver was on the floor, dangling from the cord. Wade picked it up and returned it to the cradle.

"Naughty cat." Mrs. Burleson frowned at the cat. Unperturbed, the cat continued grooming, until the arrival of the ambulance crew. Suddenly, all types and sizes of feet and some wheels interfered with its bathing. With an irritated look, it leaped onto the chair near the phone and leaped again up onto the chair's tall back. Without hesitating, another leap and the cat settled onto the top of the curtain.

The paramedics checked Holt's condition. "He looks fine, but we'll haul him over to the clinic and let one of the doctors decide if he needs more doctoring, some rest or you send him back to work."

Chapter Eighteen

The morning of the shop hop Theo was up long before daylight. She had explained in depth to Tony and the boys and to Maybelle what she expected for the day, including having no time for any of them. Even so, she had spent the whole night wide awake, worrying. There was no sense telling herself again that worry never solved anything. Thousands of worries traveled through her brain every day. She considered herself fairly smart, but she was still an expert worrier. Even as a small child her grandmother had dubbed her "worry wart."

Theo did the best she could with her hair, which always picked the most inconvenient days to totally frizz and go all wonky. She stared at it. Poked at it. Then she sighed, accepting her hair for what it was, and headed to the shop.

The morning actually went well, better than she expected. There were regular shoppers in and out chatting and making their purchases. All the preparations for the actual shop hop seemed under control. Ruby had called to confirm the time for lunch delivery and the makeshift cutting stations looked like they would work perfectly.

All that changed the moment the chartered bus pulled up. Suddenly there was chaos in the shop. The powder room toilet backed up. The second toilet, the one upstairs in her office, wouldn't flush. Theo was forced to send her customers, a horde of middle-aged women, elsewhere while she tried to get the plumber on a Saturday. DuWayne Cozzens, the plumber, sounded like he found the situation amusing. Nevertheless, he promised to come as soon as possible.

Ruby and her little girl arrived with the lunches. While she unloaded the boxes filled with gourmet sandwiches, some of Blossom's best cake and bottles of water, Theo got to hold the little girl. She promised to be as gorgeous as her mother and was just as sweet.

The delightful lunch provided by Ruby had a calming effect on most of the women. They continued shopping and taking turns at the cutting table and at the eating tables. Theo breathed a sigh of relief. She had a successful event, businesswise, and had made at least enough money to pay the plumber.

Suddenly she heard a commotion in the far corner of the shop. The screeching and thudding sounded like one of the fights between her sons. As Theo made it from the workroom to the corner of the fabric salesroom, she saw two women, much larger than herself, fighting over a bolt of fabric.

"You're not taking all of that!" A tall quilter wearing an elegant black and gold patchwork jacket blocked the aisle.

A chunky woman in a blue sweatshirt had both arms wrapped tightly around a lovely floral fabric. Her lower lip moved forward like that of a two-year-old just before the tantrum started. "I am, too."

"No!" The tall woman without the fabric made a fist, hauled back her arm and punched the other woman squarely in the jaw. As the chunky woman starting falling, releasing part of her grip to break her fall, her attacker snatched the bolt of fabric. "You can't have it all."

"Stop that!" Theo hurried to help the woman on the floor and turned to the taller woman. "Give her back the fabric." Theo had never been involved in a brawl in her whole life. The closest she'd been was when she separated her sons if they got too carried away when they wrestled with each other. That was comparatively simple. Growing up sheltered and without siblings, she hadn't learned to bite, kick or throw a punch. The two women fighting over the fabric seemed like professional prizefighters or cage wrestlers, or whatever they were called, in comparison. Not to mention that their extra six to ten inches in height and fifty pounds in weight made her feel smaller than ever.

Theo quickly realized she didn't stand a chance. Sassy attitude and no skills versus anger, avarice and size.

The tall woman with the stolen bolt was clinging tightly to her purloined treasure with one arm and pounding the shoulder and cheek of the other woman with her fist. The chunky woman was grappling with the bolt of fabric, setting her elbow into her opponent's throat. Theo guessed she'd been in a fight before. She seemed quite adept.

Theo stepped in again, trying to stop the fight and rescue whichever woman she could now hear wheezing for breath. For her trouble, Theo was struck by a fist slamming into her nose and an elbow in her stomach. Stunned, she staggered backwards and fell, crashing into a freestanding display. The display had looked like a butler holding a tray. It had been designed to display a lightweight product, not to be used as the landing site for even a small woman.

The display collapsed. The butler bent in half. The tall fabric thief now had full possession of the fabric and adamantly refused to return it. The other combatant wheezed, propped against the wall. Theo, now on the floor, reached up and grabbed hold of the bottom of the bolt and this time received a punch in the cheek for her trouble, knocking her glasses sideways on her face. "Ouch."

The glasses fell to the floor and the next thing Theo knew chaos erupted in her shop. Theo held her hand over her injured cheek and eye as she searched for her glasses, which had somehow gotten kicked farther away from her than she expected. She had a hand on the errant glasses when she saw newspaper woman Winifred Thornby snapping photographs of the melee. Trying to ignore the presence of Winifred, and at the same time wondering how the woman had managed to arrive in her shop at the worst possible moment, Theo jammed her glasses back on her face and returned to the fray as she tried to pull the two women apart.

For her trouble she was shoved again. Off balance, she tried to break her fall. With Theo falling, a few formerly noncombatant women surged forward to help her. The actual result was the opposite of Theo's intention. Theo was crushed to the ground with no fewer than five bodies on top of her. The air rushed from her lungs and she lay gasping for breath.

The situation escalated. More quilters, the local ones as well as the bus-tour ones, joined the fray, pushing, shoving and grappling with multiple bolts of fabric. Theo finally managed to slither away and made it up onto her hands and knees. It took several moments but she managed to find her cell phone under the broken butler display. She punched the number to dial 9-1-1. Flavio was on the dispatch desk. Theo gasped out a description of the problem.

Flavio made a choking sound. Theo had never considered that he might find her situation amusing. She could tell, though, that he was fighting back a laugh as he took the information. Tony was supposed to be off for the day but she could guess that was about to end. It made a bad situation even worse. She would never hear the end of it. The only good luck was having Maybelle in charge of the kids.

Wade was the first to arrive. The flashing lights on his car, parked practically on the sidewalk, framed him like a movie marquee. The handsome deputy stopped in the shop doorway and stared. He looked torn between concern and laughter. He looked uncertain about his next move.

Theo could only imagine what he was thinking. It was probably the first time he'd entered a room filled with women and had been ignored. As she glanced around the room, she saw quilters struggling with bolts of fabric. Gretchen was shoving a box of tissues at an elderly woman and yelling, "Don't get blood on the fabric!" The opera-singing salesclerk had an impressive voice and attitude.

Behind Wade, Theo heard the bus driver yelling, "Ladies, we have a schedule to keep!"

Coming into this chaos through the back door and directly into the workroom walked Katti Marmot carrying her baby, Pumpkin. Actually the tiny girl's name was Miranda, but she was born on Halloween and Pumpkin had stuck. Theo's spirits always rose whenever she spent time with the Russian bride. Katti loved life. She loved their trash hauler/recycler/repurposing guru. She loved her little Pumpkin. And she loved the color pink.

The baby was crying.

Katti's arrival from the back and Wade's from the front luckily had a slightly calming effect on the frenzied shoppers. Theo was able to work her way to her feet.

"Wow!" Wade managed to speak. He remained in the doorway but his shocked expression when his eyes met Theo's held concern. "Is that eye all right?"

Theo shook her head. Not only were her glasses badly damaged, but the already poor vision in her right eye was worse. She touched her face. It was definitely swelling. Her left eye was working well enough to see her husband arrive. He was not smiling. The ball cap with the sheriff's department insignia and his duty belt clashed with the jeans and paint-spattered gray sweatshirt he wore.

"Stop!" Tony's voice carried through the room. Something in

the tone brought the women to attention. They all popped up where they were and fell silent. He looked at Theo and his frown deepened. "What the hell is going on?"

Theo didn't know if she should laugh or cry. The women were frozen in place, gripping bolts of colorful fabrics. The room was in shambles. It looked like the scene of a massive storm or earthquake. She had been in the thick of it and wasn't sure herself what had happened. Feeling almost stupid, she shrugged.

Tony's frown deepened.

The slight movement of his lips released the spell. Forty women started explaining at the same time. Pointing at each other and flinging accusations. Tony beckoned Theo with his hand. When she got close enough to hear his voice, he sounded more concerned than angry. "What do you want me to do before I take you to the emergency room?"

Wade vanished, returning seconds later with a cold pack from the first-aid kit in his car. Tony nodded his approval and Theo pressed it against her throbbing face.

"Their bus will be leaving in a couple of minutes." Theo saw the shoppers headed to board their transportation out of the county. A few ladies were still having their purchases cut and order was quickly being restored. Theo tried to smile at the woman whose choice of fabrics had triggered the battle, but having a cold pack pressed to her face limited her ability to look cheerful. Theo was happy to see her paying for a lot of fabric. Money wouldn't make her pain stop, but it certainly wouldn't make it any worse.

The moment the bus pulled away, Gretchen and Katti and Susan, the extra help for the shop-hop day, began restoring order.

"Go." Gretchen shoved Theo and Tony through the doorway. "See the doctor."

Wade escorted them to the clinic. Responding to Wade's phone call, his own wife, Doctor Grace, met them at the door. "Let's see," Grace said, and pulled Theo into the examining room.

Over the years, Tony had seen all kinds of accidents and brawls. The first night he'd been on patrol, as a young cop in Chicago, he'd had to break up a fight in a bar. Not his most fun memory, but certainly not the last time there had been an alcohol-induced argument. Never in his wildest dream could he have imagined a brawl in a fabric store. All of the participants were sober. At least the women hadn't taken rotary cutters or scissors to the fight. In the wrong hands, they could be as deadly as a gun. He watched his wife disappear with the doctor.

"Sheriff?" Wade interrupted his thoughts. "How do I write this report?"

"I have no idea." Tony had to laugh. "Maybe you should wait until you can ask Theo what happened. All I saw was pandemonium."

"Those women were seriously pounding on each other." Wade shook his head. "Your wife took the brunt of it, but when that bus reaches home, I'll bet there are any number of bruises and scrapes. I saw one woman climb into the bus carrying some fabric in one hand and had a plastic bag tied over the other one. She said it was to keep the blood off her new fabric."

"It was pretty amazing to see." Tony could only imagine the news article forthcoming. There was sure to be an editorial about the fight. It would probably be elevated to the status of a riot. "How did Winifred hear about it before you did?"

"No idea. She was there taking photographs when I arrived."

Grace joined the men. "Theo will be fine."

Tony thought about kissing the doctor, he was so relieved.

"You don't think I need to take her to Knoxville, to an eye specialist?"

"No, but she is going to have one heck of a shiner and half of her face will be discolored for a while. Luckily the damage is mostly superficial." Grace looked at her husband, her face pulled into a frown. "What happened? Theo just kept saying that the shoppers got out of hand. A bunch of quilters?"

Wade said, "I've never seen anything like it. Bar fights are easier to handle."

Theo joined them. Her face was still swollen and discolored, her glasses bent, but she was smiling. "At least it was a good day for my business."

When they got to the house, the boys were awestruck. "Wow, Mom, you were in a fight?"

Tony guessed their mother had just moved up several notches closer to "The Most Awesome Mom" award.

"As exciting as that sounds, I'm going to put a fresh ice pack on my face and go lie down for a while. It's been quite a day."

The headline on the next day's *Silersville Gazette* read, "Sheriff's Wife Beaten." The photograph just below the headline showed Theo, her glasses wonky, and her face bruised and swollen. The photograph didn't show any blood, or it could have been the highlight of any gossip rag promising a lurid story. Only if the reader made it through to the end of a detailed listing of Theo's injuries and interviews with people who heard screams coming from the quilt shop and quotations from some shoppers who recounted a traumatic situation inside would they learn something near the truth of what had occurred.

"That woman is a menace." Theo looked up from the newspaper. "I will kill her."

"Please don't." Tony shared her anger and the sight of her scraped and bruised face did not diminish his opinion of her injuries. "The jail's pretty full right now and frankly, I think you'll heal faster here."

"At least it's not election year again." Theo tapped the headline. "How many people won't bother to read the article?"

Tony did not want to think about it.

If Tony could select the person he least expected to see in his office later that morning, and even more unexpectedly, looking timid, it would be newspaper woman Winifred Thornby. The two of them had an adversarial relationship. Tony didn't share more than basic information with the woman, and she loved to print disparaging articles about him.

Winifred's particular favorites were letters to the editor written from the jail. Shockingly, the inmates were not pleased with their less than elegant accommodations. They whined about the cheap soap, the thin towels, being forced to wear one-size-fits-no-one unattractive orange and white striped jumpsuits. They accused him personally of limiting personal phone calls, which lead to problems with their personal lives. The head jailor was too strict. The only person they left out of their misspelled and grammatically incorrect diatribes was the jail cook, Daffodil Flowers Smith. They might feel certain they could insult everyone else without retribution, but they ate well in the jail and knew the cook might not provide palatable food if aggravated.

Tony frowned and thought he would come right to the point. "Is there some reason you dropped by my office today, Winifred?" The few short hours since the photograph of a battered Theo had graced the front page of her paper were not enough for him to feel anything less than angered by her presence. Not enough time had passed, if there was such a thing.

Winifred hesitated. "Eunice Plover and I were not friends."

Tony didn't consider that a news bulletin. He'd be more

surprised if Winifred claimed to have a friend. "And you think I should know this because . . . ?"

Winifred's face tightened and she half rose from her seat before catching herself, and she settled back down. "The word on the street is that you are looking for people who did not get along with Mrs. Plover. I'm one of them."

"Was there a particular subject that you two disagreed upon? Or was it more of a general antagonism?" Tony had to admit he was intrigued.

"She once accused me of manipulating facts in a newspaper article in order to change the outcome of a vote about a zoning change." Winifred was careful not to make eye contact with him.

"Were you successful?" He didn't ask her if she had done it. He knew she had.

"No. I am ashamed of doing it." Winifred seemed to shrink a bit. "It was during the first year that I was in charge of the newspaper."

Tony doubted this disagreement was severe enough or recent enough to be a motive for murder. Nevertheless, he made careful notes about their discussion. If he had learned anything in his life, it was that people were not always predictable and rational. Given the right motivation, anything was possible.

"Is that all?" Tony thought Winifred looked like she wasn't through. What was coming next: another confession, or a declaration of war?

Winifred nodded and then shook her head. "No. I wanted to let you and Theo know that I deleted all the rest of the pictures I took at the quilt shop. I'm sorry about the picture we did print."

"Why?" This confession was more stunning than her claiming to dislike Mrs. Plover.

"It wasn't Theo's fault. The fight, that is, and she's always been nice to me. It just wouldn't seem right to print any more of them."

"I'll tell her." He watched as, without another word, Winifred rose to her feet and hustled from the room. Tony stared at the empty doorway. It didn't excuse her for printing the one she did. He couldn't help but believe Winifred had another agenda for her visit. But he couldn't guess what it might be.

Chapter Nineteen

Tony was impatiently waiting for the results of Daniel Crisp's autopsy. He felt like he was wasting valuable time.

If someone had deliberately killed Daniel Crisp, Tony's first nomination would go to Nina's dad. The second and third runners-up could be a tie between her brothers. Tony might have to toss his own wife into the mix, and his mother and aunt as well. He groaned out loud. Might as well get started with some surface interviews. It certainly wouldn't hurt to know where all the major suspects were around the time they guessed he'd died. Nothing like fishing without bait.

Nina's dad, "Lead" Ledbetter, grew up in these mountains, working on the family farm. The major crop of the Ledbetter farm had always been rocks. It was hard, backbreaking work and they barely grew anything. When Lead was a boy, they'd farmed with a mule and plow. When the mule died, Lead's father in desperation had harnessed the young man. It made Lead into a powerfully strong, and very determined, man. He was literally as strong as a mule. He hated farming. He hated everything about farming, from the color of the dirt to the smell of it, and, of six children, he was the only male.

Lead's father had not been an early proponent of equal rights for females, but he loved his daughters and on his deathbed made Lead swear to take care of them. He did. So, Lead inherited the family farm and five sisters. By that time, he had his own set of females to deal with: his wife and daughter, Nina.

He also had two sons, Adam and Zachary, usually called A and Z.

After his dad's death, Lead swore he'd never farm again. So, ignoring the spinning sounds coming from his parents' graves, he subdivided the family farm. He sold part of the land as several highly priced lots. Because he liked privacy, he turned the center of the tiny subdivision into a wilderness park. He kept the best lot for himself and gave Nina and her brothers other prime lots. He didn't like Nina's husband, so although it was her land and she picked the design for the house she wanted, the titles remained in his name. Until he died, and she officially inherited it, he would protect her from losing her home. Not only did Lead believe Daniel was untrustworthy, but Lead wasn't going to have some new "foreigner" move in and try fleecing one of his children, not as long as he lived.

Lead's bullheaded action turned into Nina's salvation. The divorce proceedings had been pretty nasty. The property settlement ended with Nina's father's sworn oath and supporting documents that he owned the property. He promised he would sell it to the first person, except Daniel, who offered him a dollar for it rather than have it fall into enemy hands.

The judge believed him, and that was the last time Daniel ever mentioned the land.

Tony thought his inquiry into Daniel's death would be incomplete without an interview with Lead. When he and Wade drove out to the elder Ledbetter's home, they were met with friendly words and fresh coffee. The cynical side of Tony wondered if the man was hoping to soften him up. But why? To protect his daughter, or himself?

"I suppose you've heard." Tony didn't get another word out before Lead's hands tightened into fists.

Lead leaned forward, resting his still-powerful fists on the table. An earnest expression settled on his face. "She didn't do nothin' to him. I didn't do nothin' to him either."

"Actually, I'm reasonably sure that's true. Mostly because I don't think there's any way you'd have put his body in your daughter's storm cellar. I think if you killed him, you'd have buried his body somewhere deep in the woods where he'd never be found." Tony let the words rest between them. "I'm more curious about when was the last time you saw your son-in-law alive."

"Ex-son-in-law." Lead spoke softly but clearly. "You're right, though, about the body. You think about those little girl babies of yours and consider what you would do in this circumstance. I might have entertained myself many days conjuring different and painful ways to rid us all of him. I damn sure wouldn't have left his worthless corpse in her house or yard." Lead grimaced. "You just wait. One of those tiny girls who have you wrapped around one teensy finger will probably drag home some worthless sack of dirt and want to marry it."

Tony felt a sizzle of fear. "I sincerely hope not."

"Just you wait." Lead did not appear happy about his prognostication. "As for the last time I saw him, hmm, it was maybe two or three weeks ago."

Tony wrote the information in his notebook. "What was the occasion?"

"We were both at the basketball game, watching the kids play." Lead cleared his throat. "I didn't like the man, that's no secret, and although he was a bad husband for my Nina, he did care for his kids. He remembered their birthdays and always watched their games if he was in town."

Knowing that was better than a lot of children in Park County had, Tony considered it a definite good point. "Was he sitting alone at the game?"

"No." Lead looked thoughtful, pressing his lips together. "Seems like he was sitting with a curvy, blond woman." His hands sketched an hourglass in the air. "She looked a bit put out, and as I recall, they left together before the game was over."

Tony wanted to talk to the buxom blond again. He hadn't seen her since their initial discussion. Since then several people had mentioned seeing her and Daniel together and not always in a lovey-dovey situation. "Have you seen her recently?"

Lead's head started to move from side to side and then stopped. "Wait. Yes, sir, I have." Lead's green eyes sparkled. "She was coming out of your little wife's shop. Yesterday."

Tony thanked Lead and headed back to town.

Theo was baffled. When could Lead have seen the buxom, blond wife leaving her shop? "I swear, Tony, if she was in there, I don't know anything about it. Did you ask Gretchen?" Her employee knew almost every customer by name, at least if they'd been in twice.

"No." Tony looked tired. "I'm just curious. Someone said she'd been spotted coming out of your shop and, well, frankly, it didn't seem like the kind of place she'd shop." Theo's mouth opened and he raised a hand to stifle her reply. "I know, I know, you are going to tell me how quilters come in every size, shape, color and gender."

Theo was amused. She must have been overly emphatic about something recently. Her husband looked ready to dive under the counter for protection. "I was going to say, Gretchen is coming up behind you, why not ask her?"

Tony turned.

"Ask me what?" Gretchen tucked a loose strand of hair back into her braided coronet.

Tony produced the photograph. "Buxom blond?"

"Oh, her." Gretchen rolled her eyes like a teenager and made Theo giggle. "She sashayed in here yesterday and looked around a bit. She watched the quilters for a while. Then she stopped by the counter on her way out and said to me that the dumb hicks in this town must have to sew their own blankets because they're too stupid to order one on the internet." Gretchen patted her flaxen, braided coronet and waved a hand at Theo's blond curls. "Gives us golden girls a bad name."

"Okay, how about this one?" Tony pulled out a photograph of Nancy2.

"Sure, I recognize her," Theo said. "I don't know her by name, but she's been in the shop from time to time."

Gretchen nodded. "She was in yesterday and she bought a lot of that fabric you pulled out for the sale rack."

Disappointed he hadn't learned more at Theo's shop, Tony decided to continue talking to Nina's relatives. Her brother, Adam, shared the flamboyant Ledbetter coloring—auburn hair and brilliant green eyes. Adam looked like a younger version of Lead. As far as Tony could tell, their mother's gene pool had been ignored by all of her children.

Adam, as befitted the alphabetical placement of his name, was the oldest of the Ledbetter children. Unlike his sister, he held the title to his house and land and could see Nina's back deck and flagpole from his front window. "I always promised her I'd keep a watchful eye on her. If she is ever in distress, all she needs to do is raise the flag, upside down."

Tony could easily see the top of Nina's flagpole. "No signal?"

"Nope." Adam's green eyes sparkled like bottle glass. "I can't say I'm sorry Daniel won't be threatening her anymore."

"Threats?" That word hadn't come up before now in his quest for the truth. "What kinds of threats?"

Adam looked genuinely surprised. "I'd expected she'd have told Theo about them, and you'd have gotten the full story."

"I can't say she's been terribly complimentary of the man, but she hasn't mentioned threats." Tony made a mental note to have a chat with his wife. "Were these recent?"

"Oh, yeah." The muscles in the brother's jaw jumped as he clenched his teeth. "Just a couple of days ago, just before she left for D.C., he stopped by and *suggested* she give him some cash."

Tony could read between the lines. This suggestion probably equaled coercion. "How much did he want?"

"A couple of hundred." Adam frowned. "It's not like it's a fortune, but it's the principle, and my sister is far from wealthy. She's not teaching high-school French to fill in the empty hours."

"When was the last time *you* saw him?"

"Maybe Sunday." Adam waved his hand toward the road. "He was driving down there with his hot, blond bombshell."

"And you weren't tempted to get your ex-brother-in-law out of the neighborhood?"

"Damn right I was. I wanted to grab my deer rifle and blow his damn head off." Adam pantomimed lifting and firing a weapon. "Didn't, though."

Tony would be shocked if the man had killed his ex-brother-in-law and left the body as a welcome home present for his sister. "Did you see or hear anything unusual coming from your sister's home?"

Adam considered the question, taking his time. Then shook his head. "We're close but not that close, and the view is pretty limited."

Brother Zachary lived the same distance from his sister as Adam, but in the opposite direction. He, too, could keep watch on his sister's home, after a fashion. Old-growth trees and dense underbrush in the park were visually limiting. Tony and Zachary had been in school together and played ball on the same teams. "How've you been?"

Zachary looked surprised by the question and Tony's presence on the front porch. "Fine, Tony, and yourself?"

Tony said, "Fine." Once the greetings were covered, Tony began asking him the same things he'd asked Adam. The answers were close to the same until they got to the last time Zachary had seen Daniel.

"I saw that no good—" Zachary swallowed the rest of his emotional statement. He paused, exhaled sharply and began again. "Sunday afternoon."

"Where?"

"He stood right where you're standing now." Zachary's nod encompassed the broad front porch that served as an additional, but outside, room. The room was furnished with a patterned carpet, upholstered chairs and sofa, and a large glass-topped table surrounded by ladder-back chairs. Just off the porch, on its own private brick patio, sat a combination gas and charcoal grill. It was as big as a car. Tony guessed Zachary could roast a whole pig on either side.

Zachary opened his front door and held it open. "I wouldn't let him in my house. You can come in if you'd like."

Tony appreciated the offer but refused. "What was he doing here?"

"Looking for a handout. He got all hot under the collar when I refused to give him any money, not so much as one thin dime. You want *my* guess, Tony?"

"Sure. You've spent more time around him than I have." Tony knew guesses would never be categorized as fact or evidence, but opinions were usually based on some type of experience.

"Only a couple of hours after he asked for money I was on my way to the Knoxville airport and he zoomed by like a bullet. Even as fast as he was traveling I could see he had a blond woman with him." Zachary's eyes darkened. "My guess is she was proving to be more expensive than he'd bargained for."

Tony knew Zachary was a pilot and was often away. Still, he thought Zachary had a pretty cavalier attitude toward the deceased. "Have you talked to your sister lately?"

"Sure, kind of. She was getting ready to take a school group to D.C." Zachary shifted to stand straighter and the corner of his lips turned down into a frown. "Is there a problem? Isn't she all right?"

Tony gave Zachary his best reassuring smile. "Nina's fine. However, her ex-husband is not."

"Well, now, isn't that just awful. I leave town and what, was he in an accident?" Delight rearranged Zachary's face. "How bad is it?"

"He's deceased."

"Well, you don't say. Isn't that a piece of happy news?" Zachary's wide smile made him look like he'd bet big money on the winner at the Kentucky Derby.

Tony sighed. He still had the feeling that Nina's brothers, either or both of them, would have been happy to take Daniel out into the woods, shoot him and bury him right there. There was simply no way, at least not one he could see, that they'd kill the man and leave him practically on their little sister's front porch.

Chapter Twenty

"Sheriff, I've been working on this autopsy and have a bit of news for you about Daniel Crisp." Doctor Death's cheery voice came through the speaker phone. The Knoxville pathologist loved his work. "I can tell you the man had a broken neck and there was no water at all in his lungs."

Tony was relieved. It was a personal thing with him. The whole idea of drowning was one of the worst things he could think of. If anything, his spending several years in the Navy had made the idea even more repellent than before. All those miles and miles of deep water. "Do you have anything else you can share with me?"

Doctor Death cleared his throat as though he were preparing to give a speech. "Well, yes. I think from what I've seen and the report and photographs of where the body was found, he might have simply missed a rung on the ladder and fallen awkwardly into that small space. It had to be like being crammed into a box and his neck broke."

"There is no sign of his being struck, causing the fall?" Tony wouldn't be shocked if the man had been punched in the jaw.

The doctor allowed himself a slight chuckle. "No way. I checked carefully for any indication of contact. He was already dead when the water started, and that might have been as much as twenty-four hours after his death. I'll say it again: there was no water in his lungs." The doctor paused. "However, that doesn't mean he didn't have help falling."

"However?" Tony wasn't quite ready to stamp "closed" on the file. "So, he could have been pushed?"

Doc Death agreed. "A push wouldn't have left a mark unless he was pushed with a fist or a pipe wrench. But, he could just as easily have lost his balance and toppled over. I can only tell you what caused him to be dead. Nothing else." There was silence for a moment. "If you have some pertinent information that indicates another manner of death, you will have to share it with me. Otherwise, I can indicate some uncertainty about the manner on the death certificate."

Tony massaged his forehead, trying to relieve some tension. "No information. Just a nagging suspicion caused by my personal dislike of the man."

"I'll list the manner as unknown until you decide. I would be interested to know why he was found in such a spot at his ex-wife's house." Like Tony, the doctor clearly found the circumstances of the man's death to be a bit peculiar, and he sounded irritated by their lack of information. "I've studied the pictures of the storm cellar, trying to understand what happened to him. It's not like the man went out there to visit his ex-wife and fell into an unseen hole in the dark."

Tony agreed. Thinking that sometimes people got what they deserved, he disconnected.

Tony thought he'd talk to Theo again. "Did Nina ever mention Daniel making threats?"

"Threats?" Theo repeated the word and let it bounce around in her brain for a moment. About the last thing she expected to be asked was if Nina had ever mentioned being threatened by Daniel.

"I'm sure over the years you've learned more about Nina's marriage than anyone else." Tony smiled encouragingly. "What was the latest news?"

"Nina was tired of him showing up erratically to see the children, and she was super upset when he showed up unexpectedly. There is an actual visitation schedule, which she checked very carefully before setting the D.C. trip in motion. Daniel arrived unexpectedly while she was packing for herself and the kids. I guess he really pitched a fit." Theo shook her head, setting her curls in motion. "She told me Daniel shouted and claimed she had no right to steal his children away when he had come up here expressly to spend time with his beloved offspring."

Tony assumed the words were Theo's. The intent was clear though. "Money?"

"Oh, yeah, if she gave him money, he'd let her take the kids to D.C. Only Nina doesn't have any extra cash, so she had to refuse."

Tony thought Theo's expression was close to Nina's brother Adam's. Luckily his wife hadn't followed her inclination either. He'd hate to have to arrest Theo for murdering the scum. "Did she mention anything else Daniel had said or done?" Tony would compare the two women's stories.

Theo went still. She stared at something only she could see. She whispered, "Nina told me he said if she continued to date Dr. Looks-So-Good, he'd take her to court and have her declared an unfit mother." Theo looked up into his eyes. "It's ridiculous, of course, but still cruel. He's allowed to bring any number of girlfriends, like his blond bombshell, along for a visit, and yet he would tell horrible, obscene lies about Nina to anyone who would listen."

"Did she tell the dentist?"

"Yes." Theo nodded vigorously. "I guess he was furious. The idea of her ex-husband bullying her was too much. He's smart and very nice as well as handsome."

Tony wasn't surprised by anything his wife reported. He liked his brother Tiberius's partner in their Knoxville dental practice. Tony wasn't looking forward to asking the dentist his opinion of the deceased. But again, as with her father and brothers, Tony couldn't imagine anyone who loved her leaving the body there, right next to Nina's front porch.

If it wasn't an accident, Tony had to consider if the death had been an act meant to destroy Nina. That seemed ludicrous. He thought a better possibility was someone who had followed Daniel and merely killed him where he stood.

Nina, like his wife, was smart, decent and not likely to be involved with anything deliberately dangerous. "Do you know of any problems Nina was having with anyone besides Daniel? Even inconsequential problems."

He made a note to himself to ask Nina as well, but his wife's radar was pretty good.

Theo looked thoughtful and finally said, "Recently she had a problem with the parent of one of her students who didn't think she was grading fairly because his boy's bad grades were going to limit his sports eligibility. That's hardly rational because how would someone know Daniel would be at Nina's house? Or weirder, who would think she'd care?"

Tony couldn't disagree. Still, weird things happen. "What was the name?"

"I don't know. You'll have to ask Nina."

"Anything else happen?"

Theo stared at him. Silently, and slowly, she shook her head.

Chapter Twenty-One

Tony knew Nina's ex-husband might not have been the best man he could be, but her children had lost their father. And they grieved. The wreckage caused by a simple hot-water tank would take a long time to fix. He was distracted from his thoughts of Daniel's death by another growing file on his desk and found himself thinking about unfairness, cruelty and fate.

Tony sat wondering about Eunice's death. Eunice Plover had lived in Silersville her entire life. She married her high-school sweetheart but never had children. She volunteered at the church and sang in the choir. Her bully of a husband had passed away three years prior from a long series of cardiac events and his adamant refusal to give up grease.

Eunice was an excellent cook, but favored the rich goodness of butter mixed with everything, especially sugar. Her husband's doctors convinced her to change her recipes to include more vegetables and less fat. She did, so he ate out. Tony himself had heard the man shout across the room for more fries at Ruby's café. He passed away, napping on his recliner, after a particularly large restaurant meal of chicken-fried steak, fried okra and fried potatoes followed by a slab of pie covered with ice cream.

After his death, Mrs. Plover returned to the foods she preferred—fried chicken, red-eye gravy on biscuits, bacon and butter were her favorite mealtime foods. If anyone could make green beans bad for your health, she could. She had a voracious appetite and an amazingly spacious stomach. In one of life's paradoxes, her medical records showed her cholesterol level was always low.

Eunice claimed publicly she lived for dessert. She and her best friend, Jenny Swift, competed against each other to produce the most luscious and potentially most fattening or deadly desserts. It was only a semi-friendly rivalry. No bake sale was complete without the dueling duo trotting out their finest cookies, cakes and pies. When they weren't cooking, they were inseparable. Although Blossom Flowers Baines actually was a better cook, she was much younger and smart enough to stay clear of the competition. Mrs. Plover's nephew, Jack Gates, was her official taster. He had a wide grin on his face when he told how difficult he found the task.

If anyone could supply informal information about Mrs. Plover, it would be Tony's own mother and possibly his aunt.

Tony and Wade drove out to the museum and cornered his mother. "I need to ask some questions about Eunice Plover." Predictably, Jane didn't want to talk to him about her. It frustrated the life out of Tony that his mom seemed to hear every bit of gossip and remember it, and no one told him anything. "Who were her best friends?"

"Why, Jenny Swift, of course." Jane finally surrendered after she fidgeted on her chair and moved the handle on her tea cup from one side to the other twenty or more times.

Tony gripped his pen. "Yes, I know about Jenny. Everyone, including me, has seen them laughing together. Who else?"

"She, that is Eunice, is older than she looks, you know." The moment Jane said the words, she paused, clearly realizing she had used the wrong tense. "Looked, I mean."

"And that has what to do with what?" Tony waited for his mother to catch up with him.

"Most of her friends are quite a bit younger than she was."

Jane looked like she had answered his question to her satisfaction. "Still, I would say Jenny and Eunice were closest friends. I often saw them shopping together or having lunch."

"And who else?"

"Well, if she wasn't with Jenny, I most often saw Eunice with Jack Gates. Not only are they relatives, but they've been friends forever, or as close to forever as two people with a twenty-five-year age gap can have. After his accident, he came to visit her quite often and now, of course, lives here." Jane's expression held a mixture of amusement and curiosity. "I believe he's much more popular with the ladies now than he was before he became crippled."

"When Eunice was found," Wade interjected, "it looked like she had just finished eating."

"Not to speak ill of the dead," said Jane, "but Eunice had an insatiable appetite for sweets, and it wouldn't surprise me if you told me that she had exploded from overeating."

"Speaking of not speaking ill of someone . . ." Tony frowned at his mother's words. He racked his brain for a diplomatic way to ask his next question. "I remember when you and Eunice were practically inseparable. What happened? Why did that change?"

"Does it make a difference?" Jane wouldn't look directly at either of the men.

"I won't know until you tell me what happened." Tony stared at his mother.

Jane shrugged. Then she fidgeted. She took another sip of her tea. She heaved a huge sigh. "It was one of those stupid, unfortunate misunderstandings. Her husband was a bully, and at one time she asked me for advice. I gave her bad advice instead of sympathy or any form of help."

"What happened?" Tony didn't really need to ask. He knew the pattern and could almost predict the result. "Did she end up in the hospital?"

"Thankfully, no. At least it wasn't anything quite that horrendous. What she had needed was a shoulder to cry on and encouragement. I pushed her away." Jane pulled a tissue from her pocket and wiped her streaming eyes and blew her nose. "But she never confided in me again."

"There are no children." Tony checked his notes.

Jane's expression turned to one of great sorrow. "She had one child, a girl, who died in infancy."

Tony felt touched by the fear every parent experiences when hearing such words. He buried it and asked, "And her will?"

"Ask Carl Lee Cashdollar. I'm pretty sure he's her attorney. I do remember hearing that her late husband's brother was even worse scum than her husband. Unless she has a will, his brother's children may be in line to inherit."

Like pieces of a puzzle coming together, Tony recognized the family by name and reputation. He had served papers multiple times to the children involving varying lawsuits about money and, most recently, bankruptcy proceedings. If they were to inherit Mrs. Plover's home and the valuable land it sat on, he guessed it would only be a matter of time before they squandered the inheritance. Tony felt like slapping himself. How could he have forgotten the recent melodrama in his office. It hadn't been long since Mrs. Plover came to his office complaining that her niece and nephews were trying to move her off the property so they could sell it. She was adamant in her refusal to sign it over to them. The little heathens, as she always referred to them, had been unable to attain even a counterfeit power of attorney.

"Anything else, son?" Jane rose to her feet, the royal indication that she was through talking to them.

Tony gripped his pen harder. "Not right now, Mom. But I'll be back."

★ ★ ★ ★ ★

Tony, with Wade at his heels, stopped by Carl Lee's law office. They were in luck. The overworked public defender was available.

Tony skipped the normal greetings and started right in. "Eunice Plover has died. Do you happen to know if she has a will?"

"She absolutely does. I just got back from a convention and am out of the loop. When did this happen?" Carl Lee was clearly upset by the news. "We drew it up very carefully in order to eliminate any possibility of her brother-in-law, or his children, getting a single penny of her estate. She called them collectively 'Satan's children.' "

"It's been a few days, and we're still not sure what happened." Tony wasn't surprised by the information about her will. It sounded like something he'd expect from the outspoken Eunice. "Can you tell me who does profit by her death? That's some pretty valuable property up there."

"I can look it up. Most of the property has already been deeded over. I remember several charities and a few individuals will share the remaining estate. None of them are related to either her or her late husband." Carl Lee pulled a spotless handkerchief from his pocket and wiped his eyes. "I don't understand. She seemed to be in such good health the last time I saw her. What happened?"

Since Tony didn't really know, all could tell Carl Lee was that they were investigating the situation. "If you wouldn't mind finding a copy of the will, I can wait."

Carl Lee stood. "Do make yourself comfortable. I'll go get it for you." He wasn't gone very long before he returned with a file containing a good-sized document. "Here you go, Tony."

Tony flipped through the pages, skimming the document. "If she wanted to make a new will, you know, without involving you, how would we know which one was the valid one?" Tony's perpetual indigestion made his stomach rumble.

"It's actually very simple. She could go to another attorney or write out a document herself and sign it in front of witnesses. The date the will is signed is the key to determining which one is the true one, unless someone can prove there was duress or some mental incapacity." Carl Lee cleared his throat. "Um, do you have reason to think there's another will?"

Tony shook his head. "No. I wouldn't be shocked, though, from descriptions I've heard of her brother-in-law and his children, to see the family show up with a brand-new document."

His statement brought a wry smile to Carl Lee's face. "Nor would I. When she didn't call them 'Satan's children,' she referred to them as a pack of hyenas. If they have a new will, you might want to check on the identity of the witnesses and maybe have her signature verified by an expert."

Tony accepted this as good advice. He decided to increase the patrol presence near the empty house. He didn't believe hyenas were likely to heed the tape and seals.

Tony sat in the passenger seat of Wade's cruiser. "Have you had any recent dealings with the Plover clan, father or children?"

"Funny you should ask." Wade made no attempt to start the car. "It hasn't been a week since I had to drag two of the younger generation out of The Spa. They were so drunk they were annoying the pack of deadbeats hanging out there."

Tony knew he'd regret his decision but it was necessary. "Let's drop by The Spa and see if there's any new fungus growing on the walls." He watched Wade's face. The handsome deputy didn't look happy with the decision, but at least he didn't jump out of the vehicle and run the other direction.

The Spa was the shortened name for The Spot, a seedy tavern

on the outskirts of town. The peeling paint on the exterior left only a faint pinkish shadow, the remains of a large red spot encompassing the door and part of the front wall. Dirty, dark and dismal summed up the interior of the bar and the owner wasn't any better. The owner, Fast Osborne, did not appear pleased to see Tony and Wade.

"Have any of the Plover family, father or children, been in recently?" Tony thought he would ask in spite of his disbelief he'd be given a straight answer. He was correct.

"I don't make a habit of gossiping about my clientele." Fast peered at them through the dim light of the bar. "Have you got a warrant?"

Tony grinned at the absurdity of having Fast bring up the *W* word. Fast was known throughout Park County for being one of the biggest gossips. Ever. The ladies at the senior center could talk all day and never come close.

"I don't believe we need a warrant to ask for this information." Wade slapped a cockroach crossing the bar for emphasis. Fast balled his hands into fists. Wade smiled. "Oh, I'm sorry. Was that your pet?"

"Before you two get into a fight." Tony stepped between the two men and addressed Fast. "When was the last time you saw the younger Plover brothers?"

Fast mumbled, "They *was* in here last night."

"Now that wasn't too hard, was it?" Tony's exasperation was growing. "Were they with anyone?"

"Naw, it were just the brothers." Fast gestured to a table barely visible in the semidarkness. "They just set and drank there all evening. They wasn't socializing or playing pool."

"Did you overhear anything they said?" Wade was back to writing himself notes instead of slapping roaches.

"Only thing I did hear was them whinin' about that aunt of theirs not being good enough to chip in some money for her dear departed husband's family." Fast's face indicated a fair amount of displeasure on his part. If his clients weren't getting extra cash, neither was he. "Guess she was a real tightwad."

Tony had his own opinions of men who thought nothing of spending the evening and their money hanging out in the bars while expecting someone else to supply food and clothing for their children. He managed to hold on to his temper, but it was a near thing. He tipped his head to indicate to Wade that he was ready to leave. It was a race to the door. Wade won.

Wade glanced at him when they were standing in the fine, fresher air of the parking lot, inhaling deeply. Heavy exhaust fumes were better than breathing in the bar. "Let me guess. We're off to notify the brother and the nephews."

"First, I think I'd like to get my own vehicle." Tony glanced at his watch. "This day is not getting any younger. Maybe I can go straight home after we enjoy our interview."

Wade nodded and climbed behind the wheel. "We've heard some sorry stories, but certainly nothing that I think says criminal behavior."

Tony agreed. "But it doesn't seem possible that she could accidentally ingest that much arsenic. It isn't a good way to commit suicide, either."

"However improbable, then, we're left with homicide." Wade's eyes started to cross.

"On second thought, I think we can wait until morning to accost Mrs. Plover's 'grieving' relatives." Tony felt his brain turn to mush. "Go home. Get some sleep."

Chapter Twenty-Two

The first thing the next morning, the quest to meet the rest of the Plover clan continued. Tony managed to track down an address for the late Mr. Plover's brother in a neighboring county. Tony and Wade headed out on the unpleasant duty of death notification.

Leon Plover, Eunice's brother-in-law, barely let them introduce themselves and mention her name before he began ranting about Eunice and how selfish she was and downright pigheaded she was about everything involving his family. "Whatever that crazy woman claims is a lie!"

"We're here with bad news." Tony cleared his throat, hoping to stop Leon's tirade. "I have to admit I've not heard anything to indicate you cared much for your sister-in-law, Eunice, at all, but she passed away." Before he'd climbed out of the Blazer, Tony had popped four antacid tablets in his mouth. A chunk of one still embedded in a tooth gave him something pleasant to think about.

"Oh, my sorrow. She can't be dead. That's so wrong." Leon turned his head and snuffled into his right shoulder. The T-shirt, once white, had seen better days and had no recent experience with a washing machine. "I'll miss her so much."

Tony considered what he was hearing. Leon had just told them their relationship was far from a pleasant one, but now the fact that she was deceased seemed to upset him way out of proportion for an antagonistic relationship. What surprised Tony even more was the giant contrast between Leon and his deceased brother. Eunice's husband had been well-educated and well-dressed. Either Leon was an ignorant piece of trash, or he wanted Tony to believe he was. Tony would swear it was the second option. But why?

"When was the last time you spoke with her?" According to the current gossip in Silersville, the argument about the house and money was ongoing and had recently escalated.

"Well, let's see, I was over to her place, maybe a month ago."

While they still stood in the entryway, Leon's two sons staggered down the stairs. Grown men, almost identical physically to their father, they were dressed in expensive, but soiled, clothing. They smelled like the Spa or another unpleasant bar: stale smoke, stale beer and maybe old chicken grease.

The brothers stared at the three men who stood at the bottom of the stairs. Finally, bracing himself against the stair rail, the one on the left spoke. "What's up, Dad?"

Leon managed a teardrop before answering. "Your beloved Auntie Eunice has passed away."

"Cool." The one on the right spoke, but both men grinned like they just won the lottery. "When do we get the money?"

"Now, boy, I expect there's some paperwork to do first." Leon looked to Tony for verification.

Tony's mouth opened but a different voice spoke.

"Damn." This came from the brother on the right. "I could sure use some of that cash now."

It wasn't easy, but Tony managed to hold his tongue. He fought to keep his expression impassive because he wanted to hear the whole conversation. If something untoward had happened to Eunice, these three appeared to have a motive and not much in the way of brains or compassion.

Leon scratched his belly. "I guess that's life." All hint of grief evaporated. "Seems to me, we might as well get started clearing out all that junk that's in the old woman's house."

"No, you will not." Tony shook his head. "That house is sealed and the property is off limits until further notice and until there is a determination of inheritance of some of the personal items." He didn't trust these men.

"That's not fair," one of the brothers whined.

"That's the way it is." Tony didn't know which of the men had said the words, but they all looked disappointed and angry. "If you trespass or steal anything, I will arrest you. If you even touch the doorknob, I will arrest you. If you are unaware of the change in ownership, you should know the house and land no longer belonged to Eunice at the time of her death."

The relatives stood, mouths gaping wide.

Tony repeated. "It will not belong to you."

Not satisfied by the suicide theory, Tony and Wade went from house to house in Mrs. Plover's neighborhood, knocking on doors and asking people if they often had contact with Mrs. Plover. They asked what the neighbors knew of her and if they'd ever noticed anything peculiar or unusual happening at her home. Most of their responses detailed facts Tony already knew. The older woman was well-liked and watched a neighbor's baby for an hour each morning until the babysitter picked her up, for free. She was quiet. She kept her trash contained. She waved and smiled when they drove by. Her most frequent visitors were her friend Jenny Swift and her nephew, Jack Gates.

One neighbor told a different story. It was not a new story to Tony, as the sheriff.

Tony knew from complaints Mrs. Plover made that she thought one of her neighbors, Wes Hoffman, was a dangerous man, if not a known criminal. She claimed Hoffman had broken every law in the book, and he was harming his children. Careful investigation showed the neighbor's most heinous activity was his preference for a vegetarian lifestyle. Tony had paid the man a visit at the time.

Now, months later, standing on Hoffman's porch, Tony said, "Do you mind if I ask you a few questions?"

"I thought we cleared up everything." Obvious surprise creased the neighbor's forehead. "But sure, it's fine."

"I'll ask a few questions, then we can work up to the reason." Tony thought either the man had no idea what was going on in his neighborhood or should be working on an acceptance speech to collect his award for really fine acting. "Mrs. Plover."

"What's that old bat accusing me of now?" The neighbor flung the door open as wide as it would go, ignoring the way it bounced off the wall, and rested his fists on his hips, making a display of his anger. "Whatever it is, I'm sure she'll write a letter to the editor complaining about my aberrant lifestyle."

"I gather you still don't get along?" Tony knew it was an understatement. This man was very angry. Tony made a notation in his notebook about Hoffman's anger. "What if I told you she was dead?"

"I'd say, either it's a lie or good riddance!" Hoffman practically spat the words. Almost immediately, whether from something his brain signaled or the expression he might have seen on Tony's face, Hoffman amended his statement. "Now that's not altogether true, Sheriff. While it is true that she is an aggravation of enormous proportions, it is only to me. My children and my wife like her." His breathing was rapid and shallow.

"Why do you say that?" Wade managed to ask a question before the neighbor launched into another verbal assault.

"She's one of those strong people. I don't think she's ever been sick." Hoffman stuffed his hands in his pockets and hunched his shoulders slightly, looking somewhat apologetic. Staring past the men on his front step, he looked in the direction of the Plover house. "She actually isn't all bad. A few weeks ago when we all had the flu bug, she brought us soup, even a homemade vegetarian soup for me."

"Was that before or after she called my office to complain about your withholding meat products from your children?"

"Before."

Tony thought the neighbor's expression bore a striking similarity to a five-year-old's displeasure when caught doing something he had been instructed not to do. "Did you go over to apologize?"

"Yes. I took her a plate of oatmeal-raisin cookies."

"When was this?" Tony mentally checked their timeline.

"Uh, well, it was Sunday."

"Did you get the plate back?" Wade studied the man's face before writing himself a note.

"No." The neighbor looked surprised by the question. "It wasn't valuable. It was a throwaway, a recycled paper product."

"If it turns up, we might ask you to identify it. For evidence purposes."

"Evidence? A paper plate?" The young man's expression changed as he began connecting the dots. "Say, what's going on? Has something happened to her?"

"Yes, I'm afraid she has passed away." Tony hated delivering this kind of news, even to people who claimed they didn't care.

"Impossible." The motion of his head from side to side emphasized Hoffman's disbelief. "She'll outlive us all."

Tony thought he would approach this from another direction. "All right, let's say I believe you. Being one of her neighbors, you were in a good position to see what was going on. You know, if there was something to witness." Tony was not happy with his own words. He tried a question. "If you were going to guess who might have a serious grudge against her, who would it be? Have you seen anyone unusual visiting her?"

Hoffman studied the ground for a bit and then stared at the house across the way, and then straightened and looked directly into Tony's eyes. "Yes, there was something strange."

"Tell me."

"I had forgotten all about it. A family stopped by her house not too long ago, a man and a woman and three children. I heard them all screaming at each other." Hoffman ran a hand through his hair making it go all spiky, as he carefully tried to recall the day.

"Was Eunice screaming?" It was hard for Tony to imagine the normally well-behaved woman acting like a toddler.

The neighbor concentrated on the question and eventually said, "No, actually, she was pretty calm. The shotgun she had pointed at them wasn't wavering at all."

Tony smiled to himself. He heard Wade stifle a laugh. The neighbor had clearly been so caught up in his own petty argument with her that having his neighbor lady brandishing a shotgun at someone else didn't seem at all threatening. "I think I need more information. Could you hear anything they said?"

"Why don't you two come in and sit down?" Hoffman led the way into his house. "Would either of you like some water or coffee?"

Wade declined.

Tony shook his head, and settled onto the sofa. "About the argument."

Hoffman launched into his story. "It was over a week ago now. Saturday afternoon. I was trying to watch basketball. The Tennessee girls had their hands full that day. It was quite a match." He studied his floor for a moment, hands spread as he shifted, almost like he was playing in the game. He looked up. "Wait. I just remembered I overheard her say she would not sign any paper. Ever! She had to be really screaming at someone for me to hear it over here. The windows were closed."

"Do you know what kind of paper she was talking about?"

"Not exactly. I had the feeling though that it was something to do with ownership of her house."

"Why was that?" Wade looked up from his note taking.

"You know how sound travels up here in the hills. One minute you can't hear anything being said ten feet away and then, with just a slight shift in the air or in your location, you can hear everything like they're talking right next to you."

Tony had experienced that phenomenon. He nodded. "What was said?"

"Well, all of a sudden I heard something about them wanting her to move into town, leaving the house, or else they'd lock her up." He frowned. "I can tell you that, as much as she irritated me personally, I cannot imagine her living anywhere else."

"But you don't know who these people were?"

"I should." Hoffman leaned back and closed his eyes. He made a little humming sound as he thought. Tony was content to wait. Suddenly the man's eyes flew open and he sat up straight.

"I had seen them before." Hoffman rose to his feet and went to the window, staring at Mrs. Plover's house. "After they had stopped by to threaten her, she talked about them. It was just the one time, and it made her so sad we ended the conversation. I expected feistiness and aggravation from her, not tears. I guess her late brother had three children, two boys and a girl. In her words, none of them ever amounted to a hill of beans. After their father died, they robbed their mother of every last penny she inherited and bankrupted the entire family. I think the angry man that day had to be one of her nephews."

Wade said, "No wonder she didn't want their name on any of her property."

Between her own niece and nephews and her late husband's family, Tony wondered how many would try to challenge the will now that she was dead. He was thankful for the information he'd received from her attorney, Carl Lee Cashdollar.

Tony heard a blast of static coming from Wade's microphone, followed by Rex's voice. "Sheila says to tell you that a pack of women is headed toward Mrs. Plover's house."

Wade looked to Tony for guidance. "Want me to hang more yellow tape?"

Tony wasn't sure what to tell him. "Better to err on the side of caution. If we let those ladies trample the scene and a crime has been committed, we will never solve it, and if we do, we will never get a conviction."

Wade gave a small salute. "I'll block off as much of the property as I can."

"I'll go back to the center. When you finish, come to my office. I'll see if I can find an address for her brother's children."

"Sounds like a family as much fun as her husband's."

Thankfully, it didn't require much detective work to locate the name and address. While he waited for Wade, Tony stared at the growing pile of papers on his desk and found himself wondering what to tackle next.

Chapter Twenty-Three

Theo stood near the quilt shop's front window and watched a small, old couple walking down the sidewalk. The two of them were holding hands as they walked and bobbed up and down in perfect unison. New to the area, it looked like they had quickly become acclimated. Theo guessed they'd had lunch at the senior center and then, carrying matching small, orange, thermal tote bags, they went for a short walk. No one she talked to knew their names.

Theo had managed to learn their home was a small apartment in the new senior housing complex. Theo wasn't quite sure that six were enough units to qualify as a "complex," but it didn't matter. Theo's enjoyment came from watching the pair. Husband and wife were almost identical in height and weight and, dressed in the right clothing, they looked like Humpty Dumpty and his wife taking a walk. They were quite round in the middle and had unusually thin arms and legs. His bald scalp did nothing to dispel the egg comparison.

They had come into Theo's shop one day, wandered about, touching almost everything except the fabric, then left. They ran their hands over spools of thread, small scissors, pre-wound bobbins, packages of needles. Shortly after that, Theo discovered a few small items missing. They could have simply been misplaced, but she had a feeling they had been stolen. She knew Miss Bessie had not been involved because when Bessie took something, she left something in its place. Bessie had once left a jar of mustard to replace a missing measuring tape.

Theo had not mentioned any of this to Tony, mostly because she wasn't certain. However, if they came in her shop again, she would watch them very carefully. If they were stealing, it was most likely not from need, but for fun. She wasn't in the mood to provide their entertainment.

"Sheriff, we've got someone at the front desk inquiring about a stuffed toy hippopotamus that has gone missing." Rex's voice interrupted Tony's thoughts.

Frustrated in his attempts to learn anything about former sheriff Harvey Winston's cold case, Louise Barnet, and preparing to talk to Jack Gates again about his late aunt, Tony had almost forgotten about the toy. "I'll be right there." Unlocking the small bin he'd placed it in, Tony retrieved it and took it with him. He expected to find a child waiting with a parent. Instead, he found the Grand Duchess and Richards, her chauffeur.

The chauffeur spoke. "I should have asked you about the hippopotamus when I was here the other day. It's been days since she lost it, and everyone has been searching. It's been a very difficult time for her."

Tony thought the chauffeur seemed embarrassed by his oversight. As for the Grand Duchess, she looked lost and confused, until she spied the dirty, soft toy he carried.

"Oh, thank you, sir," she whispered as she reached for the hippo with trembling hands. Tears filled her eyes. "My treasure."

Obviously recognizing the object, the chauffeur's face split with a wide smile. "Awesome."

Tony thought the word sounded odd coming from the well-spoken chauffeur and said, "There was no identification in it. Not even on the prescription bottle." Tony was more than curious.

"A word, Sheriff?" Richards stepped away from his employer.

When Tony joined him, Richards whispered, "She has several medications, but my wife is in charge of keeping them safe and hands them out on schedule." He cleared his throat. "However, the Grand Duchess likes to carry some pills she can take whenever she feels like she's going to have a spell, whatever that is."

"Mints?" Tony guessed.

"And baby aspirin," Richards replied. "Her doctor says it's fine and maybe even helpful."

Even as he nodded his understanding, Tony watched the Grand Duchess pull the heavy necklace from its hidden pocket. Her blue-veined hands caressed the huge jewels. "And the jewelry?"

"Absolutely real." The chauffeur must have noticed the shock Tony felt. "It's worth millions, but she only cares about it because it belonged to her mother." Richards grinned. "Whoever found it could have sold it and made a quick fortune."

Tony thought maybe he would not mention the value when he told the boys how happy the older lady was to have her treasure returned.

"She gave my wife a gold coin. From our Civil War." Tony expected the chauffeur to be surprised or to request its return.

"Oh, that's fine. She rarely tips but keeps gold coins for the occasion." Richards leaned closer. "Your wife must have made her feel quite good. It's been months since she handed out her last tip."

Tony collected Mike and headed for Jack Gates's house. The quickest way to learn about Eunice's family could be to ask another relative, one from a different tree. Jack didn't answer the bell when he rang. Tony considered it hardly surprising, since people were free to come and go at will, without checking in with the sheriff. Most of the citizens had day jobs, some worked nights, some had multiple jobs and a few worked from home.

It was only when he considered the county's work force that Tony first wondered whether or not Jack Gates held a job. The man was about forty, his own age, which seemed too young to be retired. For all he knew, Jack could be living on disability payments, or charity, or maybe he had robbed a bank in Kansas and paid cash for his house. People had secrets.

Tony was pulling away from the curb when Jack came around the corner on his three wheeler, pedaling with his arms and singing along with whatever music poured through his ear buds. Tony backed up and parked again. When he joined Jack on the driveway, he could hear labored breathing. The high-tech tricycle was not a toy.

"Sheriff?" Jack wheezed but he grinned. "You need me?"

"I have some questions about your late aunt."

Jack climbed awkwardly from the bike and had to pull himself onto his feet. The smile vanished. "Have you found out what happened to her?"

Tony's head moved from side to side. "No. We have certainly learned more, but nothing conclusive. There are too many loose ends to count."

"Do you mind if I sit?" Without waiting for an answer, Jack walked toward a pair of lawn chairs with his usual awkward movement. "How can I help?"

"Tell me about Eunice's brother and his children and where you fit in the family tree. How are you related?"

"My mom is Eunice's baby sister. You might not have even heard she has a sister." Jack shook his head and his face pulled into a frown. "No one ever hears from Mom. She's a throwback to another era."

"How do you mean?" Tony wasn't sure he'd ever heard the term used.

Jack sighed. "Maybe fifteen years ago now, she returned to live the simple life of ages past. Her words, not mine. What that actually means is she decided to go off into a wilderness in Montana and live in a hut she constructed herself. No telephone or electricity, no indoor plumbing, no wheelchair ramps."

Tony guessed that was the deal breaker for visits from her son. "Why?"

"I have no idea. She always loved the outdoors but, really, winter without plumbing? Who thinks it's a fun life?" He stared into Tony's eyes. "I can't honestly say if she's still alive. I got a card before Christmas, which arrived two, maybe three months ago. I don't expect to hear anything from her again until mid-August, when I should get a birthday card."

There was a question Tony felt he needed to ask, but he hesitated. "I know little about what happened to you, physically." He paused. "I heard somewhere that you were injured in an accident. Did your mom leave before or after your accident?"

"After." Jack's face held no noticeable expression. "Mom helped me through the initial period after the accident. As soon as it became apparent that I would have a certain degree of mobility, she took it to mean I would not need more mothering and took off for the woods."

Tony had nothing to say. He could barely comprehend the scenario. It was the polar opposite of dealing with his own mom.

"You must wonder about my family." Jack smiled and the expression held no bitterness, only sorrow. "We're a family of nut cases. Half are hardworking, and the other half are people always looking for a handout. I moved back to Silersville because I like it here and also because I adore my Aunt Eunice. She has always treated me like a whole person."

Chapter Twenty-Four

Theo slid out of bed. As she stood, she swayed on her feet, nausea taking over her entire system. "Oh, no." She collapsed onto the bed clutching her head and waited for the room to stop spinning. "I can't be sick this morning."

"Are you all right?" Tony, already showered and dressed in his uniform, stood in the bedroom doorway holding one of their little girls. He did not come closer but watched her from across the room. "I don't want to hand over Kara until I know what kind of illness you have."

"Don't bring any of the kids near me." Theo pressed her face into a pillow and took a deep breath and managed to fight down the next wave of nausea. "I don't remember the last time I felt this sick."

"Do you want me to see if Mom can watch the kids?" Tony dodged the inquisitive child trying to stab him in the eye as he stared at Theo. "Do you need to go to the doctor?"

"I don't know." Theo moaned. "I can't decide whether I'm going to pass out, throw up or be okay."

She realized there was no amusement in Tony's expression when he looked at her. Theo knew he was generally good with first aid, but she couldn't tell him exactly what was wrong. She wasn't sure herself. It was a combination of symptoms, all unpleasant.

"Thank goodness you've been spayed." He mumbled. "At least we know you're not pregnant again."

Theo groaned, delighted she wasn't pregnant and too ill to take umbrage about being compared to a pet. "Yes, that is the bright side." She managed a deep breath as she sat on the bed and was encouraged when the room didn't spin. "I think I'm going to be okay."

Theo made it to the shop and even managed to get some of her work done, but now she felt herself getting sicker with every passing moment. She had not felt this bad in years, if ever. She hated to take advantage of Tony's mom and aunt, but she knew she could not take care of her children in her current condition. Maybelle was headed to Knoxville with her family for the day so she called Jane. Predictably, her mother-in-law was excited about having all four children in her care.

It had been forty years since Jane had cared for four children at one time, without help. And those had been her own children. Somehow, Theo thought it was different with your own children. At this point, Theo really didn't care who minded her brood. If Attila the Hun offered to babysit today, she would agree, positive it would be just fine. At least Jane had her sister to help with the wild bunch.

Theo picked the boys up from school, and headed out to the museum. It was a dump and run operation. As the boys climbed out of her bright yellow SUV, she mumbled, "Help your grandmother with the girls."

Chris and Jamie gave her "the look," and rolled their eyes. Their father gave her the same look when she tried to micromanage him. She tried not to do it but the only way she seemed to be able to deal with all of her conflicting responsibilities was to overthink everything.

Jane and Martha had evidently spotted her vehicle coming up the road and hurried outside to help. After a quick glance at her face, they greeted the boys and each took a baby girl out of her car seat. "We can keep them as long as you need us to."

"Thank you both. I'll let Tony know where they are." Looking forward to a little privacy, and some sleep in her own bed, Theo headed home.

The road seemed to be wavering before her eyes, and she heard an odd ringing in her ears. She ignored the symptoms and concentrated on keeping the car's wheels between the center yellow line and the ditch on her right. It seemed more difficult than usual because her eyes did not seem to be focusing properly. She tried blinking almost continuously, fighting to see where she was going. Her hands gripped the steering wheel, starting to cramp up because she squeezed so hard. This wasn't the way to her house.

She was lost.

"Sheriff?"

Through his radio, Tony immediately recognized Rex's voice. Of the various people who worked dispatch, Rex was the most experienced and the calmest. Today, even Rex's voice held a note of dismay. Tony automatically tensed. "What's the problem?"

"We have a call about an older lady hiking with a couple of boys. It seems she has fallen and appears to have broken one arm and possibly her pelvis. That was the official report."

Tony didn't need more information to guess the next part. "Where are my mom and sons now?"

"They're all still up on the ridge. You know, the one that runs along behind the folk museum. The ambulance is on the way to them, but I can't find your wife. She's not answering her phone and according to your aunt, when I talked to her, someone needs to go get those boys. She says dealing with the twins is all she can handle."

"If *you* called my aunt, how did you know about mom falling?" Tony was also confused by his aunt's statement about dealing with the boys and the twins. The boys were pretty easy. Throw lots of food at them and let them entertain themselves. They were growing like kudzu and would probably eat cardboard if they got hungry enough.

"One of your boys called in on your mom's phone." Rex said, "I don't know which one it was but he gave better, clearer information than most adults."

Tony wasn't sure if he was more alarmed by his mother's injuries or the news that Theo was not answering her phone. She always had it with her now, in spite of his telling her she could probably leave it in the kitchen while she went to the bathroom. For a long time, she didn't carry it at all or she would leave it in weird places. He lost count of the number of times he'd find it under the newspaper or in some drawer. Since Halloween, she had practically been welded to it.

"I'm on my way." Tony jogged out to the Blazer. He would deal with getting the twins from his aunt, but that would have to wait until he learned more about his mom's condition. Flipping on the light bar and siren, he headed out of town.

It was only a couple of miles, but the twists and turns in the narrow road slowed him somewhat. By the time he turned onto the dirt road that ran up the ridge, he could see the ambulance ahead of him. He heaved a sigh of relief. In their small county, emergency medical services were rather limited. In short, they could only handle one emergency at a time. Two if they shared the ambulance. His mom was lucky. At the last curve, he pulled off the road, leaving plenty of room and not blocking the ambulance's way. Without seeing her, but hearing of the type of injuries she had, he was sure his mom would be taken to Knoxville. He climbed out of the Blazer and hurried along the road.

Sure enough, the ambulance, the paramedics, his deputy

Mike Ott and his sons filled up the small clearing. The boys spotted him and headed toward him at a dead run.

"Grandma fell." Those words were the only ones he could actually understand. The two boys were talking a mile a minute, simultaneously, and showed no signs of pausing to breathe. Tony just let them chatter on. He could see the EMTs working on his mom. It would take a while to stabilize her and pack her up for the transport. He worked his way around the crowd, the boys in tow, until he could see his mom's face. Her expression, although filled with pain, indicated more than a little aggravation aimed, he was certain, at herself.

"Mom?" Tony gave her a hard look. He covered his deep concern with his own irritation. "Didn't you say you gave up mountain climbing when you got your Medicare card?"

A slight gasp from a paramedic, one obviously unfamiliar with the patient or her youngest child, snapped Jane's glare onto the newcomer.

"I did say it," she confessed to the paramedic and lowered her lashes to cover her eyes. "I didn't mean it, though."

Tony felt a combination of fear and outrage. "I suppose, now *I* have to break the news to my brothers and sister." He was genuinely not looking forward to making those calls. As the only one of Jane's children who lived in the same county as she, it often fell upon his broad shoulders to attempt to ride herd on the most independent, irritating—and fragile—member of the Abernathy family.

With a motion of her hand, Jane waved away his concern. "What's really bad is Theo's not going to trust me alone with my own grandchildren anymore."

"Maybe, maybe not." The mention of his wife's name brought back his own concerns about her. He stepped away, leaving the paramedics to deal with his mom. Theo's phone rang six times, then went to voicemail. This time he left a message. "Theo, honey, I'm up in the hills behind the museum. Mom's taken a fall and will be headed to the Knoxville hospital. Should I bring the children to your shop?"

He waited five minutes, which should have been plenty of time, then he called the shop number. Gretchen answered, "Theo's Quilt Shop."

"Sorry to interrupt you, Gretchen, but Theo doesn't seem to be near her cell phone."

"She left here over an hour ago to go home. She didn't call you?" Gretchen sounded very concerned. "I've never seen her sick like this before. I offered to drive her, but she made me promise to stay in the shop and disinfect everything I could think of. She told me she was taking the children out to stay with your mom."

Mumbling something that neither one of them could understand, Tony disconnected. He checked for a missed call. Nothing. He hurried over to Chris and Jamie. "I don't suppose you know where your mom went?"

Many adult heads turned in his direction, eyes wide.

Chris grinned. "Home. She gave the girls to Aunt Martha."

"We're ready to leave here." The ambulance driver looked aggravated. "Can you all move out of the way?"

Tony glanced around. Deputy Mike Ott was gone. He'd evidently decided to leave Jane in Tony's reluctant care. He and the boys were standing well out of the way. Nothing was blocking the ambulance's departure. "It looks like you're good to go to me."

The paramedic sitting in the back with Jane gave Tony a thumbs-up and mouthed, "This driver is all about a power trip. He just loves an audience." Then he pulled the ambulance doors closed and they drove away, lights flashing but no siren.

"Why don't you know where Mom is?" Jamie turned to his father. The boy seemed more distressed now that the ambulance had driven away, taking his grandmother.

Tony's stomach rumbled with the increased acid caused by his worry. "I don't know, son. Gretchen said she went home sick. She's probably just not answering her phone. Let's go by the house and check on her. Okay?"

"Okay." Jamie sounded less than optimistic. "I hope she's there."

As they headed to the Blazer, Tony considered the seating arrangement. "Chris, you ride shotgun."

"Can I ride in the cage?" Jamie's brilliant blue eyes sparkled with excitement. The prospect of adventure erased some of his concern about his mother.

Tony hated to disappoint him. There was only one seatbelt in the steel mesh prisoner transport area. "I'm afraid not. I'll need to put one of the car seats in there. You'll need to ride in the center of the back seat.

"Bummer." Jamie accepted it reasonably well and climbed into the Blazer and buckled up. "I bet it's Lizzie who gets locked in."

Minutes later, they returned to the museum. Martha, carrying both girls, was beyond frantic and did not wait for them to get out of the car but hurried out the door and over to the Blazer. "Where's Jane? What's happened? What were all the sirens for? Can you make these girls stop crying? I'm losing my mind."

Tony climbed out of the vehicle and started explaining the hiking accident to his aunt, even as he took the loudest little girl, Kara, from her. He was instantly rewarded by a charming toddler smile. The smile was immediately followed by the unbelievably loud rumbling sound of a small sewage system emptying into a diaper. Kara's smile widened. "Proud of yourself, little one?" Tony wanted to laugh, but the news he had come to deliver was serious.

He pushed his aunt toward a bench and waved for her to sit. She shook her head. "Okay, here's the deal. Mom's broken some bones." Tony summed up the traumatic events on the ridge. He couldn't think of an easy way to tell his aunt. "The ambulance is taking her to Knoxville. They think she has a severely broken arm and her pelvis is at the least cracked, maybe broken."

"I have to go." Martha immediately handed him Lizzie.

Tony jiggled Lizzie and tried to shush her, but the little girl kept crying, and the next thing he knew Kara was screaming as well. Conversation was impossible. Between the sounds of the girls and the speed at which his aunt was moving, Tony barely managed to ascertain that he should lock the office but that Celeste, the museum's combination curator and relief snack bar operator, would take care of the rest.

He had to admire his aunt's efficiency. Martha had collected her purse, and Jane's, and picked up her jacket and was out the door before he could say good-bye.

The twins' screams increased in volume.

"Tony?" Fumbling with her cell phone, Theo wasn't sure who she was talking with, her husband or some other male in the sheriff's office.

"No, Mrs. Abernathy, it's Rex. Are you in need of help or looking for your husband?"

"Both." Theo tried to lift her head. Her neck didn't feel connected to it. It sort of wobbled about. "Can you get a message to him?"

"Sure."

"Ask him to pick up the boys from his mom."

"You haven't heard," said Rex.

"Heard what?" Theo decided her brain felt mushy, kind of like a wet sponge.

Instead of answering her question, he asked one of his own. "Should I call the doctor for you, or an ambulance?"

"No. I don't need an ambulance and I don't think there's anything the doctor can do unless he shoots me to put me out of my misery. I simply have some kind of bug. Now what haven't I heard?" She leaned her forehead against the wall but instead of it giving her some support, she could swear it was moving. It looked odd, like it was her car-door interior. Weird.

"Jane has busted her arm or her pelvis or both. I don't have exact information, but I do know she's in an ambulance on the way to Knoxville." Rex cleared his throat. "No one's said how it happened."

"My children." Theo blinked against the invading darkness and struggled to stand but was trapped in her chair. Bizarre. She tried leaning her forehead against the other wall. It wasn't there. As she lost consciousness, she thought she heard Rex say, "Okay."

Tony heard Rex's report of an odd conversation with Theo. According to Rex, he thought Theo sounded extremely confused and wasn't sure if she was at the house or where she called from. He was sure he heard her being sick to her stomach.

"Is Mom going to be okay?" Behind the lenses of his glasses, Chris's big hazel eyes were filled with worry.

"She should be. It's probably just one of those twenty-four-hour bugs." Pushing the question mirroring his own concerns aside, Tony glanced at the gas station he was approaching and noticed a man hurrying out of the building. He looked Tony in the face as he shoved past an old man and pointed a double-barrel shotgun at Tony before climbing into a black pickup parked by the door, the engine running. When the pickup blasted out of the parking lot, almost running into Tony's vehicle and took off like a bat, Tony swerved to avoid being hurt by the vehicle. It didn't even have a flash of silver on the bumper.

Flipping on the light bar and siren, Tony kept his eyes on the pickup racing ahead of them and talked to Rex on the radio. The black truck churned up the vegetation on the narrow strip of earth between the pavement and a ditch as it swerved over the center line and then back over to the shoulder. Tony sincerely hoped none of them would meet an oncoming vehicle. If the pickup struck another vehicle head-on at this speed, they'd all be in trouble.

Ignoring Tony's pursuit, the pickup wasn't slowing. The business end of a double-barrel shotgun emerged from the small back window and caused Tony to ease off slightly on the accelerator. Tony, even more sincerely than wanting no accident, hoped the felon wouldn't shoot at the small heads of his passengers. He didn't want to scare the boys, but he couldn't allow them to be targets. "I want both of you boys to bend forward or slide way down in your seats so your heads aren't visible." He wondered if he should tell them to unbuckle their seatbelts and get on the floor. He discarded the idea because of the danger of their skidding into a ditch and having the Blazer roll over.

"Okay." Both of the young voices sounded serious.

Rex's voice supplied information. The two men in the black pickup had indeed robbed the gas station seconds before encountering Tony on the road. Wade and Sheila were on their way from town.

Tony considered the situation madness. What were the odds of someone robbing a gas station with a shotgun? And what were the odds of the idiot doing it practically in front of the sheriff? Tony didn't know exactly what the men had done, but knew, at minimum, it had to be armed robbery. Now Tony couldn't believe he was driving with his children immediately behind an obviously dangerous felon. The little girls were sound asleep in their car seats, Jamie was buckled in between them and Chris scrunched down, wide-eyed in the front passenger seat and listening to the constant radio chatter.

"Your mom is going to have a fit." Tony stared at the road ahead, forgetting for the moment that Theo was missing.

"Maybe she's too busy throwing up to care." Chris, no dummy even if he was only twelve years old, started laughing. "Your mom is going to have a fit, too. Can grandma still ground you even if she's in the hospital?"

"Probably," Tony muttered. "Don't tell her, okay? Either of you. Hearing about this will not make her feel better."

"Okay." Two small voices repeated.

He knew it was wrong to have the boys in the Blazer. He knew it would be wrong to let the armed robber run loose in the county, and it would be equally wrong to push the boys out on the side of the road. The little girls in their car seats were well below the level of glass in the windows. The boys were not. For that matter, no one was safe.

"Good," Tony said. "Keep those heads down and don't pop up to look until I say so."

"Yes, Daddy." Two quiet voices whispered in unison, sounding younger than usual.

Tony felt guilty. It wasn't Theo's fault. When he'd last talked with her, she had been so busy throwing up it was impossible to have a conversation. It certainly wasn't his mother's fault. Broken bones in her arm and hip, particularly at her age, were nothing to mess around with. It was blind dumb luck that put them into this situation, and he could only hope it wasn't going to get worse.

Tony even considered simply pulling over to the side of the road and stopping, letting the bad guy get away. But as recklessly as the man was driving, too many other innocent people were endangered. Tony was sworn to protect and serve, but the truth was, he would have chased the bad guy anyway.

He hoped the scream of the siren and his lights flashing would warn everyone else on the road. This two-lane road would intersect with another one in only a mile. The updates on his radio gave him hope that Wade and Sheila could reach it first.

Coming around a sharp turn, Tony saw a road block in the distance. Heaving a deep sigh of relief and a prayer of thanks, he slowed down and stopped, using the Blazer to close the road. Unable to go forward or turn and go back, their felons were trapped. Tony sat and watched until Sheila closed the back door of her vehicle, locking the handcuffed men inside.

"That was awesome, Dad." Chris's voice held a note of joy mixed with excitement.

"Do not *ever* tell your mother." Tony gave thanks for being bald. His arriving home with instantly snow-white hair might be considered suspicious.

Theo gradually became aware of light. She wasn't quite sure where she was, though. There was so much white light it was almost blinding. The sounds made her think she had fallen asleep with the television on. Someone was talking, a woman, but it sounded like nonsense. Before she could form a good idea of where she was, her eyes closed and she slid back into unconsciousness.

"Theo? Theo." Each time she heard her name, it seemed to be spoken in a louder voice. Finally, desperate to make the voices stop she said, "What?"

"How are you feeling?" The voice was female and sounded more Southern than the local Appalachian accent. Although it was familiar, Theo drifted off again without identifying it.

Sometime later, but Theo had no way of knowing how much later, she heard the voice again. She recognized it this time. Grace. Doctor Grace Claybough sat on a chair next to her bed. Theo found this very confusing. There was no chair in her bedroom. "Where did the chair come from? Did I buy that?"

Grace laughed. "No. It's our chair." She reached over and took Theo's hand. "You're at the clinic."

Theo struggled with her eyelids. They felt so heavy, she wondered why they were taped down. Did it have something to do with being punched in the eye during the shop hop? "Why the clinic?"

"You came here on your own. You told Nurse Foxx that you were dying and preferred to do it here." Grace smiled again, this time with more sympathy. "You said you didn't want to frighten your children."

Theo gave up the struggle with her eyelids and left them closed against the light. Grace's story sounded vaguely familiar to her. Maybe something she'd seen on television. "Tell me the truth. Am I dying?"

"No."

Theo believed Grace. Or at least she wanted to believe her. "I feel wretched." In her head she could hear children's voices, but not her children. Her eyes flew open again. "What happened to the children? Are they safe?"

Grace patted her arm, and Theo became aware that she was attached to an IV.

"The children were not with you." Grace smiled again. "I gather you left them with your mother-in-law. The children are all fine."

Theo had the sense Grace wasn't telling her everything, but she didn't know what to ask. She didn't have the energy to think.

THE GIFT QUILT—MYSTERY QUILT
THE FOURTH BODY OF CLUES
PUTTING IT ALL TOGETHER

Very carefully measure your completed blocks. They should be 15-1/2″ by 15-1/2″; if smaller than that you will need to trim the blocks to the largest common size and adjust your sashing strips accordingly.

Sew one 2″ by 15-1/2″ strip of fabric (C) on two opposing sides of four blocks.

Sew one 2″ by 15-1/2″ strip of fabric (C) on only one side of the remaining eight blocks.

Sew one of the single strip blocks to each side of the double strip blocks making sure (C) is on the outside edge. Make four rows of three blocks. Press all seams to (C). Set aside.

Sew a 2″ square of fabric (D) on the end of remaining 2″ by 15-1/2″ strips of fabric (C). Connect three long strips with the squares and finish each strip with a square. Sew one of these new strips between the rows of three blocks with sashing. Add one strip to top and bottom. Press all seams to (C).

Measure the length and width, at top, bottom and middle. Use the average to cut two strips 4-1/2″ of (A) to length and two strips to the width.

Sew the long 4-1/2″ strips of fabric (A) on each of the long sides of the pieced center. Press to (A).

Sew a 4-1/2″ square of (D) to each end of the width long strip. Sew to top and bottom edge of the quilt.

Pat yourself on the back and do the happy quilters' dance.

Quilt as desired and bind with remaining 2-1/2″ strips of (D).

Chapter Twenty-Five

The Valentine's Day party and silent auction at the museum were going ahead, without Jane. The report from her sister, Martha, was that Jane was resting comfortably and she absolutely did not want any visitor with the flu, especially not her daughter-in-law. She would depend on her sister and children to save a slice of pie for her, if one of them had the high bid.

Tony approached his aunt. "How's the voting?"

"It's wonderful. Look around. People are practically fighting to get to the bidding sheets." Martha grinned. "I've already had to add additional pages on the sheets. Each one only has room for twenty bids. Some have already gone onto the third auction sheets, and they have a minimum one-dollar increase."

"Have you collected some pie samples for mom?" Tony felt like a greedy, ungrateful son, but he didn't want to have to share his samples with anyone.

"Yes. I fought my way through the crowd and snagged some for each of us. I'm eating mine and putting hers in the freezer. My sister can enjoy them when she gets home."

Tony nodded his approval and watched young Alvin Tibbles, Martha's renter and biggest fan, helping with the event. At least, he was helping when he wasn't smiling at the teenage beauty making goo-goo eyes at him.

Tony waved at artist Olivia Hudson, who was sitting in her

wheelchair out of the main stream of traffic. He headed over to chat.

"We haven't seen you for a while." Tony pulled a folding chair closer to her and sat. "You decided to celebrate from your wheelchair?"

"Oh, yes." Olivia gestured to the crowd pushing and jostling to get close to the silent-auction items. "I know my limitations. The eager shoppers would trample me without looking back to get a piece of the winning pie."

"It *is* pretty rough over in the sample corner." Tony agreed. "A small gray-haired woman slugged me in the stomach with her elbow and snatched the tidbit I was reaching for. I'd be removed from office if I punched her, but I considered it for a moment."

Olivia laughed. "Luckily, my husband is not only large but he doesn't hold an elected office. He was ruthless and brought me several wonderful samples."

Tony showed her his small empty paper plate. "Does he work for hire?"

"No. I'm afraid you'll have to fight your own battles."

Tony stood. "Unless I can get you something, I'll head back to the fray."

Olivia wished him good hunting and rolled her chair over to chat with Jack Gates.

The wheelchair friends had much in common, Tony thought. Olivia had prosthetic legs, but she didn't like being jostled and always used the chair in a crowd.

Today, Jack sat in a chair out of the chaos of the party. With his slow, awkward gait and an anxious, hungry crowd, he was safer seated than balancing, even with a cane.

Tony's attention was attracted by a hand-held horn blasting from the doorway. Roscoe.

"Everyone, we're about to launch." Roscoe's arm motions

looked like the third base coach sending a runner home. "Come on."

The crowd, having stripped the pie-sample plates to the last flaky crumb, headed outside to the area blocked off for their safety. Roscoe and the professor, his wife, launched a new, small trebuchet, one that would sit comfortably in the bed of their new pickup. The swinging arm tossed small, red, paper bags containing an assortment of chocolates and mints into the cheering crowd.

Although she felt much better than she had the previous day, Theo didn't feel like risking a relapse by eating pie, so she concentrated on visiting with friends, standing upwind of the food.

The combination silent auction and garage sale seemed to be a success. Theo often heard that it was hard to sell books at a garage sale, but the recently frozen books, now without bedbugs, were so cheap they were almost free. The stacks were definitely getting shorter.

A couple standing near her caught her eye and she watched, fascinated, as Quentin Mize smiled at the tall, slender woman standing next to him. Amy. Poor posture and messy dishwater-colored hair pulled into an unflattering ponytail prevented Amy from attracting much attention. Theo thought her posture was intentional.

Amy worked at the post office. After she divorced her lazy bum of a husband, she had paid off their debts and made a quiet, solitary life for herself. For extra income, she made homemade scented soaps to sell at craft bazaars, as well as knitting fine scarves and baby blankets. Theo had heard from Amy's landlord and landlady that even though the young woman lived on the second floor of their house, the mice made a racket in comparison to their renter.

The opposite might be said of Quentin. He owned land, valuable land, he'd inherited at a young age. His ramshackle trailer rested under a curtain of kudzu along with a shed held together with ancient dirt. Theo wondered if Quentin had taken Amy up to see his property and, if so, had she enjoyed viewing the broken-down rust farm he lived in? It didn't matter. Even though they were an interesting combination, it was not as unexpected as the relationship between goofy Roscoe and the university professor.

The crowd returned to the barn. Moments later, the lights dimmed gradually until only the illuminated "Exit" signs were visible. The crowd made noises of confusion and concern. Theo waited where she was rather than trip over someone standing near her.

"Happy Valentine's Day!" shouted a man with a deep voice. At his words, the overhead lights came back on. A moment of stunned silence was followed almost immediately by chaos and the room filled with laughter.

Theo pushed her way through the crowd, looking for a place where she could see what was happening. When she squeezed past the egg-shaped synchronized couple Theo had watched on the sidewalk, she stopped. Her eyes went wide and she was afraid her mouth dropped open.

The noise of the crowd vanished as almost everyone in the building leaned forward, staring openly. Theo noticed many more mouths than hers were ajar. And they were watching and listening.

Theo accidently had the best view of anyone. Three feet away from her, Not Bob was dressed as Cupid. The tall, well-built man wore a flowing white toga exposing one muscular shoulder. Tiny little wings made from iridescent gold fabric were attached to his back, and he carried a golden bow and arrow. The arrow had a rubber sink stopper on the end where the point should be. Theo thought he looked more like a Roman senator than Cupid except for the wings and the mischievous and adoring gaze he focused on Sheila. The smile was charming. It made a nice contrast with the pair of well-worn work boots peeking out from underneath his drapery.

He tossed handmade paper valentines to the crowd as he walked toward his goal.

Unblinking, Sheila appeared frozen in place near the refreshment table, holding a ladle containing pink punch. Some punch splashed on the tablecloth nowhere near a cup.

Cupid approached Sheila, and knelt somewhat clumsily, almost pulling the toga from his shoulder. The small party crowd watched in awe as the oversized cherub groped in the folds of his gown, searching for something. At length he retrieved a small, round box. He said something to Sheila that no one could hear but her. Although Theo and, she assumed, the rest of the spectators knew what he was asking.

Sheila still didn't move. Theo didn't think Sheila had breathed since Cupid arrived.

"What if I say no?" Sheila's question was barely audible but Theo was close enough to hear.

Cupid seemed undeterred. He reached out and took Sheila's left hand and whispered something most of the audience could not hear, but again, because she was almost right next to them, Theo did. "If you say no, I'll give you a few weeks to reconsider." Cupid paused. "And at the St. Patrick's Day celebration, I can predict a huge leprechaun in your future."

This time Sheila laughed. Ignoring the ladle she still held, Sheila bent forward, wrapping her arms around his neck, and kissed Cupid. In his kneeling position, he was shorter than she was and she held him in place. Pink punch dripped from the ladle onto his back, narrowly missing the wings.

Theo looked up at Tony, who had appeared like magic next

to her. "I guess that means yes."

Tony's voice was low and almost mournful. "I hope that's all it means."

"Why, what's wrong?" Theo was shocked by his lack of enthusiasm. She'd always understood he liked the man and thought he would approve of the relationship.

Tony released a heavy sigh. "What if he decides to move away from Park County? She'd go with him."

Unable to suppress it, Theo burst into laughter. She was thankful the stomach flu had been of short duration because she would hate to miss this moment. "So, it's really all about you?"

"You got it." Tony winked at her. "Who do you think put him up to the Cupid costume?"

"Tell me. How *did* you get him to wear a Cupid costume?" Theo also wanted to know where it came from.

"I merely suggested to him, if he proposed in a public spot, Sheila wouldn't be able to say no. Plus, there would be all kinds of witnesses to back him up when she said yes."

"That wouldn't stop her from saying no at a later time." Theo knew it was not her business, but she couldn't help being concerned.

The mischief in his eyes was replaced with a serious expression. "I never would have suggested it if I thought there was any possibility it wasn't what she wanted. Well, the proposal; maybe not the tiny little wings."

Theo studied the Cupid as he slipped a ring on Sheila's finger and received another kiss. "Well, personally, I think the tiny little wings are very fetching. Where did he get the costume?"

"We got Mrs. Fairchild, the retired home economics teacher, to help make it." Tony grinned. "We didn't ask you, mostly because you have no time. Plus, we weren't sure you wouldn't, however inadvertently, give it away."

Theo wasn't sure whether she ought to be offended or applaud him for his clear thinking. "I think it's a lovely costume. And you're right. I didn't have the time." She gave her husband a quick kiss and got in line to congratulate the newly engaged couple. She had to admit she was curious about the ring. There had been no flash of light, as from a diamond, when it was revealed.

Sheila was more than happy to show it off and explained the ring had been custom-made to Cupid's specifications. Rather than having the stone sit above the band, it was embedded into the metal band so it would not snag anything or make putting on the gloves she often wore while working a difficult process. The stone, as it turned out, came from his grandmother's ring. Somehow the jeweler had managed to retain the sparkle and fire of the diamond, even in the unusual setting.

When Theo stepped forward to give Sheila a quick hug, Sheila whispered, "How could I refuse to marry a man who would wear a toga and gossamer wings into a room filled with my friends and neighbors and co-workers, many of whom have guns on them? He's certainly got guts."

"His shoulders aren't bad, either." Nina had joined them in time to hear most of the conversation.

Theo looked behind Nina and noticed a very thoughtful expression on Doctor Looks-So-Good's face. It made her wonder if the man was looking for ideas for his own proposal. "I personally think the wings make the whole ensemble work."

"They are pretty cute." Sheila's smile was radiant, but she sighed. "I guess I'll never know about the leprechaun costume."

Tony was delighted to see Roscoe and the professor standing near the punch bowl. Because Sheila had vanished, along with the ladle, the professor stepped behind the table and began serving the frothy, and decidedly pink, punch with a teacup.

"Sheriff? We need your help." The professor smiled and offered him a cup of punch.

"How can I help you?" Tony accepted it. He was always struck, in a very pleasant way, by what a fascinating couple they were. It would be hard to come up with a less likely scenario than a college professor married to the man who still held the county record for the most years in the fourth grade.

"It's about Baby."

Tony hadn't seen the young black bear for several months. "Is she hibernating?"

The professor nodded. "She didn't sleep much last winter, so I expect she'll be waking up soon. Our winters are not very long here."

Roscoe's head bobbed, an echo of his wife's movement, but his expression could only be described as intense.

Since the bear wasn't a pet and lived outdoors in the woods, Tony was curious. "Is that a problem?"

Roscoe's head bobbed again like a dashboard ornament, and the professor took over the conversation. "What we need, or would really like, would be for you to check on her from time to time while we are out of town."

Surprised to hear they were going away, Tony felt his eyebrows rise, and wondered himself why he thought they should not leave. "Sure. When are you leaving?"

Roscoe grinned widely, exposing his new dental work. "We're driving down to Florida to watch some of the spring-training games. We thought we might go down a little early and look around a bit. You know, sightseeing. Visit the ocean and whatnot."

Baseball, Tony knew, was one of the activities the couple shared a passion for. Roscoe himself was an umpire, but not in the major leagues. "Just let me know before you leave and I'll drop by from time to time. What exactly am I supposed to do?"

The professor said, "If she's stirring, or wandering about, make sure she has water. You can just fill the bowl next to the old tree stump. She usually checks it for grubs. Maybe you can put some fresh berries near it for her. She loves strawberries."

The professor's expression and detailed list reminded him of Theo issuing instructions about their children if she was going to be gone. The list always included what they could eat and what they were allowed to do. Half of him was irritated by Theo doing it, as if she thought he wasn't smart enough to know how to care for them, and the other half of him was relieved to know exactly what the plan was. Besides, if it went awry, it wouldn't be his fault. "And if she decides to leave?"

"She's not a prisoner. She's not a pet. We've never kept her caged or tethered in any way. If she wants to leave, she can. We would just like to know where she goes." Tears welled in the professor's eyes.

Roscoe snuffled a bit. "Mostly, I guess, jest make sure she ain't makin' herself a nuisance somewheres. You know, so she don't get herself shot."

For everyone's sake, Tony found himself hoping the couple would return before Baby awakened. "I'll check on her."

Theo watched as Claude Marmot, trash collector and recycling guru, carried his baby girl through the crowd like she was a little princess, bringing her to greet Theo. Predictably, the ruffled dress and diaper cover were both in shades of pink. Katti, his wife, trotted along next to the pair, her hands busy tightening the rose-colored scarf holding back her own hair. She was laughing.

In a moment of madness, Theo had once asked Katti what it was in Claude Marmot's online resume and courtship that had hooked the cheery Russian woman. Theo was sure the young woman must have had several offers. While her features were simply average, her attitude about life was delightful. Theo remembered Katti had the sweetest smile on her face when she said, "He looked nice."

Claude did have beautiful hair and pleasant features whenever he bothered to get cleaned up, which was not often. Before Katti entered his life, he had shaved only intermittently and his favorite T-shirts often failed to reach as far as his belt. He was as furry as a bear. At this event, he wore clean blue jeans and an extra-long shirt. Pink.

"He said he didn't care much about colors and pink was fine with him." Katti had chattered on. "And he said he didn't need a housekeeper but he wanted someone he could hear breathing near him in the dark. He was lonely."

Unexpectedly, Theo had felt the sting of tears. She had given her friend a quick hug. And now neither of them was lonely, and their tiny daughter kept them laughing.

Chapter Twenty-Six

Tony had been called over to the jail side of the building to check on a, thankfully, minor problem. He was on his way back to his office when Rex contacted him. "Sheriff, Wade says he's located Daniel Crisp's wife Nancy1, and she's not alone."

"Where is she, or where are they?" Tony was elated. Maybe they could finally get some answers that made sense about what happened at Nina's and why Daniel's dead body was found in the storm shelter.

"Evidently all of the wives we know about are having lunch together at the Riverview." Rex's normal professional, unflappable voice rose a bit. "Can you imagine what they have to say to each other?"

"No." Tony was determined to find out who discovered Daniel's marriage addiction. "Have Wade keep them together. I'll be there in minutes."

When he arrived at the Riverview, he peeked into the dining room and he studied the five women at the table. Nancy1 was definitely the strongest personality, even if she wasn't the strongest physically. Tony would give the muscle title to nurse Nikki.

When Tony asked Nancy1 to join him and Wade, she politely declined. "I've got no secrets from my, um, co-wives, or whatever they are."

"All right." Tony sincerely hoped he wasn't making a mega mistake. "Tell me how Daniel died."

"I wanted to surprise him, you know, make the traveling man less lonesome. He always sounded kind of lost when he was away, sleeping in motels." Nancy1 even managed a slight blush. "I borrowed my brother's old Buick and followed him. He never saw me. I did lie to you, though. I brought my dog, Precious, along because I expected to be staying with him."

A series of expressions raced across her face. Tony decided anger was the main one. "What happened?"

"He stopped in Dalton, Georgia. At her house." She pointed to Nannette. "And then the next night, he was in Cleveland. With her." She indicated Nora. "I was mad enough to run over him, but he never saw me. It was terrible." Her eyes overflowed. "He broke my heart."

Tony felt positive the tears were real. He felt sorry for all of the women Daniel Crisp had misled. "Did you go home?"

Nancy1 shook her head. "I slept in the car and just kept following him on and on. I couldn't believe what he was doing. He stopped in Knoxville and Maryville and stayed with women in both places. When he headed south, I hurried to get home before he did."

"Were you angry?" It was a stupid question and Tony knew it.

"You better believe it. I wanted to wring his scrawny neck. But I didn't." The smudged mascara on her cheek didn't hide her anger. "No wonder he couldn't afford to buy me a nice ring."

"So what *did* you do?" Tony felt as though he were listening to a radio soap opera. A glance at Wade's face showed the same dazed and glazed expression he guessed was on his own face. Who does things like this?

"I *fixed* his favorite dinner." Nancy1 smiled through her tears. The light of triumph gleamed in her eyes.

"What did you add to it?" He doubted she had poisoned Daniel.

"I have these pills for my back and I just added a couple to his beer. I wanted him to be quiet." She winked. "It worked great. He slept like a baby all night long."

Tony wasn't shocked. In fact, he rather admired her technique since the man came to no harm from it. "And then?"

"The moment he passed out, I got into his cell phone and found a bunch of numbers he called a lot, and I started calling them."

"That had to be very interesting." As understatements went, Tony was rather proud of it. "What did you learn?"

"Oh, I learned how hard he works, traveling and all, and how he tries to be a good husband even though he travels. I heard several versions of the same damn story." Her lips had a bitter twist by the time she finished. "Jerk."

"And then?" Wade leaned forward like he was watching a championship basketball game. His eyes traveled from wife to wife.

"I guess you don't think any of us are very smart." Nancy1 gestured to include all of the women at the table. "It didn't require no rocket scientist to guess where he'd be the other day. He is good with his kids, all of 'em. So, we thought we'd throw him a little surprise party."

"And did you?" Tony wondered if Daniel had mentioned that his children were going to be away. What was the man's agenda?

Nancy1 laughed heartily. "Oh, yeah. I dropped him off at the house and went back to town to bring the others up."

Tony looked around the table. Every one of the five women smiled cheerfully back at him. He saw nothing in any of the faces that indicated any guilt.

Nancy1 continued her role as spokeswoman. "We carpooled up to the ex-wife's house and when we made the turn, there he stood on the front porch looking down into this big hole, holding the lid. When he looked up and saw all of us together, he about peed in his pants."

The smiles widened on the wives' faces. They nodded their agreement with their spokeswoman's description.

"When we stopped and started climbing out of the two cars, he flipped around so fast he was a blur. I mean it. It looked just like somethin' in the cartoons. Then he kinda moved his arms, like this." She demonstrated outstretched arms rotating, making circles.

Tony could see it in his head. Nancy1 could certainly tell a good story. "And then?"

"He fell backwards into that hole. When he didn't climb out, we all went and looked at him down in that pit. I'm telling you, he shoulda been on fire."

"Was he dead?" Tony thought they were getting to the crucial moment.

"Oh, yeah." She giggled. "We had Nikki check. She's a nurse, you know, and she said he was gone."

"So you all just got in the cars and left him there?" Wade blinked like he was coming out of a trance.

"Oh, yeah." Her smile held neither malice nor concern. "A little present for his ex-wife."

Tony knew there was little or nothing he could charge any of them with. Certainly nothing in the autopsy indicated he'd been attacked. "So, why did you all come back here today? Just to meet for lunch?"

"Money," Nikki whispered. "As it turns out, he wasn't worth much, personally or monetarily, but I was cleaning out the stuff he left at my house and found an insurance policy, payable to me. The amount's not much, but still I need a copy of the death certificate to file a claim."

"And you suggested the others check for similar windfalls?"

"Yes. We are all part of the same weird family and while we're all here, we thought we'd have lunch. The bad news is we all thought he was special and that he loved us." Her expression suggested she now thought he was closer to being something nasty stuck to the bottom of her shoe. "The good news is, since it turns out none of us is actually a widow, none of us is on the hook for paying for a funeral."

As a good news/bad news situation, Tony found it grounded in reality and practicality. It made Tony wonder, though, who would eventually pay for a funeral—or if Daniel Crisp would actually have a funeral. If there were one, its expense would most likely fall to his parents. His personal vote, if he had one, might be scattering the ashes on a burning campfire.

Chapter Twenty-Seven

Tony happened to be in the dispatch center chatting with Rex when Mrs. Dixon called 9-1-1. The veterinarian's wife spoke clearly and calmly. "My little group of dog trainers and I want to report a possible fire. We're up on the hill just past the old cemetery. There's a plume of smoke coming out of the woods to our east, and I know there are only a few houses in there."

Rex proceeded in his normal manner, competently getting the information they needed without any sense of melodrama. "Does the fire seem contained?" Rex's question was for Mrs. Dixon.

"What would that look like?"

"A single plume maybe? Like smoke being funneled up a chimney." Rex was typing as he spoke. He'd already alerted the volunteer firemen to head to the fire station. "Trash burning in a barrel?

"Not exactly. It doesn't seem to be growing very quickly, anyway, and nothing like fire engulfing anything or leaping from tree to tree. What is really more bothersome is we saw someone running away from it." Mrs. Dixon was not overwrought, just thoughtfully reporting what she saw.

"Arson?" Rex was actually talking to Tony. Mrs. Dixon overheard.

"Probably." Tony and Mrs. Dixon spoke at the same time.

Tony identified himself.

Mrs. Dixon sounded amused when she said, "I thought I had an echo."

"Can you stay there until we arrive? The fire engine will be heading out in less than a minute."

At the same time Tony started talking to Mrs. Dixon, Rex had called the first responders for the fire department. From Rex's window, Tony saw volunteers leaping from their vehicles and running into the fire hall.

"Oh, sure." Mrs. Dixon sounded very calm. "We might make our way over a little closer to the fire just to keep an eye on it, in case it starts getting worse."

Tony was torn between thanking her and asking her not to get involved. The thanks won. By the time he disconnected, the roar of the fire engine and the blare of the siren could be heard, faintly, in the dispatch center. He hurried out of the building.

Wade's vehicle was ahead of Tony's Blazer as they headed out of town, sirens blaring, and up the hill. Tony watched carefully for any signs the fire was growing, as well as any sign of someone running away.

As she had said he would, Tony found Mrs. Dixon and her group, past the cemetery and heading toward the plume of smoke. Wade went past them, then pulled off the road and parked on the shoulder. Tony parked right next to Wade. They climbed out of their vehicles and watched the dog parade.

Mrs. Dixon led the way with a black and white dog at her side. The spotted canine of unknown heritage had floppy, black ears and a jaunty black tail curved up over its mostly black back. The tip of the tail was white. Behind her came Boston, not with Mouse, his shepherd, but leading a dun-colored dog with a stripe of black along his spine. After Boston came Kenneth Proffitt with a large red and white spaniel, and bringing up the rear was young Dillon Teffeteller with a medium-size shepherd mix.

"That's quite a dog parade," said Wade. "Mrs. Dixon is giving all of them a good workout and something positive to do with their lives."

"Are you talking about the men or the dogs?"

"Both. Mrs. Dixon is clearly no stranger to training either or both of them. I'll bet they're all too exhausted by dinner to do much more than eat and sleep."

Mrs. Dixon was an attractive fortyish woman with prematurely gray hair. She approached Tony's car, and pointed toward the back of the fire engine. "It's just past there."

Lacking a better place to park, Tony and Wade left their vehicles where they were and headed in toward the fire engine on foot. "Can you four stay here for a little bit? I'd like to talk to you."

Mrs. Dixon said yes and none of the men attempted to correct her. They nodded in almost perfect unison. The dogs sat at attention, apparently willing to remain there for an extended period of time.

Tony and Wade made the short hike to the fire department vehicle in only a couple of minutes. Fire Chief Cox pointed to a small pile of burnt wood and wet ashes. Mixed in was some copper tubing and shattered glass. "Another still."

"What do you think?" Tony feared that one of these fires was going to burn out of control and destroy homes and forests. "Is this someone's idea of an anti-alcohol campaign or someone cutting down on the moonshine competition?"

"I don't know." The chief left a smudge of soot on his chin as he rubbed it. "It's crazy either way. The stills so far have been very small like this one and Orvan Lundy's. Not much competition."

Tony returned to Mrs. Dixon and her tribe. "Did you see anyone?"

"Yes. Someone was hustling away from the fire area and into

those woods on the right." She pointed to a gap in the trees. "I couldn't say if it was a man or a woman." Mrs. Dixon spoke, and the three men's heads bobbed their agreement. "I'd say fiftyish, with curly, blond hair under an orange ball cap. Maybe five and a half feet tall, a hundred and seventy pounds. Was wearing a tan canvas jacket and jeans."

After making note of everything she'd said, Tony looked at each man in turn. "Did you see anything else, anything different?"

Boston nodded. "Sunglasses."

"Was this person carrying anything?" Tony didn't want to offer any suggestions that might incorrectly influence his information.

Four solemn faces were turned toward him. Four heads shook in denial.

Tony thanked them for their help, and he and Wade made their way back to the scene of the fire. The dog trainers' description of the person did not ring any bells. It didn't make any sense, though. Who would come into a county and not only know the location of the stills but be prepared to blow them up? The only thing that made any sense to him was someone trying to knock off the competition.

"Wade, I believe you have some inside contact with one of the local distillers of not quite fine alcohol. I'd like you to ask around and see if there are rumors of a takeover or a new bigger operation."

"At least that would make sense." Wade stared at the charred rubble. "What other reason could there be? Somebody either is totally against alcohol for personal reasons or is trying to corner the market."

"The description certainly doesn't fit any of the local legal liquor providers."

★ ★ ★ ★ ★

"How does Mouse like the new dog?" Having followed the group back to the veterinarian's home, Tony stood with Boston, watching the trainee dog play with the German shepherd war veteran.

"I think Mouse finds it amusing to watch me and the squirt do our training." Boston's voice was soft, but the shepherd's ears pricked up. "Mouse isn't young anymore and generally enjoys his routine of sleep, eat, sleep, exercise and more sleep. When I'm working with the squirt, he's usually dozing with one eye open."

"He doesn't offer advice?"

"Not to me." Boston's whole face lit up in a true smile, maybe the first one Tony had witnessed on the man. "One time Mouse told the squirt to go back to work."

"How did he do that?" Tony didn't doubt it happened.

"Mouse just lifted one eyelid and then showed a couple of teeth as he cleared his throat."

"Very effective, I presume."

"Oh, yeah." Boston grinned. "They play together. It's amazing. When either of them is training or working, it's like a switch gets flipped. Neither one seems to have trouble with the changes."

"And you?" Tony liked to blame his late father for his inborn desire to make things right, or at least better. It didn't matter if it wasn't part of his actual job description. "Are you enjoying the training?"

Without their customary shadows, Boston's eyes sparkled and he nodded.

Tony needed no other answer. Months earlier when Boston first showed up in Silersville, his eyes had held only loss, confusion and anger. Maybe the younger man would never be again whatever his former self had been but today, at this moment, he was happy. It was a vast improvement. Tony remembered his dad had always liked to say, "Today's the only day we have, so use it wisely."

"What is the other dog's name?" Tony returned his attention to the trainee.

"Squirt," Boston said. At the sound of his name, Squirt turned to look at Boston.

Tony grinned. Surprised. "That's really his name? I thought it was a description. What have you trained him to do so far?"

Boston looked thoughtful. "First, I had to train him not to fear me. These dogs we're working with have all been rescued from someplace. Then, some of the basics, you know, come, sit and stay."

Tony thought of their family dog. Daisy could come and sit but she wasn't good at staying. "And what's next in their training?"

"We'll teach them to pick up things, you know, like a dropped pencil. And fetch the cell phone. Flip a light switch." Boston's voice grew soft. "And just be there in the dark."

Tony had heard very similar words to describe Marmot-the-varmint's reason for searching for an internet bride. Loneliness.

"Sheriff?" Rex's voice on the radio sounded angry rather than his normal calm. "A neighbor called to ask someone to go out and check on Old Nem. Something about vandals and his chickens."

Tony was already halfway there so he headed out the road toward Old Nem's farm. He found the old egg man standing by the side of the road not far from his farmhouse. Nem was wheezing and trembling as he stood there. One hand was pressed to his heart and the other rested on a dented mailbox on a post. Tony stopped, flipping his lights to flash and climbed out.

Poor Old Nem was shaking so violently, the mailbox was moving. Tony was shocked by the old man's expression.

"Sheriff?" The questioning sound of Nem's voice sounded as though he wasn't quite sure he recognized Tony.

Tony hurried closer so he could check on the old man. "What's wrong?" Tony wondered if he should help the old man into his vehicle to sit.

"Them devil kids."

Fury replaced Tony's concern. Not at Nem. Without any details, Tony knew exactly who Nem meant. Karl's Bad, a smart aleck, over-rich, under-disciplined young movie star, had been causing problems for Tony's department for a couple of weeks. It felt longer. The "star" was living in a rented cabin during a film shoot. His personal security staff almost outnumbered Tony's whole department, including the jail staff, Ruth Ann and the cook, Daffodil. With the exception of the bodyguard named Bear, the star's entourage was just a pack of thugs. "What did they do, Nem?"

"They was a-tryin' to run over Miss Elizabeth with one of them four-wheeled motorbikes."

"Where was this?" Tony knew Miss Elizabeth. The vintage speckled hen liked to wander about looking for tasty bits. It wasn't unusual for her to investigate trash tossed from a passing car. Tony hoped she hadn't been in the middle of the county road. With Miss Elizabeth's penchant for jaywalking, it was amazing the old hen was still alive.

"She was right there." Nem pointed toward a field. His whole arm shook. "In *my* corn field. They was a-chasin' her back and forth and laughin' like crazy people."

Tony felt a surge of glorious satisfaction. The corn field was definitely private property and the owner, Nem, had been an eyewitness. Surely they would be able to charge Karl's Bad, the wonder boy, with trespassing and destruction of personal property. Their prosecutor, Archie Campbell, would probably love to prosecute the young movie idol, if for no other reason than getting his own face in the newspaper. Tony called for Wade to join him. "Bring your camera and gear. We're going to make some tire impressions."

Chapter Twenty-Eight

Once they started looking for him, it didn't take Tony and Wade long to locate the visiting movie star. Karl's Bad stood proudly next to a bright blue, souped-up, four-wheel-drive vehicle. It even had his face painted on the hood in silver and black. Subtle.

Tony pretended to admire the vehicle and spotted some corn stalks caught up on the front end. He took a picture with his cell phone. "So this belongs to you?"

"Yeah. It's all mine, and no one else is allowed to touch it." The proud owner ran his hand over the roll bar as if petting a dog. "It was custom made, just for me."

Tony snapped a few more photographs. Then he talked into the recorder, mentioning the date and time and had the star say he understood that Tony was recording everything. Tony used his most professional voice. "I'm investigating a case of vandalism, trespassing and animal cruelty. Would you like to come with me on your own or in handcuffs?"

The star shrieked into the microphone, "I know what you're up to." The steady stream of profanity and angry words pouring from the young man didn't abate.

Tony hoped the battery was fully charged. The brat had a lot to say.

"You think you can frame me? My publicist will have a field day. By the time he's through with you, you won't be able to get a job picking up poop after the dogs at the pound."

The star lost the last semblance of control and lunged toward

Tony with a long blade that looked like a machete that he grabbed out of a sheath in the ATV. Tony kicked the star's right leg out from under him and watched him land in a heap.

Wade stepped in and fastened handcuffs around the celebrity's wrists, neatly pinning them behind his back. Karl's Bad swore but Wade just let the angry words cascade over him. Nothing the wonder boy said apparently bothered him at all. In fact, it looked like Wade rather enjoyed it. It meant the little pervert was scared.

Bear, the bodyguard, stood off to one side near an expensive sedan. The big man held his empty hands away from his body. He was smiling.

There was no doubt that the movie star would be back on the road before Tony and Wade could finish their paperwork. Tony didn't care. He wanted every infraction documented. He had plenty to keep him busy, but a busy schedule couldn't be his excuse for allowing anyone, local or visitor, to destroy private property and threaten citizens. There was no doubt in his mind that the movie star would think little more of running over Old Nem than he would Miss Elizabeth. It was only by chance he hadn't already done so.

After hearing both bad things about him, especially from Tony, and a few starstruck comments in his favor, Theo finally got to meet Karl's Bad, the Wonder Kid. She didn't think it was an apt description. Theo found him less than wonderful and, at twenty-one, not quite a kid either.

Karl's Bad had long brown hair, blunt cut and hanging past his shoulders, but at least it was clean and shiny. In every picture and every time she'd seen him in town, it was always parted on the left, even when he wore it in a ponytail. Another "always" was the ear bud he had in his left ear—presumably he spent his day listening to something important, either a phone call or a message from his manager. His skin was pale pink and although a nice blue, there was a vacancy in his eyes Theo knew Tony found disturbing because he'd tried to describe it to her. Theo thought the young man could've been a store mannequin for all the normal expressions he possessed. Tony had told Theo he had seen rage and then nothing but emptiness. She believed him.

Theo thought if the young man smiled, he could possibly be cute in a genderless way. It was not exactly Tony's style. Comparing the two of them made Theo laugh out loud. She didn't see a muscle on Karl's Bad anywhere, just scrawny arms and legs and big ears sticking through strands of brown hair.

A few wispy whiskers sprouted on his chin and above his upper lip. The average middle-aged woman could grow a better beard than he could. Theo had never seen one of his movies and couldn't help wondering if he looked better on the big screen. It was hard to imagine he would be even mildly impressive, even if his target audience was young girls. It was also hard to imagine he was capable of memorizing and delivering words in a script. Clearly his talents were wasted on her.

Theo wasn't sure if his lack of appeal was because he really had none, or if it was because she was too old at almost forty to see the gifts he was purported to have.

One of Tony's deputies, Darren Holt, was stepfather to drop-dead gorgeous teenager Karissa Sligar, now officially adopted, with her last name changed to Holt. Tony had always found the girl to be intelligent and grounded in reality. When she babysat for his kids, she was both popular and in control.

When the young movie star invited Karissa to a party, she had refused, albeit a bit reluctantly, and then she told Darren, who told Sheila, who told Tony. Karl's Bad, the wonder boy, had suggested to Karissa there would be drugs and alcohol for everyone who came to the party, and she should bring a few of her girlfriends along. But only the good-looking ones.

Concerned about the situation, Tony and Sheila met with Karissa at her mother's salon. Prudence had called and asked him to stop by. "Now my daughter has changed her mind and wants to go to the party. She's been reinvited." Prudence sounded angry and frightened. "Please talk her out of it. I don't trust any of them. They're like rats."

Working on being in Prudence's good graces, Tony had practiced and no longer called the Klip 'n' Kurl a beauty parlor, or at least not all the time. He liked to prove his ability to learn, at least when it suited him. "Karissa, what made you think you could get yourself re-invited to the party?"

"Oh, that's easy. He gave me a number to call when I was ready for an adventure." The teenager rolled her eyes. "So I called."

"An adventure?" Tony repeated. He could imagine the allure of a youthful celebrity to a young person. "That sounds like more than a party. Have you heard of other girls from your school being invited?"

"Kind of. There's been some talk, but my closest friends don't have the required looks. You know what he said?" Karissa's voice rose with each word. "He said he couldn't afford to be seen with any substandard girls. By his standard. Like suddenly he's God?"

"If you don't like him or trust him, why go?" Tony knew Karissa was a star in the school drama program. She wasn't a good enough actress to keep him from believing she had a plan. "What are you suggesting?"

"I'll go to the dumb party and act all impressed." She fluffed her hair. "Sheila can fix me up with a wire and you can arrest him if he offers me some drugs. I saw something just like it on television last night. It gave me the idea."

"Television?" Tony felt out of step.

"I will not." Sheila jumped in. "You don't know what you're suggesting. It's not a good idea."

Karissa's lower lip jutted out and anger lit her lovely eyes. "I don't like him or his friends, or the way they act like everyone who lives in Park County is a dumb hick who never saw a real movie star before, and all the girls should be grateful of his and his posse's notice."

Tony shook his head. "No. You can't do it. It would be unprofessional on my part to allow you to go where we can't protect you, and just plain dumb on yours to consider it."

"With or without a wire, I'm going." Karissa's chin stuck out. "His chauffeur is picking me up after dinner. I'll be fine."

"No, you're not." Prudence grasped her daughter's arm. "It's crazy and dangerous."

"You can't stop me." Karissa tossed her head.

"Don't try me." Prudence leaned closer. "I didn't win the arm-wrestling championship because I'm a ninety-pound weakling, and I'll bet Darren will loan me some handcuffs. I'll lock you in your room."

Tony was wondering whether he'd have to arrest Prudence or Karissa.

Sheila whispered in the quiet created by the mother and daughter trying to stare each other down, "I'll go instead." She smiled. "We're about the same size so I can wear one of your outfits, and if your mom does her hair and makeup magic on me, I doubt they'll notice. At least not right away. All those illegal substances really alter reality, and I'll bet they keep it pretty dark."

Darren was talking to Sheila's back. "We'll be sure and keep you in our sights."

Sheila's response was a quick glance up at Darren and a nod. She was not smiling.

"I don't like this." Tony wondered if they were rushing into danger. "You can't wear your vest under a teenager's party dress. There's just no place to put it."

"I know."

"Sheila, if there is any problem, or you feel at all uncomfortable, get out. Or run to the bodyguard named Bear." Tony could only hope letting her go to the party wasn't going to be a monumental error in judgment.

"I'll wear a wire and carry my best purse."

Tony knew the purse she referred to. It wasn't very big. The pocketbook had enough space to hold a quarter and a tube of lipstick. The rest of it contained a tiny gun.

Prudence, practically in tears because she was so grateful her daughter would be forced to stay home, went to work on Sheila. "You men go away. We don't have much time to turn Sheila into Karissa."

Only fifteen minutes later, Tony returned with the wire they would attach to Sheila. He was amazed by the transformation. He knew Sheila's hair was long and blond, but seeing it brushed out and curling around her face was a striking contrast to her normal neat braid. The teenager's party dress exposed way more skin than her uniform.

Tony thought Sheila looked vulnerable.

Wade, entrusted with her codes, had gone to collect Sheila's special purse. He came through the back door of the salon and handed it to her. "Damn, Sheila, you *are* a girl! Has Not Bob seen you in a dress?"

Prudence suggested, "Someone, quick, take a picture."

Tony felt the weight of responsibility too strongly to be amused. "I don't like it."

"The limousine is on the way." Darren radioed from his assigned post.

★ ★ ★ ★ ★

Maybe half an hour had passed since the fake Karissa was picked up in the limousine. Listening to every word, Tony heard Sheila try chatting with the driver to find out how many other girls he was collecting, but got nowhere. Probably to entertain herself, and keep Tony and Darren from following their desire, which was to stop the car and jerk her out, she began to sing.

At first the words sounded like nonsense to Tony but the tune was familiar. Then he understood what she was saying.

"I'm going to be the only girl. Get me out of here. These doors have to be opened from the outside."

"Sheila?" Tony spoke into the microphone. "What can you see?"

If it were anyone else in the car, he'd have sent Sheila with her rifle up into the woods above the cabin with Wade to be her spotter. With any luck, she'd find herself a great vantage point and take a strategic shot if there was trouble. Locked inside the car, she was helpless. So were they.

"The limo is just making the last of the turns." Sheila's voice was steady. "I can see the front door on the cabin is opening. Looks like five guys coming outside. Karl's Bad is in the center of the pack."

"Where's Bear?" Tony hoped his description of the man and his trustworthiness were spot on.

"He's part of the escort. Wait. Now I don't see him." Sheila hesitated. "The limo has stopped."

Through his binoculars, Tony saw Bear working his way around to the far side of the limo, away from the entourage. At least Tony's gut instinct about Bear and what line he was not prepared to cross seemed to be about to pay off.

"Sheila, Bear's headed your way." Tony spoke into the microphone. "When the door on your left opens, get out. Go with the bodyguard." Silence.

The sound of gunfire coming through Sheila's microphone was unbelievably loud. Tony was about to charge forward when he heard Sheila's voice again. "I've disabled the limo."

Tony heard the high-pitched sound of Karl's Bad shrieking. Then complete silence. "Sheila?"

Nothing.

Chapter Twenty-Nine

"Sorry sir. Everything is fine." Suddenly Sheila's voice came through the microphone. "I had to make sure I didn't need to take a shot. I can't talk and breathe at the same time. My new hero is Bear. He punched the Wonder Boy in the jaw and got me out of the car, and then he shot the car and we ran into the woods." Sheila continued a commentary, not terribly complimentary, about the actor and his pack of toads. "We'll stay out of sight until you can come down and pick up the trash. Who would think I'd miss wearing that uncomfortable vest?"

Tony, Wade and Darren arrived at the cabin before she finished speaking.

As soon as the three county cars came to a stop, forming a road block, Bear shepherded Sheila from the woods and into Darren's car.

Karl's Bad had still not noticed the switch. He called Karissa by name and bleated his innocence and devotion. "Come out, wherever you are."

Surprising no one, the wonder boy feigned shock that they would believe he'd ever harm Karissa or any other girl. He fired Bear on the spot for punching him, and then threatened to sue the former bodyguard for abandoning his job. "You were supposed to keep *me* from getting hurt." He bleated like a sheep when the limo driver hurried to tell his side of the story, incriminating the star. He'd been ordered to pick up the girl and keep the doors locked and the barrier glass between them closed.

Newspaper woman Winifred Thornby, having been tipped off to follow them, snapped a photograph of the limousine, the bad boy and his toads. Not a single photograph was taken of Sheila or Bear.

Tony didn't think the feud between himself and the newspaperwoman was over, but he thanked her for her part in the little melodrama.

Tony stuck his head into Darren's car. "Sheila, are you really okay?"

"Yes, sir." A brilliant smile and nod was her response. "Can I go home? I feel extremely underdressed."

He handed her his cell phone. "You'd better call your fiancé right now. Evidently you promised to meet him for dinner, and he's been plaguing dispatch looking for you and calling the cell phone you left at the Klip 'n' Kurl. Prudence told Holt the thing hasn't stopped ringing since you left."

"Oh, no." Sheila laughed. "I couldn't tell him, and no one else could know, either." Her fingers flew over the surface of the cell phone.

Seeing one of the toadies attempting to slither away from the scene, Tony stepped in his path, assisted by Bear. Not a happy day for toads. Tony wasn't sure what, if anything, he could charge the crew with, but he didn't care. He'd wanted Karl's Bad, the wonder boy, out of his county and the residents safe. Now he would have. For the moment.

Deputy Darren Holt had one of the young men handcuffed, leaning against Tony's Blazer. "Holt, dump that one into Wade's car and take *our* Karissa home."

Darren hustled to follow instructions.

Minutes later, the parking area in front of the cabin was empty except for the fatally wounded limousine and Tony's

Blazer. Tony stood next to Bear, watching the last of the crew headed down the hill. "I'm afraid you're out of a job. My guess is he's probably not going to take you back."

"Man, it felt so good to help a nice person." Bear grinned. "I hated my job. I hated waking up every day feeling like I was a bad guy because I was paid by scum. Worse than scum, because I'd do anything for money. Standing there listening to garbage spewing out of his mouth was getting harder by the hour."

"Did you know what they planned?"

"Not exactly, but I knew it wasn't going to be good." Bear clenched and unclenched his fists. "Your deputy shocked me, though. I thought I was going to snatch a teenager who would try to fight me. I expected screams and fingernails, maybe a kick or two." He blinked. "Instead, I heard her say my name and 'let's go,' like she was expecting me."

"I told her to run to you if there was trouble." Tony exhaled sharply. "I had to hope I wasn't wrong about you."

"Oh, man, that makes me feel so good. Clean, you know?" Bear turned his face away and hid his expression.

Tony waited in silence for a little while, watching the procession of vehicles. "I recently fired a new deputy. He was two months into a six-month probation."

Bear straightened and stared into Tony's eyes. He listened attentively to every word. Hope lit his eyes. "The cost of living better here than in California?"

"Oh, yeah." Tony had to smile. "On the other hand, the incomes are lower, too. What's your background?"

"Played college football and earned a degree in education." Bear shook his head. "I wasn't good enough myself to play professional ball, but I can coach."

"Arrests? Drugs?"

"No, sir." Bear smiled. "Neither of those."

"And your wife?" Tony thought this might be the deal breaker.

"Do you think she wants to move to Tennessee?"

Bear hesitated only a moment. "She'd love it. That is, as long as we have access to good doctors for our kids. We've got a little guy whose special needs make him a medical frequent flyer. He's why we need the extra money."

Tony could tell the man wasn't complaining, just stating the facts. "There's a children's hospital in Knoxville."

"That sounds real good." Bear pressed his lips together as if he was trying to keep from laughing.

"Okay then. Come in tomorrow and fill out all the paperwork. If everything checks out, you'll have a six-month probation before going to the academy in Greeneville." Tony felt relieved that it might be just this easy to find a competent deputy. "I'll bet you don't have wheels to get you back to town."

"You'd be right. Can you give me a lift? I've got to call my wife."

Tony's smile disappeared when he turned back to face the front of the cabin. He hated the idea this was going to turn into a media mess. The lurid headlines about Karl's Bad being arrested were bound to create some kind of backlash. He just didn't know if his department was going to look stupid or heroic.

It was up to Winifred now.

First thing the next morning, Tony took Daisy to the vet's office for her regular shots and checkup. He wasn't surprised to see Boston and Mouse in the waiting room. He sat near the pair and smiled when Daisy slithered close to Mouse and started licking the shepherd's ear.

"Mouse all right?"

"Yeah, he's good. Just needs a little maintenance, you know. I think I'm getting the hang of living here," Boston said. "I like working with the dogs and Mrs. Dixon."

"I'm glad to hear it."

Daisy looked up and gave Boston's hand a quick lick.

Boston appeared to relax. "I know I'm not alone, and my life's an old story. The classics, I guess, never go out of style. I enlisted in the Army and gave my girlfriend a ring. She was all 'I'll wait forever and love you until I die.' "

A flicker of wry amusement lit his face, showing Tony a glimpse of the boy he had once been. The smile vanished as quickly as it had come and was replaced by bitterness.

"Either forever is shorter than it used to be or she lied. I came home all screwed up, you know, and found she had married my brother. They have a baby girl."

"So you left." It wasn't a question.

"Yeah. I thought I'd leave them to each other. I still had to take care of Mouse, so we just walked away. There's something wrong in my head, you know. It's not just that I can't hear out of this ear."

Tony watched him tap the left ear. "You still can't sleep inside?"

"Not really." Boston ran a hand over Mouse's back. "It's coming though. I made it inside several nights in a row during snowy times. I didn't sleep, but I keep trying. Now at least, I start out inside and then some time in the night I have to go out. Mrs. Dixon set me up with a bed and a shower and a place to lock up my stuff. Not to mention a mailing address."

"And money?"

"I'm okay now." Boston's smile flickered again. "It helps to have a mailing address and it is quiet out here. I get disability payments and Mrs. Dixon has chores for me to do. You know, I shovel, mow, paint fences. Clean dog kennels. She's good people."

"And her husband?"

"Oh man, he's awesome. Mouse needed his shots, and the man won his trust. Dr. Dixon doesn't talk much, but you can see his heart is good and he and his missus are sweet on each other. I like them both."

After her visit with the veterinarian, Tony dropped Daisy off at the house and went to work.

He'd barely made it to his desk when the phone on it began to ring.

"Sheriff, I think we found your missing Dahlia." A man's deep bass voice boomed through the earpiece on his phone.

Even though Flavio had informed Tony there was a caller on the line for him about Blossom's missing sister, he was startled by the powerful voice. "Who are you and where are you?"

"Oh, sorry, Sheriff, I'm detective Gabe Johnson. I gave my name to the man who answered the phone and guessed he'd passed it along. I'm here with a man you'll want to talk with. We're in Southport."

"Southport?" Tony's geography was only fair and thought it quicker to ask. "Are you near Nashville?"

"Not even." Johnson burst into laughter. "We're not far from Wilmington over on the coast of North Carolina. I'm giving the phone to Mr. Sawyer."

"North Carolina?" Tony couldn't imagine what Dahlia was doing there. "Is she all right?"

In contrast to Johnson's voice, Mr. Sawyer sounded like he was whispering. "I met Dahlia the other evening, or some woman of that name. According to Gabe here, she matches your description of the missing lady. Dahlia seemed real nice. She was unhappy with her husband and said she was going to visit her sisters."

Although he was confused, Tony was glad Dahlia wasn't injured somewhere. "Did she give a reason for being in North Carolina? As far as I know, her sisters, at least most of them, live here in East Tennessee."

"No, sir. When she wasn't crying in her beer, she spent her time listing everything her husband had done to annoy her in the past ten years. I'm a bartender, and a lot of people think I get paid to listen to them." Mr. Sawyer's voice developed a pronounced whine. "I don't."

"And when she left, do you know where she went?" Tony pulled a worn road atlas off the shelf and opened it to North Carolina. His finger followed the highway until it reached the end of the road.

"If you're asking if she was okay to drive, she was definitely not, but she said she was staying in the motel next door and had walked over." He coughed, sounding a bit like he was covering a laugh. "Then I watched her stagger back to her motel. She had to stop about halfway there and leave her dinner and drinks in a shrub."

"When was this?"

"Like every night for a week now." Irritation filled Sawyer's voice. "It's time for her to go home."

If Tony had to guess, he would guess that Dahlia had been so busy being mad at her husband, she didn't even noticed her surroundings until she was faced with the Atlantic Ocean. She had gotten on Interstate Highway 40 and hadn't stopped until the road ended.

Glad one mystery was solved, Tony finished the call and notified Blossom.

His next duty was a sadder one.

Tony had agreed to take Jenny Swift to the Plover house to pick out an outfit for Eunice Plover to wear to her own funeral. With seals on the doors because not all of the evidence had been sorted through, he couldn't let her go alone. He was sure Jenny had a set of keys to her best friend's house, but took the ones they had found in Eunice's purse, just in case.

The drive was quiet. Neither of them felt like making small

talk. Parking in the driveway, he followed Jenny as she led the way around to the kitchen door. Her hands were shaking too hard to get the key into the hole.

Tony took the key from her. Seconds later the door was unlocked. Jenny stepped inside.

"Oh, no! How did she get my pie plate?" Jenny's voice was more of a scream than a question.

The last thing Tony expected when he agreed to escort her into the house was this. Tony watched as Jenny frantically ran into the kitchen and stopped in front of the counter next to the sink.

"What pie?" He glanced around the room and saw an empty pie pan sitting on the kitchen counter. It was beige ceramic with the words "world's best pie" written around the outside in blue script.

"That's my favorite pie pan. Eunice gave it to me for my last birthday. I made a lemon meringue pie in it and gave it to Jack Gates. He was supposed to be the one who ate it. Not her! Never her!" Her words ended in a wail. "I've killed her. I've killed my best friend."

"Wade, get Doc Nash up here now." Tony spoke into his radio even as he pulled the hysterical woman away from her friend's belongings. "Don't touch anything."

Tony glanced around. The last time he'd been in the house, Mrs. Plover's body had been taken to Knoxville, and he and Wade were combing through the house, looking for something, anything that might explain the woman's death.

The clean pie pan sat on the counter the entire time. He remembered seeing it in photographs of the kitchen.

With only a few words, Jenny Swift's hysterical statement changed everything he knew about the case.

Mrs. Swift did not appear to be listening to him, so he moved her away from the doorway and forced her to sit on a ladder-back kitchen chair. Her eyes were glassy, and he could tell from her short, quick breaths that she was about to hyperventilate.

"Jenny. Try to take a slow deep breath."

She blinked at him as if she couldn't see. Then her voice, reedy and quiet, whispered, "I don't feel at all well. Can you help me?"

Wade, accompanied by Doc Nash, rushed through the doorway.

The doctor immediately hurried to Jenny's side. "What's going on?" He stared at Tony.

Tony would've answered if he could've come up with a reasonable statement.

"We're going to need an ambulance. She has a history of serious cardiac problems." Doc Nash kept his stethoscope pressed against Jenny's chest.

Complying, Tony radioed for assistance. He stepped out of the way and signaled for Wade to join him. "She says she killed her friend with a pie."

"A pie?" Wade looked as confused as Tony felt. "Why would she kill her friend?"

"More to the point, why did she just find out?" Tony watched the doctor even as he said, "I think she said the pie was for Jack Gates."

"That's bizarre. He doesn't live anywhere near here."

"No, he doesn't. But, I have seen Gates and Eunice together at different events. They're relatives."

Wade continued to watch the doctor trying to stabilize Jenny. "He's a lot younger than she is. Not that that means anything."

Tony nodded. "I hope we can talk to Jenny soon."

"And if she did kill Mrs. Plover, will we be able to find any evidence?"

Tony's perpetually irritated stomach rumbled. "Just to be on the safe side, although it is closing the barn door after the horses have gone, we'll replace the seals as we leave."

Soon the kitchen was filled with the ambulance crew joining the doctor. Tony and Wade stood in the dining room. He remembered their mission. They had come for clothes for Mrs. Plover.

An oxygen mask covered her nose and mouth as Jenny stared into his eyes. "Jenny, can you describe the clothes you wanted to get?"

He thought he could do that small service for the deceased.

Gasping for breath, Jenny told him what to get, and where he would find it. She passed out and the doctor went to work again.

Tony gathered the clothes.

Chapter Thirty

Jack Gates answered their knock on his door and stood in his doorway, using the door frame for support. "Sheriff? Wade?"

"May we come in?" Tony said.

"Sure, sure." Walking with his swinging-dragging gait, Jack led the way into his living room. A wheelchair sat empty in the adjoining dining area. "I hate that chair," he volunteered without being asked as he waved Tony and Wade toward the sofa. "What's up?"

Clutching his notebook, Tony settled onto the sofa. "Do you mind answering a few questions?"

"No. Not at all." Jack lowered himself onto a partially raised power recliner. He pushed the buttons on the control and the chair shifted Jack's seating position. "What's this about?"

Tony said, "We're trying to chase down some loose ends. Can you tell me about a pie Jenny Swift delivered to you?"

"Oh, sure." Curiosity filled Jack's face but he shrugged. "She brought me a pie maybe a week ago now. Recently, she's been very generous to me."

"What kind was it?" Wade said.

"Lemon meringue." Jack sighed heavily. "It's my all-time favorite dessert."

Tony heard "favorite" and saw unhappiness. "You don't look pleased to have received it."

"No. I was pleased, but . . ." He sighed again and his hands twitched on the armrests of his chair. "I have recently developed some health issues that prevent my enjoying that much sugar."

"Jenny didn't know?"

Jack shrugged. "It's not the kind of news I thought to spread around. It's not a *secret;* it's just not the kind of thing that comes up in casual conversation."

"So when she brought the pie, what did you do?"

"I thanked her profusely, which made her happy, and I ate a small slice, you know because it is exceptional pie and willpower is *not* what I'm best at. After she left, I took the rest of the pie up to Eunice's house. She has, er, had a voracious appetite for goodies." Jack sighed heavily. "I thought she'd enjoy it."

"What about you?" Tony asked quietly. "Did you enjoy the pie?"

"Why, yes. It was delicious." Jack looked intrigued. "Should I not have? Is there something you're not telling me?"

Tony didn't answer directly. "Any sense of feeling ill afterwards?"

"Ill?" The expressions chasing across his face began changing from polite to concerned to suspicious. "Why? Was there something wrong with the pie?"

"We believe so." Tony heard himself and grimaced. "It sounds so bizarre, but we have reason to believe there was arsenic in the pie, and that's what killed Eunice."

Jack laughed. "Nonsense. If there was, wouldn't I have died, too?"

"I don't know. You are a good-sized man and ate a small piece. Maybe that's all the difference necessary between feeling fine and a fatal dose. Maybe her slice was larger."

"I hate to speak ill of the dead." Jack's eyes filled with tears. "But my aunt was prone to overeating, particularly sweets. I can imagine she might have eaten the entire remaining pie. What I can't imagine is why you think Jenny would bring me a pie full of poison in the first place."

Tony and Wade went to visit Jenny in her hospital room. Even though she was attached to an IV and several monitors, she looked close to death.

"Will you tell us what happened?" Tony watched as Jenny's eyelids lifted halfway and then closed again. He heard her sigh and waited.

"I had barely delivered the poisoned lemon meringue pie to Jack when I came to my senses. I ran back to his house just in time to see him pull out of his driveway. I was frantic until I saw him return. He seemed fine, but all night I stayed awake and watched the house." Tears seeped beneath her eyelashes.

Tony handed her several more tissues. And waited while she wiped her eyes.

After dabbing at her eyes, she compressed the tissues into a ball in the palm of her left hand and her fingers tightened around it. Jenny's eyes closed again as a shudder ran through her. She inhaled and then, as she exhaled, her eyes opened and she stared directly into Tony's. "I went over first thing the next morning, terrified he had died. When he opened his front door and I saw his face looked absolutely normal, I was so relieved. He was laughing as he talked to someone on the telephone. I said I would come back later."

"Did you think he hadn't eaten the pie?" Tony made notes about the times.

"I thought maybe I hadn't used enough poison, or maybe that it was too old and had lost its power." Jenny blinked away more tears. "What happened?"

Tony didn't think it would matter if he gave her an answer. "Jack has developed diabetes and did not want to tell you and hurt your feelings, so he took the pie. Later, he gave most of it to his aunt."

"Oh, my." Understanding completely, Jenny lay back against the pillows. "My dearest friend, Eunice, could never resist overeating desserts."

Tony guessed he had about a hundred more questions to ask her, but the doctor signaled his time was up. Jenny needed rest.

A few hours later, Tony received a call from Doc Nash.

"Jenny Swift was returned to her house and when I went to check on her, no one answered the ringing doorbell and the door was locked. I'm very worried. She should not have been alone." The normally calm physician sounded almost panicky.

"I'll send Wade and then I'll join you both. We should be there in a few minutes." Tony was talking to Wade even as he headed to his vehicle.

When they broke into the house, Tony and Wade and the doctor found Jenny Swift stretched out on her couch unconscious. Next to her was an empty glass and a handwritten note.

Tony picked it up and began to read. "I've always hated the idea of suicide. Someone taking over God's decision about how long we should live. And the horrible tragedy the family is left to bear. Their pain is mixed with undeserved guilt. But there are only a few members left in my family, and I pray they will forgive me. I killed the wrong person.

"To Eunice's myriad friends, I am sure that this confession will not ease your pain, or compensate for your loss. Nor mine. She was my best friend. The pain of knowing what I have done is beyond belief.

"To my intended victim, Jack Gates, I suspect we will both meet again in the depths of hell. If you have not already informed the authorities of the reason I hate you so, I will explain it to them now.

"Jack Gates killed my daughter. And I have hated him every

moment of every day since then. My dear friend Eunice knew you only as her nephew, and she possessed the greatest, kindest heart. A couple of times I tried to tell her why I thought so little of you. I don't know whose idea two of you taking a cruise was, but for some reason it became the final straw. I heard you both laughing about the fun you would have. My daughter has been dead for twenty years and instead of the grief fading, lately it has grown stronger. I could no longer tolerate the sight of you. I suppose you feel sure that you have won this final battle between us. Only time will tell."

By the time Tony finished reading the note, the paramedics had managed to revive the woman. She was still desperately ill, and he knew she might not make it.

The look she gave him was one of heartbroken disappointment. She wanted to die. She couldn't speak because of all of the medical equipment; the tears streamed from her eyes and soaked the cushion under her head.

A few hours later, Tony and Wade stood by Jenny's hospital bed. She was in a different room this time. The doctor had warned them to make the visit short. She was greatly improved, but was not out of the woods yet.

"We found your note." Tony read her rights to her, mostly so she'd realize they could not ignore her actions.

Jenny's voice was barely audible. "Ask me anything you want."

"Where did you get the poison that you filled the pie with?"

"My old house is filled with it. Even the antique wallpaper in the attic is known as arsenic green. It really does have arsenic in it. I loaded the pie I intended for Jack. I soaked the wallpaper with lemon juice, and I added spoons and spoons of the poison still left in tins and boxes in the attic. It was once commonly used for many purposes. You could say, I guess, my murder weapon of choice was an antique." She moved restlessly on the hospital bed. "I put it in my tea, but I guess I didn't use enough on myself."

"What made you decide to give him a poisoned pie?" Tony was baffled. He had seen Jack with both Jenny and Eunice many times, and all of them seemed totally happy and agreeable. "What changed? Your note indicated he'd killed your daughter?"

"I hated that my friend trusted him. Just because someone is a relative does not mean they are good people. He was 'oh, just so nice,' and 'deals bravely.' Do you know why he has trouble walking?"

Tony couldn't imagine what this had to do with a poisoning. "Some accident when he was much younger."

"Some accident indeed—when he killed my daughter." Jenny's fingers clenched the edge of the sheet. "He was driving under the influence of something. I don't know if it was drugs or alcohol. I don't care. It made him lose control and his motorcycle tipped and slid under hers. She and her motorcycle went over a railing and down a steep canyon into a river. She drowned, trapped under all that weight." Jenny struggled for breath, almost like she was drowning, too. "I didn't ever tell Eunice it was her nephew I blamed. I'm not sure I knew of their relationship in the early days when she and I became friends. All those years ago. I was completely distraught at the time. I suffered from horrible depression and could barely even lift a hand. My new best friend visited me, made me laugh, made me live and introduced me to quilting as therapy."

"And Jack Gates?" Tony hadn't heard this story before.

"He didn't live here then. To be honest, I'm not sure when I realized who he really was. When he moved into the house across from mine, it took a while before I was positive it was the same man. Eunice loved her nephew and was happy and excited he'd moved to Silersville."

"You didn't tell your friend who he was, to you?"

"Oh, I tried to tell her, but I guess I didn't try hard enough. I could see his front door from my kitchen window. When he started riding that bike, I hoped he would crash or be hit by a truck."

Tony hated hearing of her tragedy. "I'm so sorry."

Jenny struggled to speak. "I'm not asking you to be sorry. I'm telling you why I wanted him dead."

"Where was the accident?" Tony couldn't remember even having heard about it.

"They were in New Mexico, riding through the mountains." Jenny sighed. "At the time lots of people told me that his being crippled was punishment enough and I should forgive and forget." She buried her face in her hands and sobbed. "I could never forget. He killed my little girl."

Although Tony felt deep sympathy for the woman, he had to have the facts. "Why didn't you ever mention this before? This is not the kind of thing that usually stays secret in a community like ours."

"It's been such a long time now. As I said, at first I wasn't sure it was the same man," Jenny explained. "He didn't live here, only visited a few times with my daughter, and then only briefly."

"Do you know where he grew up? Or where his family is, other than Eunice?" Tony wondered if there were relatives somewhere he needed to notify. Her eyes drifted closed. And for a moment Tony thought she had fallen asleep.

"He and Shannon, my daughter, lived in St. Louis. I don't know anything about his family, except I did meet his mother and father at the wedding. Shannon and Jack got married here. Your dad performed the wedding." Her eyes opened and met his. "He would be so disappointed to know what I have done."

The doctor signaled that it was time for them to leave.

Tony nodded his head, even as he thought about the twenty

years since the tragedy had taken place. He would've been peeling potatoes on an aircraft carrier; at least that was the story he liked to tell. He was saddened and disappointed by what he had learned. He touched her shoulder gently. "And now you've killed your best friend."

Tears seeped into the pillow. "I will never forgive myself."

Tony stood in the back of the church waiting for the funeral service for Eunice Plover to begin.

Jack sat in his wheelchair near the front, next to an empty pew reserved for the family. He seemed weaker each day. Tony had stopped to talk to him, explaining the poison. "She never meant to kill her friend."

"I understand." Jack studied his hands. "Jenny was heartbroken. I might have tried to kill me, too." He looked up. "Her daughter was the other half of my soul. Neither of us can forget, or bring her back. Could Jenny think *I* wouldn't have preferred death to my life filled with guilt and half a body? I got what I deserved."

Tony left the man to deal with his grief.

The remainder of the church was packed with only friends and neighbors. Tony didn't find it surprising, because he knew the only known relatives, besides Jack, were off somewhere trying to find an attorney who could break Eunice's will. Not a chance.

What had proved to be the breaking point with the greedy family was learning that she didn't even own the house she lived in. It had been sold to a charity, for a dollar, with the provision she could live in it for the duration of her life. She even continued to pay the taxes. That news had broken their spirit. Much as Jack's spirit had been broken by the knowledge that his aunt died for something he accidentally destroyed in his reckless youth.

The last greedy relatives scuttled off in the darkness, like cockroaches, taking with them the ceramic planter filled with tulips from the front porch. It was the only thing not locked inside or nailed down.

Tony's cell phone vibrated and he stepped into the foyer. "Yes?"

"Sheriff, there's another still on fire. This time Chief Cox thinks he knows where the arsonist is." Flavio's excitement caused all of the words to arrive in one breath.

Tony sorted it out. "Where should I meet him?"

"He'll be going through the intersection, just a block from the church. He says for you to follow him and that you can't miss him. He'll be in a big red truck."

Even as Flavio spoke, Tony heard the fire engine and ran to his vehicle. Rather than create any disturbance at the funeral, he decided not to pull Wade or Mike out of the church. He fell in line behind the firemen. The shrieking sirens of the fire vehicles and his Blazer brought the curious out in force.

By the time they reached the burning still, the culprit was gone. Tony squinted at the pile of rubble. "I thought we might catch him this time." Chief Cox nodded. "So, whose still is still standing? There can't be many more."

"I have no idea," Tony said, his dream of another closed case shattered. "I had no idea there were this many to begin with."

Theo felt all recovered after her bout with the very bad flu bug. She arrived at her shop a little late in the morning and parked in the rear. Using her key, she unlocked the workroom door and, turning her back to it, pushed it open with her rump. The twins each held one of her hands and were walking well, but not breaking any speed records as she backed through the doorway.

Theo was so busy concentrating on the girls and juggling her purse and their lunches that when a horn honked right behind her, she jumped up in the air and squealed. Caro stood just inside the workroom, behind her gaily festooned walker, and she got so tickled by Theo's reaction, she started laughing like crazy and honking the walker's horn again and again.

Theo wasn't sure whether to be happy her friend was laughing or pull out the stern face because she could have had heart failure. The vote was instantaneous. Theo joined in the laughter, and laughed so hard she had to sit down. Kara and Lizzie, evidently believing the party was for them, laughed and clapped as well.

Within a minute every person in the shop, even the strangers, were at minimum having a fit of the giggles. Others were laughing hard, gasping for breath. Joy is contagious. Life was good.

ABOUT THE AUTHOR

Barbara Graham began making up stories in the third grade and immediately quit learning to multiply and divide. Her motto is "every story needs a dead body and every bed needs a quilt." She writes because she cannot "not write." Barbara is intrigued by the problems and situations her imaginary friends manage to get themselves into. She refuses to accept any blame for their actions or misfortunes.

A prize-winning quilter, she enjoys combining her fabric addiction with her predilection for telling tall tales.

Married to a man who can do math in his head (very useful to a quilter), she has two perfect sons, a perfect grandson and granddaughter. She has a delightful daughter-in-law and is "not the worst mother-in-law in history."

3/16

Silver Falls Library
410 S. Water St.
Silverton, OR 97381
(503) 873-5173

DISCARD